BLOOD Ties

A Sequel to Family Lies

June E. Hudy

Copyright © 2012 by June E. Hudy.

ISBN:	Softcover	978-1-4797-2101-6
	Ebook	978-1-4797-2102-3

All rights reserved. No part of this book may be reproduced or transmitted in any form or by any means, electronic or mechanical, including photocopying, recording, or by any information storage and retrieval system, without permission in writing from the copyright owner.

This is a work of fiction. Names, characters, places and incidents either are the product of the author's imagination or are used fictitiously, and any resemblance to any actual persons, living or dead, events, or locales is entirely coincidental.

This book was printed in the United States of America.

To order additional copies of this book, contact:
Xlibris Corporation
1-888-795-4274
www.Xlibris.com
Orders@Xlibris.com
122287

ACKNOWLEDGEMENTS

I want to express my appreciation and thanks to the following people for making this novel become a reality:

To my friend Carol for the hours she put in, reading, editing and proofing; to Lynn for her help and insight into the trauma of kidney failure; to my family for their support to see this novel published and to my husband for his patience and understanding while I quizzed him about health issues and spent hours on the computer.

Finally, I want to thank my readers for purchasing my books and their encouragement to write this sequel.

Thank you, one and all!

Chapter 1

Southern Alberta

"I have decided I would like to get in contact with my biological father," Shane spoke softly, as he laid his soup spoon on the table and looked up at Amy.

Amy also laid down her spoon and sat back in her chair. She couldn't believe her ears! After all this time, Shane wanted to get in touch with his father? She took her time answering. When she spoke, her voice had a tremor, "So what brought this on now? Are you unhappy with your family and life at the ranch? Are you and April having problems?"

"No, nothing like that. It is just with April having our first child soon, I started thinking about our family history, and my biological father is part of that history."

"Even if he has never acknowledged you all these years?"

"Maybe he doesn't know I exist," Shane replied as he picked up his spoon again and proceeded to finish his soup.

Amy didn't know how to answer that. She knew Shane's father, Dave Knight had denied that she was carrying his baby. She had gone to him when she found out she was pregnant, but he wasn't interested in being a father. Would he feel any different now? After all the years, Amy did not want to go there. She was happy with her life; her life with Ivan and their two children, Laura and Abe, and finding her son Shane. She had never dreamed that she would ever see the child she had to give up when she was sixteen years old, much less have him as part of her family. She felt so blessed and she wanted nothing, absolutely nothing to spoil that. Amy knew she could not stop Shane from seeking his father, but she didn't have to help him in his search. So picking up her soup bowl and picking up Shane's and the children's, she headed to the sink. Depositing the dishes, she turned to Shane and said, "Shane, you are a young man with a wonderful future and a family on the way. I think you would be making a mistake to look for your father, but it is your choice. I don't want to see you hurt, but I certainly don't want to be like my controlling mother. So I will just warn you; be prepared to get rejected. You don't know how Dave will react if you contact him. Possibly his wife and family know nothing about you, so be forewarned."

Shane came over and put his arm on Amy's shoulder, "I know you are concerned about our family, but I have to do this. Not for myself so much, but for my children. They have a right to know their biological grandfather. You and Ivan will always be special and have a top place in my heart but I have to do this."

"Well, I wish you luck, but please tread carefully. You and April are very special to us. Ivan considers you his son you know."

"Yes, I know and that will never change. I don't plan to replace you and Ivan in my life; just add someone else."

Amy sighed and patted Shane's hand, "Okay. Do what you must. Just know that I don't ever want to see that man again. When he would not support me when I needed help, I just wrote him out of my life and I want it to stay that way."

Shane grinned, "There! That is the Amy I know and love. You are the best Mom a guy could ever want. You can be sure I will always be your son first."

"Okay, okay, get out of here. I have work to do. Ivan will be back from Lethbridge before I get these floors washed. When are you expecting April back from her Mom's?"

"She hopes to be home tomorrow. They have been out shopping for baby clothes, so I hope the closet in the baby's room will hold everything. I know how April's Mom can be when it comes to shopping!"

With that remark, Shane kissed Amy's cheek, ruffled Laura's hair and tickled Abe as he passed them at the table and headed out the door. He was whistling as he stepped into his truck and headed down the driveway.

* * *

Amy watched Shane drive away. Turning from the window, she surveyed her little family at the table and tried to hold back the tears. Things had been so good for so long and now Shane wanted to 'rock the boat', so to speak. Any kind of change always upset Amy and especially when it concerned her family.

Ever since Amy had come to work on the Collins' Ranch several years before, her life had completely changed. Getting away from Medicine Hat and moving to the ranch west of Milk River had taken a lot of courage, but Amy was never sorry she had made that move. It was there she found the son she had been forced to give up and found Ivan, the love of her life. Through a misunderstanding she nearly lost Ivan but their strong love and the caring of Shane's adopted Mom brought them through the crisis. They now had a wonderful, strong marriage.

Shane had been raised by the owners of the sheep ranch that Amy came to work at when she left Medicine Hat. She never dreamed that she would find out that Abe Collins was actually her biological father. She found that out after she realized that Shane was the baby she gave up for adoption eighteen years before. Finding her son was the most stupendous thing that could happen in her life. She had then realized her mother had duped her for years, telling her that her father was dead. Eventually, she was able to make peace with her mother, though the fact that she had deprived Amy of her father for all the years was very hard to forgive. It was only through Ivan's help and love, that she was able to forgive. Through him she had found peace in his church and the fellowship of the church women. "Please God," Amy implored aloud, "don't let anything ruin things for us now."

Taking Abe from his high chair and shooing Laura into the bathroom, Amy decided it was best to leave things in God's hands. Maybe this would all blow over. At this point, she wasn't going to mention anything to Ivan. He might not understand Shane's reasoning. Amy was having a hard time understanding it herself.

Sending the kids out to the fenced backyard to play, Amy dug out her scrub pail and went to work on her floors. There was still work to do in spite of everything that was discussed that day. There would be time to worry about things when the work was all done.

Chapter 2

Southern Alberta

Shane was smiling as he headed onto the main road and shifted into high gear. "Well, that went better than I thought it would," he spoke aloud. "My Amy Mom never ceases to amaze me." Shane knew that contacting his father would upset Amy, but he was hoping to give her some time to digest the fact that he had to do this. He was sure if she thought about it enough, she would realize why he was doing it.

Shane would be forever grateful to the Collins' who raised him, but finding Amy, his natural mother was the most awesome experience of his life. While discovering Amy was his mother, he also found out that Abe Collins, the man he called father, was actually his grandfather. So the Collins were also part of his family history. He just had to make Amy see that Dave Knight was also part of that history.

Because of April and the child she was carrying, Shane knew he was doing what had to be done. Shane smiled as he thought about April. What a wonderful wife she was. She was so much like Amy, willing to learn anything new and experience everything pertaining to life on the ranch. When they found out she was carrying a child, April went right out and purchased a crib and started getting a room ready for the baby. She had a bout of morning sickness, but was now doing great. She literally glowed with her pregnancy, while getting bigger every day. The baby was due within the month and Shane could hardly wait. They had decided to wait to find out if it was a boy or girl, both agreeing that the suspense was very exciting. The next while would be very busy, so Shane knew he wouldn't be looking for his father until things settled down. They also had to get through harvest in the next month. So far he hadn't mentioned anything to April and didn't want anything to upset her while she was expecting. There would be lots of time later.

Seeing his turnoff, Shane shifted down and turned up his road. Dust was flying as he picked up speed, making him think again that they were in need of a good rain. The pastures were starting to dry up and the dugout in the lower pasture would soon be dry. He might have to move the twenty head of cattle he had there if they didn't get some moisture in the next week. They were fortunate that they had a good water supply at the buildings and a creek running through the upper pastures, but it was getting low too. He would hate to have to haul water to the cattle. If the drought continued, he might have to start feeding them too. Shane didn't want to think about that. Ivan would be in the same boat, Shane acknowledged. I will discuss it with him next time I see him, Shane mused as he topped the hill and headed down into the ranch.

Halting in front of the barn and corrals, Shane stepped out of the truck to be greeted by Lad and Sampson, his two cattle dogs. Lady had passed away while Shane was away on his mission with his church. When he returned he had decided that he needed two dogs so purchased Sampson as a young three month old pup. Lad was very jealous at first but soon accepted the young dog and between him and Shane, they managed to teach Sampson his job. He wasn't anywhere near as good as Lady, but not many dogs were. Lady had the marvelous instinct of being able to pick out a sick animal or know if something wasn't quite right in the pasture. Lad was her son. Though not as good, he excelled in moving cattle. He had been trained on sheep as that was what the Collins ranch raised for years, but the sheep were sold off to finance Shane's mission. Lad soon took to herding cattle and even surprised Shane.

Being a Mormon and a young man, Shane had been expected to go on a two year mission with the church. After his adopted Mom died, Shane made the decision to go and he never regretted it. His mission was to Italy and he learned so much about life in that country. Coming home was also a wonderful experience. Though he had a great time on his mission, he was ever grateful to live in Canada and have the freedom of Canadians. The next great experience of his life was meeting April and persuading her to marry him. He just could not think of life without her by his side. He was so looking forward to her return from her parents, which made him remember; he had promised to get the lawn mowed while she was gone, so had better get to it. Shane was whistling again as he headed to the garage to dig out the lawn mower. Lad and Sampson frolicked by his side, each wanting attention. Shane reached down and petted each one before he opened the garage door and stepped inside.

Chapter 3

Regina, Saskatchewan

Dave Knight set down the morning paper and looked at his wife Alice across the cluttered breakfast table. "Did you say something?" he quizzed as he picked up his coffee cup and drank the now cold coffee.

"I think sometimes I might as well talk to the kitchen stove, for all you listen to me," Alice answered, "You get your nose in that paper every morning and don't hear a word that I say."

"You know with my job I have to keep up on current events here in the city. I don't want to sound ignorant when a resident phones me about some problem and I don't have a clue."

"I'm sure you could look after all that at the office. We never seem to have anything to say to each other any more. Ever since Sarah left home, you don't seem to want to talk to me. I am feeling neglected. Thank God for my job where at least the people talk to me."

"I'm sorry. I guess I wasn't thinking. I do miss Sarah around here. She was always chatting away. Things are pretty quiet here without her."

"Especially when you tune out anyone else talking," Alice groused as she got up from the table, taking her cup and plate to the sink. "As I was saying, I will be late tonight as I have a conference with my staff at 5:00 PM. There is hamburger in the fridge and potatoes scrubbed ready to microwave. I made a salad. I should be home by 6:30 PM. I'm off now, so you have a good day."

Dave waved good-bye and returned to his paper, but he found he couldn't concentrate. The things Alice mentioned got him to thinking. Yes, he did miss Sarah . . . a lot. She was into her fourth year of university and had decided to move out on her own just a few months before. The house seemed so quiet without her constant chatter and her laughter. She always had friends over, though no steady boyfriend. She said she didn't have any time for a boyfriend with all the studying she had to do. Dave could believe that. He was sure he would never want to be a pharmacist. They had so much to learn with new things cropping up all the time. Sarah used to discuss a lot of it with Dave and he really missed that since she moved. They did text back and forth, but it was not the same as hearing her voice every day. Lately, Dave had been phoning her but she seemed busy so they didn't talk long.

So I guess Alice is right. I have been a drag, Dave acknowledged. I sometimes wish we had adopted more than one child. They had adopted Sarah when she was four years old. She had been in foster care for all four years of her life. She had some health issues as a baby and was never adopted. Dave and Alice had wanted children of their own but Alice was unable to have a child so they decided they would get an older child. That way they didn't have to deal with formula and potty-training. Besides the waiting period for a baby was at least five years but an older child was more readily available. He and Alice had married young and planned to have children early so adopting an older child seemed the right thing to do.

When they first laid eyes on Sarah, it was like there was a definite connection. She looked so sad and scared and their hearts went out to her. She had Dave's blond hair and blue eyes and was tall like Alice. No one ever questioned that she wasn't their child. Of course Sarah knew she was adopted as she remembered coming home with them from her foster home. Alice stayed home from her job as social worker for the first while after they had Sarah so she could become confident in her new home. Alice was able to keep up to date on her job through the internet connection. She took Sarah with her when she needed to go into the office. At that time, Dave was still working in maintenance with the city of Regina. A few years later he was offered a job with the water works and had gradually worked his way up the ladder. Now he was in charge of things. He was very content with his life. The money was good and they had the funds between their two jobs to put Sarah through school. They owned their own home and each had a new car. Life was good. I just hope that I can get over this feeling I have that things are going to change, Dave thought as he got up from the table and took his plate and cup to the sink. He would load the dishwasher when he got home from work.

Chapter 4

Regina, Saskatchewan

Sarah wasn't feeling well. "I must be working too hard lately," she said aloud as she buried her head under her pillow. It was 6:30 AM and she had to be in class at 8:00 AM. Sarah moaned and finally managed to sit up. Rubbing her forehead to try to alleviate the headache starting, she slipped her feet into her slippers and shuffled her way to the bathroom. As she gazed into the mirror she was shocked at the swelling of her face. Her skin looked funny too.

"Man, what is going on? Did I eat something that didn't agree with me? I never should have let Judy talk me into going to that Asian restaurant. Maybe I am allergic to something they use in their food. I don't need this," Sarah lamented as she slipped off her pajamas and stepped into the shower.

It was 7:15 AM by the time Sarah managed to dress, drink a quick juice and grab a bagel as she picked up her school bag. At the door to her apartment she decided to wear her sturdy walking shoes as she planned to go grocery shopping after school. She picked up a shoe and opening the laces tried to put her foot into the shoe but the shoe was too tight. "Now what is going on?" Sarah moaned. "How come my shoes are tight? I can't believe this! I will have to wear my sandals."

Even her sandals were snug but she managed to get them on. "Well, now that does it," Sarah spoke out loud. "No more Asian food. Looks like it must be loaded with salt. What else would cause my face and feet to be so bloated?"

With that Sarah closed her door, locked it and headed out to her car just as the traffic was starting to pick up on the streets of the city.

* * *

Alice was grateful she didn't have a busy schedule at work for the morning. She was having trouble focusing on her work. Something was definitely wrong with Dave. He was not himself the last few weeks and she just did not know how to reach him. He wasn't happy about Sarah moving out on her own she realized, but Sarah needed the space. Sarah was a good daughter and always stayed in touch and had been calling and sending text messages to both of them so why did Dave seem so sad? Surely he must know that a parent cannot hang on to their children forever. Alice set down her coffee cup and stared out the window. She had often wondered if they had done the right thing by only having the one child. If they had adopted two, Sarah would have had a brother or sister. Maybe things would have been better for her and maybe easier for Dave now to let go. But it was too late to rectify that. Maybe someday when Sarah gets married and has children of her own, Dave will be happier, having some grandkids to spoil. Alice smiled to herself. She wouldn't mind a few grandkids to spoil either.

Turning back to her desk Alice picked up the file laying there and glanced at the heading. Another family in crisis. Sometimes her job was very depressing; so many unhappy people and the little children always were the ones to suffer. With a sigh, she opened the folder, just as her phone rang.

Chapter 5

Regina, Saskatchewan

Alice arrived at the hospital just as Dave drove up. They dashed inside in time to see Sarah whisked into the emergency room. Stopping one of the ambulance attendants, Dave asked, "What happened. What is going on?"

The attendant glanced at them and said, "I imagine you are her parents? She was in class and she suddenly passed out. The instructor called for the ambulance when he couldn't wake her."

"Is she going to be alright?" Alice asked.

"You will have to talk to the doctor about that," the attendant stated, as he checked his watch and headed out the door.

Alice and Dave hurried over to the nurse's station. The nurse behind the desk was on the phone so they impatiently waited until she was off, then Dave asked, "What can you tell me about Sarah Knight that was just brought in by ambulance. We are her parents."

"I'm sorry, Mr. and Mrs. Knight. We don't have any information yet, but if you will have a seat in the waiting room, I will see that the Dr. talks to you as soon as he can. We will want you to fill out some forms as well."

Dave and Alice had to be content with that and taking the forms, made their way to the waiting room. There, they sat side by side and were holding hands. Neither one of them liked hospitals and their precious little girl was now in emergency. Tears streamed down Alice's face and Dave put his arm around her and hugged her tight. She buried her face in his shirt and mumbled, "Oh Dave, I am praying so hard that there is nothing seriously wrong with Sarah. So you think she is just working too hard?"

"I don't know. I just had a feeling this morning that something was going to happen. I can't explain it, but just a feeling in my gut. However, she is in good hands. Dr. Klein is the best. He will get to the bottom of this, I am sure. We have to be strong."

"I know," Alice sniffled as she straightened up and reached for a tissue. "It's just so hard to think of all that could be wrong. Sarah has always been so healthy ever since she has been with us. I know she had some health issues before we got her, but she had a clean bill of health when we adopted her."

"I know. I hope it is just working too hard. That is easy to solve. I kick myself for letting her move out. Maybe if she was still with us, we could have kept better tabs on her."

"Oh Dave, you can't smother her. She needs to stretch her wings and be a responsible adult. You can't control her life."

"I know. It is just so hard to have her all grown up. I wish I could zap her back to my little girl."

Alice reached over and patted Dave's arm, "I know. However, let's deal with one thing at a time. When this is all over, we have to have a long talk about you and your problem."

"What problem? I don't have a problem," Dave answered, but he smiled and took her hand.

* * *

"Hi Sarah!" Dr. Klein took Sarah's hand and pressed it when she opened her eyes, "How are you feeling?"

"Do you really want to know? Well, not too good. I feel like I was hit by a truck. What happened?"

"Actually, you were in class and you passed out. The instructor couldn't wake you so called the ambulance."

"Oh no! Mom and Dad will be frantic. I hope no one told them."

"They are here in the waiting room. I will let them in as soon as I am finished, but first I need to ask you some questions. How long have you been feeling sick?"

"Actually, I have been tired a lot lately, but it really hit me last night. When I woke up this morning, my face was puffy and splotchy, and then when I tried to put my shoes on, I couldn't. My feet were all swollen."

"Okay. I want to run some tests on you today. Right now, I will let your parents come in and then we will see what is what, okay?"

"Okay, though I wish no one had told my parents. They will be freaking out, especially my Dad."

Dr. Klein smiled, "Yes, I am sure he will be. You are his little princess."

* * *

Dave was not prepared for seeing Sarah with an IV in her arm, her face swollen and pale. With a lump in his throat, he leaned over Sarah and said, "Hello, Princess. How are you doing?"

Sarah opened her eyes and softly answered, "Hi Dad. I am just peachy as you can see. I think it was something I ate at that Asian restaurant. I must be allergic to something in their food."

"Hi honey," Alice stepped forward and took Sarah's hand, "Do you really think that is causing your problem? I have eaten there many times and never had any problems. I think Dr. Klein is going to run some tests this afternoon to be sure."

Sarah struggled to sit up and tried to swing her legs off the bed. "I can't be missing that many classes. Can you tell Dr. Klein I will come back this afternoon after my classes are finished?"

"I will do no such thing," Alice answered firmly, "You are staying here until those tests are done. You can make up the classes later. This is no laughing matter. Something has made you very sick and we have to get to the bottom of it."

"Better listen to your Mother," Dave added, "I also think it is important to find out what is going on. You might pass out again in class. I am sure you don't want that."

Sarah sighed and settled back on the pillow. "I guess you are right. I still don't feel very well and I am so tired. Sometimes I feel like I can't breathe. I think I could sleep for a week."

"Well, just relax and rest. We will be right here if you need us, okay?"

"Thanks, Dad. You too, Mom. You are the best parents a girl could ever ask for. I love you both so very much." With that, Sarah closed her eyes and drifted off to sleep.

Dave and Alice tiptoed out of the room so they could fill in the forms and talk without disturbing Sarah.

Chapter 6

Southern Alberta

Shane stepped out of the saddle and let the reins slide from his hands. He knew Bud would stay where he was. He had purchased the horse as a three year old at a horse sale in Lethbridge. He was started under saddle but still very green. Shane had enjoyed finishing the training and Bud had become very attached to him. He would never leave Shane stranded. That was a good thing on a cattle ranch, especially when you are miles from the ranch buildings.

"Well, Bud," Shane stroked the horse on his sleek neck, "What do you think? Is it time to move these cows to the upper pasture?"

Bud flicked his ears back and forth and stuck his nose on the front of Shane's shirt. Shane laughed and patted his nose. "You are an old flirt, Bud. You always know how to get around a guy. I would like nothing better than to stand here all day and gaze at the wonderful view before us, but April will be expecting me for dinner, so we had better get our job done."

With that, Shane swung into the saddle, whistled for Lad and Sampson and headed down the hillside toward the cows and calves grazing in the flat. When they spotted the approaching foursome, the lead cow knew what was up and started heading up the draw toward the gate. "That old girl sure saves us a lot of aggravation, doesn't she?" Shane commented to Bud and the dogs. "Now we just have to watch for stragglers. We will make it in time for dinner after all."

Shane always found himself smiling when he thought of his wife. She was getting close to her due day, but was feeling well and so excited about the baby. Shane was just as excited. He could hardly wait until he could hold his son or daughter in his arms. Thinking about his mother Amy, he thought about how hard it must have been for her to give her baby up at birth. He just could not imagine having to do something like that. It would break his heart. By rights, he should be annoyed with his biological father for not supporting Amy back then, but he didn't know his side of the story; and there always are two sides. He hadn't tried to find his father yet. He was waiting until April had their baby and harvest was over. Then he would talk to April about it and start his search.

"Come on, you critters, I don't want to be late for dinner. Lad, get that stray over there!" He whistled and Lad raced off to round up the calf that had stopped to investigate a badger hole.

* * *

April finished sewing the hem of the curtains she had made for the baby's room. She had debated for a long time about the color, but decided that blue could go for either a boy or a girl. The material she chose had stars and moons on it, with little angels in between them. She loved the material and hoped Shane would too. He always told her that he was happy with anything she was happy with. He is such a good husband, she thought and will make a wonderful father. I am so blessed to have him for my eternal partner. He has had a lot of sadness in his life, but triumphed over it all. I am so glad that he had the opportunity to know his biological mother. Amy is so special. We can count on her for anything; advice, help, pointers; anything. She seems to have everything under control. As she cut off the thread, April thought about Amy and Ivan. They had such a good marriage and two great kids. Amy was such a good role model. Shane thought the world of Ivan too, so things were good on the two ranches. Ivan and Shane worked together in haying and harvest time so that was nice, April mused. Now she only hoped that she could hang on and not have the baby until after the harvest was in. It would only be another week of so if the weather held. Her due date was in two weeks. Patting her tummy, she spoke aloud, "So are you listening? Don't get in a big hurry to see this old world. Let Daddy get his harvest done first."

Smiling, April rose and rubbing the small of her back, set her sewing aside and headed out to the kitchen to check on dinner. Shane would be home soon and she had to set the table yet.

Chapter 7

Southern Alberta

Amy set the pail down she was carrying and mopping her brow, gazed off to the west, checking for clouds. It was a beautiful day and had been nice all through the harvest for the men. Amy's garden had done exceptionally well during the summer and had produced an abundance of vegetables, which she had been sharing with Shane and April, being as April was limited to what she could handle during her late pregnancy. Amy had processed and frozen bags of peas and beans. She had pickled jars of cucumbers and now the tomatoes were starting to ripen. She still had to make some beet pickles as they were Ivan's favorite. It was a lot of work, but Amy loved every minute of it. Her mother never had a garden and Amy had often wondered what it would be like to grow her own vegetables. When she came to work at the Collins' ranch years ago, she got her first taste of gardening and she loved it. Ivan said she definitely had a green thumb, whatever that meant.

Picking up her pail and heading to the garden, Amy hoped the kids would stay playing in the fenced in yard until she was finished picking peas. Laura was a good help, but Abe always said, "me 'elp" and then proceeded to pull up the vines and everything. She hated to discourage the kids from coming to the garden as she wanted them to experience the joy of growing too, but Abe was a problem. Next year, he would be older and understand better, she hoped.

As she started to pick the peas, she thought of Shane and April and the little bundle they were expecting. April was due soon and Amy could hardly wait. Just imagine . . . . me a Grandmother, she thought. That is exciting! She really hoped nothing would spoil the happy occasion, like Shane contacting his biological father. He hadn't mentioned it lately so maybe he had second thoughts. Amy was hoping for that. She was not ready to deal with that man, now or ever. The last she heard, he was married and lived in Regina, working for the city or some such thing. She thought she heard he had a daughter, which would make her Shane's half sister. Knowing how Shane felt about family, he would be sure to want to get to know her. Amy shuttered. It was just too much to think about the consequences. Let us hope it never happens. Amy put it out of her mind and finished picking the peas. It looks like there will be another picking if the frost holds off, she acknowledged as she picked up her pail, just as Laura and Abe came bounding up to the gate.

'Me 'elp! Me 'elp!" Abe chorused as he jumped up and down by the gate. Laura pulled at his arm and tried to stop him from climbing the gate.

"Not today, my little munchkin. Mommy is all finished. Now we have to go and shell the peas. You can help with that."

Laura pouted, "Do I have to? Daddy said he found the kittens at the hay barn and I want to go see them. Can I, Mom?"

"Me too! Me too!" Abe shouted. It seemed like he always talked in doubles.

"Yes, Laura, you can go but just for a little while. I do not want you out by the barns when the men come in with the machinery. Abe, Mommy needs your help shelling the peas, okay?"

"'kay, 'kay," Abe nodded his head and took Amy's hand.

* * *

Ivan was frustrated. He only had about thirty acres to finish combining and he broke a belt on the feeder house of the combine. Now it meant a trip into town and wasted time. He glanced over to where Shane was auguring the grain from the truck into the bin. Maybe he could get him to run to town while he got the old belt removed. Ivan jumped down from the combine seat, limping a bit when his left leg took the pressure. "Okay, arthritis, you can leave any time now. I don't need you," Ivan complained as he reached down and rubbed his knee. He had noticed his knee giving him a bit of trouble at times over the last year, but had been good lately. Must be a change in the weather coming, Ivan reflected as he put on his gloves and walked to the left side of the combine.

Shane arrived just as Ivan started to release some bolts. "What's up?"

"Broke a belt. Do you think you could run to town and pick up a new one, while I get this one off?"

"Listen, why don't I do the grunt work and you go to town? You know exactly what belt you need and I can be doing this."

"I won't argue with you. My knee is kicking up again and I could use the rest. Thanks. I will be back as soon as I can. Maybe call Amy and April and let them know we might be late for our supper."

"Will do. Tool box in the combine?"

"Yep. Just by the door. Okay, I'm gone."

Ivan got into the truck parked just off the field and headed to the access road. He sure hoped the dealership had the belt in stock. Lately they didn't seem to keep as much inventory on hand. They always said they could have parts in a day or so. Ivan didn't want to wait a day or so. With just thirty acres left, it would be nice to have it finished and get the straw on the field baled before the weather changed. It was just his luck to have a break down. The feeder house belt was very common so he was confident it would be in their stock.

Turning onto the main road, Ivan increased his speed and turned on the radio. Tapping his fingers in time to the music, he let his mind wander. Of course the first thing to come to his mind was his little family. He never dreamed that he would be a happy married man and the father to two great kids, not to mention having a stepson who had always been special to him. He had a silly grin on his face when he thought about the new baby coming. Him, a grandfather? Wow! He could hardly wait to see that baby. He didn't care if it was a boy or girl. He was sure Shane didn't either. They all just wanted a healthy baby and Mom. April was a great girl, Ivan mused. She fit in so well with everyone and Amy and the kids adored her.

Amy . . . now there was one great lady. She isn't afraid to tackle anything, even if it is too big a job for her. Ivan chuckled as he remembered her first attempt at milking a cow. Amy was determined if they were going to live on a ranch and have all those cows, they should be able to milk one and not have to buy milk. He tried to tell her that they were range cows, not milk cows, but he finally gave in and brought one into the barn for her. The cow had lost her calf a day or two earlier so had lots of milk. Ivan tied her up in a stall, put a pole behind her and then let Amy in with her pail. What a commotion! Amy ended up on her backside, the cow's foot in the pail, manure on her face from the cow's tail and a look of astonishment on her face. Ivan remembered laughing so hard, he had tears running down his face but Amy was not amused. Being Amy, she got to her feet, got the cow's foot out of the pail and proceeded to manage to get a bit of milk into it, while the cow was bawling and trying to lay down. When she exited the stall, Amy had a smug look on her face as she marched past Ivan with her trophy milk. However, that was the end of the milking. To this day, they were still buying milk at the store.

Ivan slowed down, stopped for the main highway, and turned left toward the town. Enough pondering and better concentrate on my driving, he thought. With the crazy drivers out there, a person had to be on their toes all the time.

Ivan was now anxious to get his belt and return to the ranch to finish the field.

There would be time enough to reminisce when the fall work was done.

Chapter 8

Regina, Saskatchewan

The traffic was heavy just like the weather, with storm clouds threatening to burst any moment. Just the way I feel this morning, Dave thought as he maneuvered his way through the traffic to the hospital. Dr. Klein had phoned Dave at his work that morning, asking for Alice and him to come to the hospital to review Sarah's tests results. He didn't give them any hint to what the results were and that had Dave worried. Nothing could happen to his little girl. He wouldn't let it. His whole life centered on her. Surely, it was just something minor that needed the parents input before he prescribed a treatment plan. Braking for a stop light, Dave noticed that his hands were trembling. Okay; calm down, he told himself. Getting all upset isn't going to help Sarah. I have to be strong for her. He tried to smile when he thought about how anxious she would be to get out of that hospital and back into class. Boy, I sure pray that is going to happen for her. I have a bad feeling about all this. Dave wished he had eaten something for breakfast as his stomach was in knots and he could feel the beginning of a headache coming on. Alice always did tell him to start his day with a good breakfast, and then he wouldn't get these stupid headaches. He don't know if that is true, but this one is going to be bad, he can tell.

He found an available parking spot in the lot and headed into the hospital. Alice was already there, waiting for him.

"Did Dr. Klein give you any clue as to why he wants to see us?" Alice quizzed him, as she gave him a hug.

"Not a word; just could we come to the hospital to review Sarah's test results. It sounded like it was important."

"Yes, that is the feeling I got."

"Have you been in to see her?"

"No. I just peeked in and she was sleeping, so I decided to wait for you here. I didn't know what to tell her if she asked why the Dr. wanted to see us, so thought it best if we meet with him first."

Dave sighed, "I agree. What on earth could we tell her, and it would just worry her because we were called up to the hospital."

Taking a seat in the waiting area, Alice answered, "That's right. I have already notified the nurse that we are here and she will let Dr. Klein know. Why don't you sit down?"

Dave stopped pacing and took the seat next to Alice, "I don't know if I can sit. I am so worried. I just know it must be bad, if Dr. Klein thinks we had to come here."

"Dave, don't get yourself all in a stew. Remember that is not good for your stomach. I sure wish you would get that checked out. I think you have an ulcer and worrying will only aggravate it."

"I know. I know." Dave leaned back in the chair and closed his eyes, feeling the headache getting worse. He knew he was making himself sick and that was not going to help Sarah. He willed himself to calm down. Alice reached over and stroked the nape of his neck. It was very soothing and he was starting to relax when the nurse said, "Dr. Klein will see you now."

* * *

Dr. Klein had a very busy morning, and when the nurse ushered the Knight's into his office, he was just managing to have his first cup of coffee.

"Good morning. Please excuse the mess here on my desk. I am swamped these days. Can my nurse bring you anything? Coffee, juice?"

"I'm fine for now," Dave thanked him; "We don't want to take up much of your time when you are so busy. Just let us know what treatment you are prescribing for Sarah and we can get her out of here and home."

"Well, that is why I wanted you both here when we discuss this. I know this is going to be hard to hear, but Sarah is a very sick young woman. She is going into renal failure."

Alice gasped and grabbed Dave's hand. Dave was confused. "What is renal failure?"

Alice answered for Dr. Klein, "It means her kidneys are shutting down. Doctor, what does this mean in the long term?"

Dr. Klein glanced at the shocked look on Dave's face and answered quietly, "For now, we are going to start some dialysis, probably twice a week to start but eventually, I feel she is going to need a kidney transplant."

Dave got up from his chair and slammed his fists together, "I knew it! I just knew in my gut that something was wrong. Will she be able to continue with her studies? She is so looking forward to graduating."

"With care and lots of rest, she should be able to function reasonably well for a while. It is hard to make a prognosis as each individual case is different."

Alice rose and coaxed Dave to return to his seat. "Have you told Sarah yet?" she asked the Doctor.

'No; I thought we would do that together unless you would rather tell her on your own."

"I think it would be better if you were there too," Dave stated, "I know it is going to be extremely hard to see her face and not break down." Dave put his head in his hands and big sobs wracked his body. Alice leaned over, tears in her eyes and rubbed his back.

Dr. Klein rose, picked up Sarah's file and said, "When you are ready, you can meet me in Sarah's room. I am going there now to check her over. Take your time. I know this is extremely hard for you." With that Dr. Klein left, closing the door gently behind him.

* * *

Sarah was sitting up in her bed when Dave and Alice walked in. Dr. Klein was writing in her chart.

"Come in folks. I think there is a young lady here who wants to see you," Dr. Klein said as he hung the chart on the foot of the bed.

Forcing himself to look cheerful, Dave leaned over and kissed Sarah, "How are you feeling this morning?"

"Pretty chipper. Don't I look chipper?" Sarah laughed, "Hi Mom. Boy, you two are taking lots of time off work. It must be nice to be the boss and be able to do that!"

"Being the boss does have its quirks," Alice replied as she reached over and hugged her daughter, "You are looking a lot better today."

Dr. Klein cleared his throat and started, "Sarah, I asked your parents here today because we have something to discuss with you and I thought you might need the support."

Sarah settled back on her pillow and looking at Dr. Klein, replied, "I know what you want to discuss. You see, I am going through for a pharmacist, and we take a lot of background that is purely medical. I looked at my chart. I know what renal failure is."

"So you peeked," Dr. Klein, laughed, "Aren't you the smart one! So do you have any questions, then?'

"Yes. How soon do I have to start dialysis and when can I go home?"

"Right to the point. I like that in a person. Well, I would like you to have your first dialysis in the next day or so, then weekly for a while and see how that works out. As far as going home, I don't think you should live alone for a while, until we see how things go. However, you should be able to leave the hospital today. When you come in for your first treatment, we will install a PICC line, which will remain in. It is so much better than having to put in an IV every time."

Alice spoke up, "It is good she can come home with us for a while. I will take some days off work to be with her."

"That makes me very happy, to have my little girl where I can look after her," Dave said with tears in his eyes, "No one ever put anything over on you, princess. Are you sure you are feeling well enough to come home?"

"Sure. I just feel tired and I know I have a nice, soft bed in my old room. Actually, I am looking forward to having Mom's home cooking for a while." She reached over and gave Alice's hand a squeeze.

Alice squeezed back and with a break in her voice said, "You never cease to amaze me. I was prepared for you to be devastated with this news and you are taking it better than your father and I. I am so proud of you."

"And with that, I am gone," Dr. Klein looked at Sarah, "I will file your release papers. You will be notified when to come back for dialysis. Okay?"

"Thank you, Dr. You have been very kind. I imagine we will be seeing lots of each other in the next months."

"That is true, Sarah. Now you take care," and with that, the doctor left the room.

"Well," Dave said as he sat in the only available chair, "Let's have a chat about how you know so much about renal failure and fill your old Dad in."

Chapter 9

Southern Alberta

April had just put the finishing touches on the quilt she was sewing for the baby's bassinette when she felt the first pain. She dropped the quilt on the table and grabbed her stomach. "Oh, no!" she moaned, "You were supposed to hang on for another week. Then Daddy will be finished harvest." She rubbed her stomach as the pain subsided. Maybe it is just false labor, she hoped. She picked up the quilt and did the last few stitches, then bit off her thread. Picking it up, she lumbered to her feet and headed to the baby's room. Everything was ready for the baby, but she really was hoping that harvest would be finished before the event. Shane had mentioned only this morning that if the weather held, all the straw would be baled and stacked within the week. They had been very fortunate with no rain in the last while and no major breakdowns. The pasture could use some rain, so the men were torn between wanting the rain and wanting to finish baling.

April was heading to the kitchen to put on the kettle when the second pain hit her. This one was exceptionally strong and she cried out while grabbing the doorframe. Okay, April contented, I guess this is not false labor. Grabbing the phone, she dialed Shane's cell. She had just talked to him at lunchtime, so he sure will be surprised, April chuckled.

Shane answered on the first ring, "April?"

'Yep, it's me. I think we have a baby on the way . . . Shane? Shane? Well, did I lose connection?" April dialed the number again and Shane picked up, "I'm on my way; sorry. I just heard baby and jumped in my truck. Are you okay?"

"I'm fine. Don't have an accident getting here. I will be ready when you get here."

"Okay, I am south of Ivan's but should be there within ten minutes. Have you called Amy and your Mom?"

"No, but I will. You just get here safe." April hung up and dialed the Johnson ranch.

"Low . . . . Low."

"Abe honey, put Mommy on the phone, okay?"

"'Kay, 'kay. Mommy, mommy!"

April could hear Amy in the background lecturing Abe about picking up the phone. The little toy that could talk back fascinated him and no amount of talking to him had stopped him from answering. April had to smile. She had a younger sister that was the same way.

When Amy came on the line, she sounded a little frustrated, "Hello, Johnson ranch."

"Hi Amy; it's me. Shane is on his way home. I think it is time."

"Oh April, are you okay?"

"I'm fine. Shane will be here within a few minutes and I am all ready to go. I just have to call my mom and she will meet us at the hospital. Are you going to be there, too?"

"I certainly will, as soon as I can make arrangements for the kids. I'll see if I can get hold of Ivan."

However, she didn't have to; Ivan drove into the yard. Jumping out of his truck, he hurried to the house. "Shane took off from the field in such a hurry, I knew it was time, so thought I had better get home to be with the kids so you could go to the hospital."

"You never cease to amaze me. I was just going to call you. Are you sure you can stay with the kids?"

"Of course. Just call me when I am a grandpa," Ivan noted as he gave Amy a hug.

"That is a deal, and I will be a grandma. Wow!"

Amy grabbed her purse, glanced in the mirror as she hurried by and ran out to her car. I hope I get to the ranch before Shane and April leave and then I can ride with them, Amy decided. That way I can help April with the breathing.

* * *

April was really in labor. The pains were coming twenty minutes apart and strong. Amy was glad she was in the vehicle with Shane and April, so Shane could concentrate on driving and she could comfort April. She was doing very well, laughing between each contraction and commenting on whom the baby would look like. Shane was saying he hoped the baby had her nose and sense of humor. She was answering that she hoped the baby had his hair and eyes. Amy thought that was good they were concentrating on the fun part instead of the pain.

As another wave of pain hit April, Amy pressed her hand and encouraged deep breaths and huffing. Soon it was over. "Right on time," Amy said, "fifteen minutes apart. Let's hope your water doesn't break until we get to the hospital. That can be messy."

April laughed, "Well, that I sure can't control, can I? We are almost there so I don't think we have to worry. I hope Mom made it there already."

"I'm sure she is there," Shane replied, "She is so excited about her first grandchild; I just hope she didn't get stopped for speeding on the way there."

"Me too," laughed April, "She would never live that down with her sewing circle."

As they turned into the hospital grounds, they could see Millie, April's mom and Jack, April's dad standing by the door. They waved and hurried forward as Shane pulled into the parking lot.

* * *

It was 10:30 PM when Ivan got the final call from Amy that he was now a grandfather. She had been calling him every hour or so to keep him informed of the progress. It was taking a bit of time, being the first baby, but she had done well, bearing the pain and keeping a good sense of humor.

"Well, Grampa, you grandson has finally arrived. Seven pounds, five ounces and twenty inches long. He is adorable."

"So we have a grandson. That is terrific! How is April and the baby?"

"Both are doing well. April is still in the recovery room. Shane is with her, of course. I think he is the happiest guy in town tonight. He was suffering right along with April with every contraction, but is in awe of that baby. He keeps checking him to see if he is real, I think. I think I know someone else that did that too."

"Who, me? Never!" Ivan smiled to himself, "I was just hoping for good ranch hands when I get old and crippled."

Amy laughed, "You are so phony. I can read you like a book; you were worried sick when I was in labor. I love you, you big goof."

"Love you right back. When do you think you will be home?"

"We will be coming home as soon as Shane can tear himself away from his little family. April's parents left a little while ago."

"Okay, see you when you get here."

Ivan set the phone down and leaned back in his chair. He was a grandfather! Now that was something he never thought would ever happen. He never thought he would ever be a father either. He smiled as he thought about the two sleeping in the bedroom upstairs. What a blessing it was when Amy came into his life. He nearly lost her through a silly misunderstanding, but their love for each other brought them through it. Thank you, God for all my blessings, Ivan prayed silently. Please Lord; let nothing change that.

Chapter 10

Regina, Saskatchewan

Sarah didn't want her parents to know how she actually felt. She knew her dad was having a hard time dealing with things lately and seemed to be always on the edge of cracking. Her mom had enough to worry about with her dad and her job. She dealt every day with family problems.

She had a long talk with Dr. Klein before she left the hospital. Dr. Klein understood her worry about them and said she could talk to him any time about things that bothered her. Right now, she was concerned about her schooling. What if she couldn't return to class? It would mean the last four years of studies wasted. She so wanted to graduate with the rest of her class. Dr. Klein assured her if she got on dialysis, she should be able to continue for now. He also informed her that she would eventually need a kidney transplant and she should get on the list. He then told her that a family member was usually a good candidate for a transplant. Sarah didn't tell him she was adopted. It really wasn't the time just yet. She was going for her first dialysis in the morning, so would see how that was.

Alice knocked on Sarah's door and poked her head in. "Like some company?"

"Sure, come on in, Mom."

"It's not me; it's one of your classmates," Alice answered as she stepped aside. A tall, dark man stepped into the room.

Sarah struggled to sit up in the bed, "Oh, Hi Jesse. I didn't expect company. Excuse the way I look."

Jesse sat down on the only available chair, 'You look just fine to me. Your Mom was filling me in on your problems. I am so sorry to hear that. You go for dialysis in the morning?"

"Yes, first thing. It takes about 3 hours. I don't know how I will be able to keep up with my studies and take dialysis at the same time."

"You know, I had a sister on dialysis for over three years. She was on the transplant list, but nothing came up to match her; then eventually she started to fail, so I donated one of my kidneys."

"You did? That is so awesome! Did you notice any difference with yourself, only having one kidney left?"

"Not at all. Once I was healed up and back to normal. Moreover, the good thing is my sister didn't reject it and she is doing great. She is nursing in Saskatoon."

"So maybe there is hope for me?"

"Absolutely. And until you can get back to class, I can give you copies of my notes. You have your text books here?"

"Yes, Dad stopped by my apartment and picked everything up for me."

"Great! I will talk to the instructor, see if there is anything you should be aware of, and get back to you. Do you have a cell phone number I can call, or should I just call the house?"

"No, I will give you my cell number. This way, Mom and Dad don't have to be disturbed every time someone calls me."

"Okay, I will copy my notes from yesterday and today and get them to you tomorrow. You take care. Dialysis isn't that bad, they say. Just take something to read, as it does take a while. Maybe a good time to do some studying."

With that, Jesse stood up and headed to the door. Just as he reached there, Sarah said, "Thank you, Jesse."

Jesse turned and winked at her. "No problem," he said and went out, closing the door behind him.

Sarah lay back on her pillow and closed her eyes. Now wasn't that a surprise! She had noticed Jesse since the first day in class, but he was always with friends and didn't seem to notice her. She had spoken to him a few times and shared some supplies, but she could not remember ever having a lengthy conversation with him. So what brought on this "good will" visit? Not that she was unhappy about it. She had always liked Jesse, even from a distance and never heard any negative things about him. He got good marks and didn't seem to be high on parties like some of the others she could mention. A friendship with Jesse could be a good thing. Besides, he was cute.

Swinging her legs over the side of the bed, Sarah decided to get up and get dressed. She wanted to go downstairs for supper. She figured her mom had enough to do without lugging meals to her. She felt a bit light-headed, but stronger. Making her way to the bathroom, she stripped off her pajamas and stepped into the shower.

* * *

Alice heard the shower running and chuckled to herself. There was nothing like a good-looking young man to make a girl pay attention to her appearance. It was so important that Sarah keep a good attitude. Alice wasn't sorry she had contacted Allison who used to work in her department, after she remembered that Allison's daughter had a kidney transplant. She then found out that Allison had a son in Sarah's class. Allison was sure Jesse would be happy to help Sarah with her classes. Alice was grateful that Jesse had agreed. Sarah would not be happy to find out she had instigated Jesse's visit. However, what Sarah didn't know right now, wouldn't hurt her.

Hearing Dave's car drive up, Alice put the chops on to grill. She hoped Sarah ate a good supper.

Chapter 11

Southern Alberta

The days were starting to shorten and the nights had a nip of frost in the air. Leaves were falling in an assortment of sizes and array of color, covering the house yard. Amy was trying to rake them up, but Laura and Abe were having a blast, diving into the piles and scattering the leaves everywhere. Amy eventually gave up and joined them. Laughing, she gathered an armful of leaves and threw them high into the air. Abe shrieked and ran behind Laura.

"I'm going to get you," Amy yelled as she darted around Laura and made a grab for Abe. He took off running and was giggling so hard, he misstepped, bumped into the wheelbarrow and fell down. Amy caught him, only to have Laura grab her from behind and stuff leaves down her shirt. Soon all three of them were rolling on the ground, laughing and throwing leaves everywhere.

"Okay, enough, enough!" Amy moaned as she lay on the ground with both kids on top of her, "You are squashing Mommy."

"Quash, quash," Abe mimicked and then he suddenly rolled off her stomach and took off running toward the house. Amy glanced over and saw Ivan standing there. Abe had spotted him. "Daddy, Daddy!" he shouted as he launched himself at Ivan.

Ivan grabbed him and set him on his shoulder, "Are you picking on Mommy? Looks like you and Laura got the best of her, too."

Laura jumped up and brushed the leaves off her clothes, "We were just having fun, Daddy. Mommy tried to catch us, but we threw leaves on her. She looked so funny, Daddy."

"I can see that," Ivan smiled, "Do you think you guys can stop with the playing long enough to get cleaned up and go to town with me?"

Amy sat up. "What's up?"

"I have to go to town for some lumber to repair the corrals, as I will be weaning soon. I was wondering if you had any shopping to do, or anything else you need. I thought you might enjoy a break away. We could stop for a treat with the kids if you like."

"A treat! Let's go, Mommy. What treat, Daddy?" Laura was ecstatic.

"Reat, 'reat," Abe copied as he starting squirming to be put down off Ivan's shoulder, "We go; we go!"

Amy laughed, "Well it looks like I am out numbered. Do I have ten minutes to get myself and the kids cleaned up?"

"I think that can be arranged. I will get the car seats into the truck."

Amy hurried the kids into the house. So much for the plans she had for today, but it was a real treat to spent time as a family in town. She would pick up some groceries while there and Abe needed a new pair of boots, now that winter was in the offing. He was growing so fast. Washing Abe's face and hands, she couldn't get over how much he resembled his dad, right down to the unruly hair and pronounced chin. Laura, on the other hand, looks nothing like either of us, Amy mused. She has curly, blond hair, not auburn like mine or brown like Ivan's. Her eyes are brown though, but her nose is cute, not a honker like Ivan's or mine. Amy laughed to herself. Yes, Ivan and she both had prominent noses, so it was a good thing the kids didn't inherit it.

Laura had washed her hands and face, but neglected to comb her tangled hair. Amy grabbed the brush and to Laura's chagrin, began brushing the tangles out. "Ouch, Mommy; that hurts," Laura whined as Amy brushed the leaves and tangles out.

"Well, maybe you should try to brush it yourself every morning so Mommy doesn't have to," Amy commented as she did a final brush through and tapped Laura on the nose, "There; all done. Now let's get out to the truck or Daddy will leave without us."

Ivan had the seats all secured in the club cab truck they had purchased after they had the two children and was waiting by the door. Getting the kids into their seats, he then watched Amy coming from the house. She still looks as young as the day she came to work on Collins' ranch, Ivan thought as he watched her. Ivan remembered the struggles Amy had, dealing with the lies her mother had told her about her father and her baby and with her first failed marriage. He also remembered the struggle she had with her faith. She eventually joined the Mormon Church so they could be sealed in the temple. To this day, she still had some questions about the church, but was happy to go with him on Sunday and have the kids brought up in the church. Because of her mother and the way she dealt with her religion, Amy was very skeptical about religion in general when she first moved to the ranch. However, through Laura, Shane's adopted mother, she started to understand that religion is really the people who are involved. Amy's mother was a very bitter, unhappy woman and that was the side of religion that Amy saw.

Amy's mother had never once come out to the ranch to see them. Ivan and Amy made it a point to drive to Medicine Hat at least twice a year, so she could see the grandkids. She was living in an assisted living complex and seemed happy enough there. She treated the kids well, and they knew she was 'Gramma' but she never agreed to come for an extended visit to the ranch. Ivan felt that Amy was relieved in some ways. Her mother and she never got along.

As Amy got into the truck, Ivan also got in, reached over and gave Amy a kiss. "What was that for?" Amy smiled. "Just because," Ivan answered and started the truck.

"Kiss; kiss!" Abe echoed, and then started laughing. Laura poked him and giggled.

* * *

It was a fantastic day. They picked up the lumber first then headed to the dry goods store to look for boots. Things were on sale, so they managed to find a good pair of winter boots for Abe. They bought them a little big as they realized he was probably going to be growing over winter. Abe was proud of his new boots and wanted to wear them right away, but Ivan convinced him they were for when the snow came. From there they headed to the Dairy Queen and enjoyed a treat. Abe managed to make quite a mess, but enjoyed himself immensely. Laura, getting to the age where little brothers were gross, was disgusted with the mess he made. "Mommy, don't let him touch me with his fingers," she implored Amy, "I don't want to be all sticky."

"Don't you worry, my young lady, I will take care of the sticky," and with that, Ivan took Abe out of his chair and headed to the bathroom.

"There now, quit making a fuss, Laura. Abe is young yet and not as careful as you. I am proud of you and how grown up you have become, but we must be tolerate of other people."

"I am, but Abe is not other people. He is my brother and he is messy."

When Ivan returned with Abe, they headed to the grocery store and then home. It had been a good afternoon. Carrying the groceries into the house, Amy noticed the light flashing on her telephone. Knowing there was a message; she set the groceries on the cupboard, and pushed the button.

It was April and she sounded like she was crying, "Oh, Mom, can you come over right away? I am so scared and I don't know what to do."

Chapter 12

Southern Alberta

It was Shane and April's first fight. Not that it was actually a fight, so to speak, but a rather large disagreement. Amy hated being in the middle of it, but April sounded so upset on the message she left on Amy's answering machine. Amy had headed right over to the Collins ranch, leaving Ivan to put the groceries away and watch the kids. April met her at the door, with the baby in her arms.

"Oh, Mom; I thought you weren't going to come."

"We were gone to town. It was a spur of the moment trip. I should have called you to see if you needed anything, but didn't think of it. I'm sorry."

'Don't be sorry. I am just glad you are here now. Just let me put the baby down and then we can talk."

Amy watched April leave the room with her son. They decided to call him Michael Shane, after April's father, whose middle name was Michael and of course, Shane after his Dad. He was a good baby so far, sleeping four hours at a stretch, so April was getting some rest between feedings.

When April returned to the kitchen, Amy asked, 'Where's Shane?"

"I don't know," April replied as tears welled up in her eyes, "We had a huge argument and he left. That was hours ago. He has some insane notion that he wants to find his real father. I told him Ivan was his father. I didn't want him running off, looking for his biological father. Do you know where Shane's father is?"

"I don't want to take sides in this, but Shane did mention to me some time ago that he wanted to look his father up. I didn't support him then, and I still don't. Even if I knew where his father was, I will not be party to seeing him hurt. His real father rejected him before he was born. Will he have changed? Who knows? I just know I don't want to see Shane hurt."

"I don't either, but he seems so intent on doing this. I begged him to leave it alone and let things be. We have our own little family. We have you, Ivan, and the kids. My family is large and supportive. I know he thinks that family history is not complete unless he has his real father involved, but look at how many children never know their real parents. He is so fortunate to have found you."

"Well, that is a long story. It certainly was by accident, but sometimes I think there was a higher power directing our footsteps back then. I just know I am so very happy to have Shane in my life and now you and Michael. I just wish Shane would be content with that."

"He seemed so angry with me because I didn't understand his need to find his father. I don't know where he went and when he is coming back. I am so scared I have ruined everything," and with that, April started to cry.

Amy rose from her chair and gave April a hug, "Don't worry; he will be back. He just needs some cooling off time. I have never mentioned any of this to Ivan as I didn't want him getting upset over all this, but maybe I had better say something now, as it looks like Shane is going to pursue this."

"I'm so sorry to dump all this on you," April wiped her eyes, "You really think Shane will be back soon?"

"I'm sure. As soon as he realizes what he has to lose. I don't think he is going to give up on the father thing, so you and I will have to deal with it. Maybe his father will deny him, and then things will get back to normal. We can only hope. I know that sounds cruel, but I am like you; I don't want change in our lives here. Everything is so wonderful."

"I second that. Things are great. I will try to be supportive when he returns. Just be prepared to accept whatever will be, as I will have to. You are the best. Love you."

"Love you too. Take care and give that baby a big hug for me when he wakes up. If you and Shane need some time alone, just bring Michael over to us. The kids will love it."

"Thanks. We will see how things go."

With that, Amy hurried out of the door and into her car. She was now anxious to get home and have a talk with Ivan. She didn't want Shane blurting something out to him before he was prepared.

Chapter 13

Regina, Saskatchewan

Dave could not be more proud of Sarah if she was his own flesh and blood. She was taking everything in stride as she went weekly for her dialysis and still kept up with her studies. The main irritation for her was the dialysis site that they had to install which made it difficult for showering and wearing some of her clothes. Otherwise, she seemed to be doing well. Of course, it helped that the cutest guy in her class was helping her with notes and information when she had to miss a class. Dave had to admit Alice contacting Allison and getting her son to help had been a good thing.

After a lengthy discussion with Dr. Klein, Alice and Dave had persuaded Sarah to give up her apartment and move back home for the time being. When she finished her schooling and her kidney issue was resolved, then maybe she could start looking for another place. Dave, Alice and Sarah had packed up her stuff and gave notice the week before. The landlord was very understanding, being as it was a health issue and didn't even demand the extra month's rent money.

Now the only problem seems to be my own making, Dave thought, as he drove into his parking spot at work and shut off the engine. I have to learn to relax and get my stomach settled down. Maybe I should see a Dr. and find out what is going on. Alice could be right. Maybe it is an ulcer. Lately, there has been a lot of talk about treating it with antibiotics. If that is all it takes, maybe I had better go.

Dave locked his car and walked toward the main doors. There is time enough to think on this later. Right now, I have a meeting in ten minutes.

* * *

Alice put the last of the buns she was making into the heated oven, and checked the temperature. Taking the pan of buns that she just took out of the oven, she headed for the counter and popped them onto the wire racks sitting there. Ripping off a paper towel, she mopped her forehead, and grabbing her cup of coffee, sat down on the chair nearest to her.

It had been a busy morning. She was returning to work in two days and wanted to get a lot of the work caught up at home. With Sarah at home again, she wanted to be sure she was eating correctly. She was doing so much better since the dialysis and Alice was praying that continued. She had a long talk with Dr. Klein only a few days ago, and he assured her that Sarah was indeed responding very well to the treatments, but he still thought that she should be on the waiting list for a kidney. She was young and a very good candidate for a transplant. Alice didn't even want to think about that yet.

Right now, Alice's focus was to be sure Sarah was taken care of and eating well. She was on a special diet because of her kidney failure. While on her own, Alice knew that Sarah had been consuming many processed meats and packaged items, which are all high in salt content, which was bad for her kidneys. Now that she is home, her diet will be far healthier, Alice contended, as she rose to check on her buns.

* * *

"Do you want to stop for a quick snack or something, before you head home?" Jesse asked, as he picked up his textbooks and looked over at Sarah.

"Why not? Sounds like a plan. Where do you want to meet?"

"You pick. I'm open to anywhere."

"How about Arby's? It's right on the way home for both of us."

"Great. See you there."

Sarah gathered up her books and making sure her desk was clear, headed out to her car. Unlocking her doors, she slid behind the wheel and laid her books on the seat next to her.

"Well, Jesse finally has asked me for something other than school work," Sarah voiced aloud as she started her engine, "I thought he would never ask. I know I shouldn't get my hopes up because what guy wants to be stuck with a girl that is having health problems? Nevertheless, it is nice that he finally decided to spend a bit of time with me. I guess a little fast food once in a while won't kill me, if I can spend more time with Jesse."

Sarah contended that she was very grateful to Jesse for his help over the last while. Because of him, she was able to stay up to date in her studies. All the information he had copied for her was a Godsend. When she had to go for dialysis, he would come by that evening with the notes for that day. He always spent time talking to her Dad and Mom, but made a point of not being alone with her. Sarah thought it was out of respect for her parents at first, but later, she thought it might be because he did not want her to take his help the wrong way. Well, she did appreciate all his help, but was grateful that he finally seemed to want to spend a bit of extra time with her.

Although her future was uncertain, Sarah was ever grateful to Dr. Klein for being sure she understood her options and what to expect. She knew she would eventually need a transplant, but was hoping that it would be delayed until she was through school. Living on dialysis for the rest of her life was not an option she wanted to think about. Thinking about the surgery was not fun either. Usually the donor was someone who had died, so that was not a pleasant thought. Although there were live donors, they were usually family member. Sarah had told Dr. Klein she was adopted. He had hinted at a family member being her donor so he was surprised when he found that out. However, he assured her that a donor did not have to be blood related, just have matching blood. Therefore, they would wait and see what happened in the next months.

Chapter 14

Southern Alberta

Shane was disgusted with himself. He had handled that all wrong. Now April was annoyed with him, and he knew Amy would be, too. Shutting the engine off, Shane stepped out of the truck, and sauntered over to the creek. Because of the lack of moisture, the once roaring waterway was just a trickle. Ivan had mentioned only the day before that he had only seen that creek dry once in his years on the ranch. Scanning the sky to the west, Shane could see clouds building up. With any luck, it would rain. Could sure use a two-day rain, Shane thought. That would give the pastures a start for the next year.

Thinking about Ivan, Shane wondered if he should have a talk with him. Maybe by doing that, it wouldn't be so hard for Ivan when I do look for my dad. On the other hand, would it be easier to try to contact my dad, and if successful, then let Ivan and Amy know. Maybe he will reject me, as Amy said he did before I was born. Then I won't have to tell anyone. I thought I was doing the right thing by discussing it with April before I went ahead with my plans. I sure didn't expect the result I got. I guess I should have approached the situation a different way. I love my little family so much; I don't want anything to change that. I hope April will forgive me for upsetting her.

Looking at his watch, Shane realized he had been driving around for hours. He headed back to his truck and climbed in. Bowing his head, he offered a prayer that April would be forgiving. Sometimes, it is only God who can solve these things, Shane thought. Praying for guidance, Shane decided to leave it all in God's hands. Only He would know the correct thing to do. As he prayed, that still, small voice spoke to him, saying, 'Go home to your wife and child.' Starting the truck, Shane did just that.

* * *

Amy arrived home from April's, only to find Ivan trying to make grilled cheese sandwiches for the kids.

"I'm glad you are here," Ivan exclaimed, "I have made three sandwiches and burned every one. The kids are not happy with me."

Amy laughed, "You have your pan too hot. Here, let me take over."

"Gladly. How's April?"

"She will be okay. We will talk later."

"Oh, it's that bad, is it?"

Amy buttered the sides of the bread, and laid it in the pan, "Well, that depends."

"Mommy, Daddy can't make good grilled cheese. He burned them all the time,"

Laura informed Amy, "Good that you came back. We needed you."

Amy ruffled Laura's hair and gave her a hug, "I need you too, so don't worry. I'm not going anywhere."

Once the kids were fed, Ivan gave the kids their baths while Amy cleaned the kitchen. Rinsing the last of the plates and putting them in the dishwasher, Amy wiped down the table and grabbing the broom, swept the floor. When she heard the patter of little feet coming, she knew the kids were ready for bed and coming for their good night hugs.

'Hug; hug," Abe chattered as he reached up his arms to Amy. Picking him up, she gave him a big bear hug. He giggled and said, "'Nough, 'nough!"

Laura was busy picking out a bedtime story. Ivan entered and taking the book, glanced over at Amy, "Your turn or mine?"

"I'm going to put a load of wash in, so could you do the honors tonight?"

"Sure. Come on kids. Let's see what Mona the cow is up to."

* * *

It was an hour later and Amy and Ivan were relaxing in the family room, when Ivan questioned, "Well, are you going to tell me what is up with the young newlyweds?"

"Oh, Ivan, I just don't know where to start."

"How about the beginning?"

"Okay. First, I don't want you to get upset. This is not a sure thing yet, but I want you to be forewarned."

"Now I am starting to get worried. 'Fess up."

"Some time ago, Shane came to me to discuss something. It was back in the summer and he said he just wanted to warn me so I would be prepared when the time came."

"Time came for what?"

"He's planning to try to contact his biological father."

Ivan stared at Amy, "Is this what happened? Is that what April was upset about?"

"Indirectly, yes. Shane finally decided to do this and mentioned it to April. She was very upset about it. She thinks he is making a mistake. I do too, but as I told Shane at the time, it is his decision. I don't want to see him hurt. If his father is still the same, he will reject him and that will hurt. I was also concerned about how you would react. That is why I never mentioned anything to you in case he changed his mind. No sense in upsetting more people than necessary."

"So where is Shane?"

"April doesn't know. He took off when they had words. She is so worried that he won't come back."

"Shane will be back; don't worry. He loves his family and that baby is his life. He is probably just off thinking things over. Maybe he will change his mind. I hope so, but for purely selfish reasons on my part. I am content with Shane as my stepson and Michael as my grandson. Will that change if he finds his real father?"

"I don't think so. Shane loves you. I think he is doing this because of the church. He feels he must have his family history correct. What do you think?"

"Well, we do stress family history, so maybe that is true. I also think he probably has a desire to know his real father."

"He will probably be very disappointed. However, I guess he will have to resolve that himself. I just hope April and he can come to some agreement on this issue."

"Me too. Nevertheless, they are intelligent young people, so I am sure it will work out. Let's go to bed. I have an early day tomorrow. I will be helping Ward's move their cattle home."

"I am so glad you are taking this well. I wish all men were as secure in their skin as you are."

"I don't know about that, but I do know I can't control Shane and what he wants and thinks. He is a talented and smart young man. He will do what is right for everyone, and I know he will always be in our lives. Don't you?"

"Yes, I know you are right. That little family is a special part of this family. I love having a family."

"I do, too. That won't change. I will have a talk with Shane first chance I get. Now, let's go to bed."

Chapter 15

Regina, Saskatchewan

Dave just knew it was not going to be a good day. It started out with Sarah's car having a flat tire. She was running late for her treatment, so Dave had to drive her, which put him late for his meeting with the Mayor. Why today of all days, Dave thought angrily. I sure don't need the extra frustration. Parking his car at the first available meter, he jumped out of the car, shoved some coins into the slot and dashed up the steps to the city hall. He had no idea why the Mayor wanted to see him. As far as he knew, everything had been resolved at their last meeting. But knowing the Mayor, she marched to her own tune, so who knows what she has up her sleeve now, Dave voiced silently as he opened the door and headed inside.

"Have a seat, Mr. Knight. The Mayor is on the phone right now, but will be with you shortly," the secretary smiled at Dave. Smiling back, he took a seat near the water cooler and picked up a magazine.

The 'shortly' ended up being over a half hour. Dave was starting to get antsy, as he knew he had lots of work on his desk. When the secretary ushered him into the Mayor's office, the Mayor laid down a file and standing, offered her hand.

"Thank you for coming, Dave. I am sorry about the wait, but I just got off the phone with the auditor. It appears we have a problem."

"A problem? What kind of problem?"

"Well, we are not sure yet, but it appears there is a discrepancy in the funds in your department. The accounts just don't seem to balance."

Dave stomach started to knot up, "When was this discovered?"

"During the last audit. We didn't say anything right away, as we wanted to double check the figures, but there definitely is a shortage. Ultimately, you are the man in charge, so I called you in."

"But, but . . . ." Dave stammered, "I don't know what to say. All my employees are long term. They do their job efficiently and many work overtime on their own time, just to keep things running smoothly."

"Well, someone is skimming funds somewhere. Have you noticed anything different about any of your staff, like seeming to have more money? Noticed any of them seem to be gambling, or drinking, or heaven forbid, doing drugs?"

"Am I under suspicion also?" Dave blurted out.

"Of course not, but you can see why I called you here to my office. We couldn't take the chance that someone in you employ would hear us on the phone."

"Yes, I can see that. Thank you for alerting me to the problem."

"Okay, this is what we are going to do. The sooner we get this ball rolling, the better." The Mayor leaned forward and pushed a file toward Dave. He reluctantly picked it up.

* * *

Wouldn't you know it! Just because I slept in, I had to have a flat tire, Sarah moaned, as she settled in the chair for her treatment. Poor Dad. It was all he needed this morning when he had a meeting at the Mayor's office. If Mom hadn't already been gone to work, she could have driven me and saved Dad. Sarah smiled at the perky young nurse that came in to hook her up to the dialysis. Everything was routine, so no need for discussion. Sarah let her mind wander as she settled back in the chair. Things were going well with her classes. Jesse was a doll and was keeping her up to date on the classes she missed. He was starting to spend more time with her and they had some interesting discussions about the course and the new things being taught. Her Mom and Dad had grown accustomed to seeing Jesse and she in the living room, their heads poured over their textbooks. Even Dad is starting to loosen up a bit, she smiled to herself. He is always so uptight. Mom thinks he is working himself into an ulcer. I sure hope not. Maybe I will have to persuade him to get to the Dr. and see what's up. He worries so much about me and forgets about himself. Mom worries about all of us. I don't know how she does it. She works full time, keeps the house and yard up and worries about me. Sarah closed her eyes and settled back in the chair, trying to relax and get the treatment over with.

Dr. Klein poked his head in to say hi, but noticed she had her eyes closed and quietly closed the door.

* * *

Alice was the first home and as she unlocked the door, she could hear the phone ringing. Thinking it was probably Dave or Sarah, she quickly grabbed the receiver and answered without checking caller ID. "Hello," She said breathlessly.

There was a pause, then, "Hello. Is this the David Knight residence?"

"Yes, it is. Who's calling?"

"Is David Knight there? I would like to speak to him."

"No, I'm sorry. He isn't home from work yet. Who is this?"

"When will he be home?"

"Listen; I am not answering any more questions until you identify yourself."

"My name is Shane Collins. I need to talk to David Knight."

"Can you leave a number where you can be reached?"

"No. I will call back when he is home, if you can give me a time he will be in."

"I expect him home within the hour, unless he has a late meeting."

"Okay, I will call back then. Thank you."

Well, wasn't that weird, Alice thought as she set down the phone. She stepped to the closet and hung up her coat, then headed into the bathroom to wash up before starting supper. What was all that about? She had never heard of a Shane Collins. Probably some guy looking for a job. However, why wouldn't he call the office?

* * *

"What a day," Dave grumbled as he kissed Alice's cheek and sat down at the table, "First, Sarah has a flat and I have to run her way over to the hospital which put me late for my meeting with the Manor. Then she made me cool my heels in her waiting room for nearly an hour, which put me way behind at work. Then our main computer decided to take today off, so everything had to be done manually, which is above most of these young people today. What kind of training are we giving these kids, where they can't even add up two columns or even use an old fashioned calculator?"

Alice rolled her eyes as she removed the potatoes from the stove and drained them, "I imagine in the future, they will be saying the same about us, Dave."

"And that's not all. On the way home, some idiot ran a red light and T-boned a half-ton truck, which made the rest of us all witnesses, so I was stopped there. I'm sorry I am late. It has just been one of those days."

"Don't worry. Sarah isn't home yet. Does she have a ride?"

"Yes, she said Jesse was going to bring her home. They should be here by now."

"Speaking of Jesse, do you think things are heating up between those two?"

"What do you mean, heating up?" Dave growled.

"Don't get your tail in a knot. What I mean is do you think they might start dating?"

'Sarah has enough to worry about without guys," Dave answered as he got up to start setting the table, "Do you think we made a mistake by having him help her with her studies?"

"Not at all. I think Jesse is a fine young man. We are so lucky he is willing to help Sarah out. They have been spending quite a bit of time together."

"Speaking of the devil, or I should say kids, I think they just drove up."

"Oh, before I forget, you had a phone call earlier. The guy wanted to talk to you and seemed persistent. Said his name was Shane Collins and he plans to call back this evening."

"I don't know any Shane Collins. Must be someone looking for a job, or to sell something. Just tell him I'm not home if he calls back."

Chapter 16

Southern Alberta

"Well, that went well," Shane told himself sarcastically, "Why did I have to sound like such an idiot? Who ever I was talking to must think I am a complete nutcase. I have to settle down."

Shane put the phone down, settled back in his chair, and picked up his glass. April had gone to visit her mother in Lethbridge for a few days, so he thought it would be an opportune time to make the call to his father. He managed to find Dave's phone number and address from the Regina phone book that his friend Jason had. He didn't tell Jason why he was interested in Regina; just he was always looking for family members. He didn't tell him the family was one he had never met. Shane had remembered Amy telling him years before that she thought his father was living in Regina. Not that she was telling him anything now. She was silent about the whole situation. He knew April had called her when they had their disagreement, but Amy had never mentioned it to him. Maybe she thinks if she ignores it, I will let it go away. Someday, she will understand why I have to do this. Ivan too. Shane rubbed his hand over his face. Speaking of Ivan, I still have to talk to him; make him understand that Dave will never take his place in my life. I owe him that much.

Getting up from his chair, Shane headed to the kitchen. Taking the skillet from the cupboard, he grabbed a couple of eggs from the fridge, and broke them into a dish. Adding a little milk, he whipped it together and poured the mixture into the pan. Looks like scrabbled eggs and toast tonight, Shane decided. April will be home tomorrow and I will be looking forward to that. I really miss her and Michael.

* * *

Shane had just finished supper and cleaning up the kitchen, when the knock came at the door. The dogs didn't bark, so Shane was sure it was someone they knew. Sure enough, when he looked out, Ivan standing on the porch.

"Well, come on in. What are you doing, roaming around at this time of night, and without your family?"

"Hello to you, too. Just thought I would come over and see how you are managing without the little family. Amy said you didn't come over for a meal while April was gone, so she wondered if you were sick or something."

Shane laughed, "I can see her thinking that. Actually, I have been trying to get the roof finished on that shelter before the cold weather sets in. It has kept me pretty busy."

"Why didn't you call? I could be helping you."

"With your bad knee? The last thing you need is crawling around on a roof. I did okay. I finished it today. April will be home tomorrow. I can't wait. I miss them so much."

"I can imagine. I miss Amy and the kids if they just go to town for the day. I do not even want to think of life without them. I never ever dreamed I would be a husband, let alone a father. I wasn't young when Amy came into my life. What a blessing she has been."

"To all of us. I am so happy that I was able to find my biological mother. I don't know if Amy has told you, but I am pursuing my search for my real father."

"Yes, she did mention it to me. Have you thought this through completely? You know that things will change in your life once you make contact with him. He may or may not be what you expect. By bringing him into your life will upset all our lives."

"I know how Mom feels about this, but I hope she can understand why I have to do this. Do you understand? My real Dad will never take your place. You have always been there for me, even when Dad . . . or I should say, Grampa Abe was alive. Nothing will change that. However, I need to do this for my kids. They have a right to know their lineage for their family history."

"Don't do this just for the church and your family. Be sure it is the thing you want to do for yourself. I was fortunate, as I never had to make that kind of choice in my life. My mother passed away when I was young, my father nearly abandoned me, but Abe and Laura took me under their wing. They wanted to adopt me, but my dad wouldn't allow it. I was never close with my real father, so even sometimes knowing who your father is doesn't make a difference. Just be sure you want to do this before you upset the apple cart, so to speak."

"I appreciate you coming over, Ivan, but my mind is made up. I have already put a call in to Regina. He wasn't home so I will try later."

"Well, good luck. You are like a son to me and I don't want to see you hurt. You can talk to me about this any time. Keep me posted, okay?"

"I will."

Ivan got up to leave, grabbing his cap by the door, "Be considerate of your Mom. She is having a struggle with this, so don't bring it up in front of her, okay?"

"Okay; I might not have any luck, and then there will be no need for her to know I even contacted Dave. This will just be between us, all right?"

"Perfect. Give April and Michael a hug for me when they get home. Bring them over for supper some night. Amy loves company."

"Will do. Have a good night, and thanks, Ivan."

"No problem. Take care." With that, Ivan stepped out the door and sauntered to his truck. Lad and Sampson danced around him, until he reached down and petted each one. When he got into his truck, they returned to the porch.

* * *

Shane watched Ivan drive away. *I am so lucky to have that man in my life. He really cares about family. When I was a kid, I wanted to be just like Ivan.* Shane laughed to himself. *Well, I guess in many ways, I really am a lot like him. We both love ranching, trucks, family, and wide, open spaces, not to mention the church.* Being as Shane was adopted by Abe and Laura, he had been raised in the church, while Ivan had joined after he was old enough to make that commitment himself. They had both gone on missions; Ivan to Scotland, and Shane to Italy. *So we do have many similarities,* Shane mused. *I just hope I can be as good a father and husband.*

Thinking of fathers, Shane looked at the time. It was 9:00 PM, so he decided now was a good time to try that call again. Picking up the phone and checking the number he wrote on the paper, Shane dialed.

"Hello, Knight Residence."

"May I speak with David Knight, please?"

"May I say whose calling?"

"Shane Collins."

"I'm sorry; Dave is unavailable. If this is about a job, I can give you his office number and you can call there tomorrow."

"It's not about a job. It is personal."

"What do you mean personal?"

"May I ask, are you David's wife?"

"Yes, I am Alice Knight."

"Please. I really need to talk with him."

"Why?"

"This is very difficult for me, and I really don't want to cause any problems, but ask him if he knew a girl by the name of Amy."

"Why on earth would I ask him that? He probably knew many girls by that name in the past years. Did she work for him?"

"Hardly. They went to school together back in Medicine Hat. I really need to talk to David about this. Is he there?"

"Just a minute. I will see if he is available."

Shane waited on the line for what seemed like forever, but eventually the phone was picked up.

"Dave Knight here. What is this about my school in Medicine Hat?"

Shane hesitated, then spoke, "Hello, my name is Shane Collins. A couple at Milk River, Alberta adopted me. My biological mother went to school with you at Medicine Hat. Her name was Amy. She gave me up for adoption as she was only sixteen years old. She told me you are my father."

There was dead silence on the other end of the line. Then there was an abrupt reply, "I only have one child and she lives here with me. Don't call here again." With that, the line went dead.

Chapter 17

Regina, Saskatchewan

"What was that all about?" Alice asked, as Dave walked into the kitchen.

"Oh, just some guy looking to get a job with the city. His mother knew me from high school, so he thought he could get a reference from me. I can't believe how nervy some people are."

"Well, he did seem a bit pushy when he called earlier. I guess you can't blame a guy for trying, right?"

"Huh . . . Yah, I guess that is true. Well, I think I will go watch some TV for a while. I am going to make an early night. I have a big day tomorrow."

"Okay. I am just going to finish here and maybe read for a while. Sarah has already gone to bed. She looked tired tonight."

Dave kissed Alice and nodded, "I noticed that too. I sure hope she is doing okay. When does she see Dr. Klein again?"

"I think next week. She is due for blood work then."

"Good. We want to stay on top of everything." With that, Dave left the room, headed into the family room and clicked on the TV. He surfed until he found a cop show and settled back in his chair.

When they say your past can come back to haunt you, no truer words were ever spoken, Dave acknowledged to himself. He hated lying to Alice, but didn't know what to say. He hadn't thought of Amy for years. Maybe it was something he wanted to put out of his mind. He vaguely remembered her coming to him and saying something about a baby, but how did he know it was his? She was running wild; who knows whom she had been with? How was he even going to explain this to Alice and Sarah if it is true?

How will he know if it is true? He couldn't even remember what Amy looked like. What if he really had a son out there? Dave shook his head. And I thought my day was bad before! This really tops it off. With how persistent that person was, would he give up just like that? Dave really did not believe it.

Checking the time, Dave decided he had better get some sleep. They were setting up the sting at work tomorrow, so he had to be on top of his game if they were going to catch the thief. He just hoped he would be able to sleep.

* * *

Alice laid her book aside and turned over in the bed. She wasn't concentrating on her story anyway. There was something fishy about that phone call Dave received. She figured there was more to it than Dave was letting on. He hardly ever watched TV after nine o'clock at night, so why tonight? It was almost as if he didn't want any more questions. Who really was Shane Collins? I don't believe that person was looking for work. He told me it was personal, but Dave tried to say it was about work. I don't know. Dave had been so pre-occupied with something this last while. He did mention some problems at work. Was this Shane part of that? Why would he call Dave here at home? Moreover, who was Amy? Some old girlfriend, or not so old? Okay, girl, get hold of yourself. Stop imagining things. You have to trust Dave. He has always been honest and forthright. Hasn't he? Alice reached up and shut off the light. She had to let it go and get some sleep. She had a busy day tomorrow.

Chapter 18

Southern Alberta

"Well, I can't say I wasn't warned," Shane spoke aloud as he set down the receiver, "He sure was abrupt. He didn't even listen or want to hear what I had to say. How can he not realize I am his son?" Shane leaned back in his chair and stared out the window. "Well, I'm not giving up that easy. The next step is to see him face to face. Maybe then he will realize I am not going away."

Shane got up and shut off the lights. Tomorrow he would check with April and if she were agreeable, they would take a trip to Regina sometime in the next week or so. Maybe if Dave saw his grandson, he would have a different attitude. "I realize his wife probably doesn't know anything about this, so I will have to see him at his work. Mom said he worked for the city, so I will go to the city hall to find out where. I bet he will be surprised when I show up." Shane laughed to himself. He thought he would be more upset about Dave's denial, but being forewarned had helped. He wasn't going to say anything to Ivan or Amy until he actually was able to make contact. Then if Dave accepted him and his family, he would have to tell them. Making his way to the bathroom, Shane washed up and headed to bed. April would be home in the morning and he could hardly wait.

* * *

"So he really is going through with this?" Amy quizzed Ivan, as she put the final changes on the chair she was painting. She found the best time to do something like that was when the kids were in bed. Abe just could not keep his fingers off the paint.

Ivan hung his jacket on the peg and headed to the fridge to get a drink, "It sounds like it. He seems set on it. I think he is strong and even if he gets a rejection, he can take it. It helps that he has April and Michael. No matter what happens with his father, he also knows he still has them and of course, us. I think we have to respect him in this decision. We don't have to like it, but let the chips fall where they may."

Amy sighed, "I know. I just was hoping he had changed his mind. Did he get in touch with Dave?"

"Not yet. I guess he phoned his house, but he wasn't home yet. I imagine he has tried again now."

"I sure wish I could be a little fly on the wall when Shane says he is his son. I bet he never told his wife he had another child."

"Maybe he is in denial. If he is, he will blow Shane off. However, I don't think Shane will let it go at that. I bet that if his father denies him, he will demand a test. If he does, will you be willing to be tested?"

"Surely it won't come to that. Why would I want to prove that Dave is Shane's father? Why would I want to help out that relationship?"

"Because you love Shane," Ivan said simply.

Amy stood up after finishing the last coat of paint on the chair and looked at Ivan, "Yes, of course I love Shane, but I'm not stupid. Why would I jeopardize what we have here, just to prove to Dave that Shane is his son?"

"Again, because you love Shane. This is important to him. He needs your support in this. Why are you being so difficult in this?'

Amy stomped out to the entry and put her paint and brushes away where the kids couldn't reach them. When she came back into the kitchen, she answered Ivan, "Because that man would not support me when I needed it. He denied that my baby was his, accused me of sleeping around, and then merrily went on his way, while I had to go to a home for unwed mothers, come back and put up with the sanctions of my strict mother. He didn't have to go through anything. He graduated with honors while I was in the Home giving birth to his child, which I then had to give up. That is why I can't forgive him." Amy grabbed a juice from the fridge and took a big drink, while trying to get control of her temper.

Ivan came up behind her and stroked her arm. Amy turned and hugged him, "I just get so mad when I think of that man."

"Amy, you have to let it go for your sake and this family. I know it was a terrible time for you and I can understand why you are so angry. I, for one, cannot understand a man not taking responsibility for his actions. Nevertheless, the Lord tells us we must forgive our enemies if we want to return to Him. Getting rid of our anger is a good place to start. I don't expect you to welcome him warmly. As a matter of fact, if you did, I might just have to punch him out, but try to not let this eat at you, okay?"

"I will try; it is just so hard. I guess I should feel sorry for him that he denied himself the privilege of known Shane while he grew up, just like I was denied because of him."

"Maybe things wouldn't have been any different. You were a minor and under the control of your mother." Ivan released Amy and took her hand, "Come sit with me for a bit. I could use a good cuddle and I think you could, too."

Amy tried to laugh, "That I definitely could use, but I am ready for bed. Why don't we do the cuddling there?"

"That sounds like a plan," Ivan responded and taking Amy by the hand and shutting off the light, he led the way to the stairs.

Chapter 19

Southern Alberta

The weather turned nasty. It was late October and the countryside had lost its color and portrayed a dull brown. The leaves on the poplar and maples had dropped to the ground, making a thick carpet under the trees. The willows along the creek looked bright red against the background. The wind was cold as Shane and Ivan herded the cattle from the upper pastures toward the paddock below the Collins' barn. Even dressed in heavy coats and winter boots, they found it difficult to stay warm. Their gloves did not offer much protection when they had to hold the reins.

"Man, it must be pretty cold. That wind just cuts right through a person," Shane commented as he pulled his winter cap further over his ears. "I didn't check the thermometer this morning."

"I did," Ivan replied, "I don't think you want to know what it said. I sure wish we had moved these cattle before this cold snap set in. I am glad we got mine sorted last week and the calves weaned. When do you plan to wean?"

"I have a truck coming next week so I thought I would skip the weaning. This way, we won't have to put up with the bawling and frustration of both the cows and calves."

"That might be a smart idea. I think I will hang on to the calves until the first of the year. I have lots of feed and maybe the market will pick up."

"Or get worse. I don't have the option of making a choice. My bank loan is due in November and I need the calf money to cover that."

Sending Lad off to pick up a couple of strays, Ivan kicked his horse Belle into a trot. "Well, let's get these critters moving along. I can't feel my feet already and my knee is kicking up. It does that every time the weather changes. It is a pain."

"Probably riding horseback doesn't help that knee either. You might have to decide that a gas burning horse is better for you," Shane commented.

Ivan grinned over at Shane, "Now, what cowboy rides a gas eating horse? They say exercise is good for arthritis and this is good exercise. I'm not ready for the bone yard yet."

"Okay, okay. Just trying to make things easier for you." With that, Shane reined Bud to the left and headed up the draw to make sure there were no strays hiding out there. He would be glad to have the cattle all home and the calves shipped before he made his trip to Regina. April had agreed to him going, but decided to let him go on his own. He was hoping she would come with him, but he did not want to push the point. If things worked out, she said she would go the next time. He would have to make some excuse to Ivan and Amy why he was away, but maybe he would be lucky and be back before they even noticed he was gone. Regina wasn't that far away.

* * *

It was on mornings like this that Amy was glad she kept Laura home for one more year. She wouldn't be six until November, and living so far out of town, it would be a long bus ride for her. Worrying about the weather would not make things easier.

Laura was quick at learning and could already write her name and count all the way to twenty. Both Amy and Ivan spent time reading to her and Laura was already trying to read to Abe. Amy had to chuckle to herself as she watched Laura sit Abe down and 'read' to him, copying Amy as she 'read' and turned the pages. Abe listened intently and when Laura was done, handed her another book with the request, "More, more."

The temperature had dropped during the night and the wind was blowing from the west, scurrying along the ground and lifting the final leaves from the trees in the yard. "I sure don't envy the men moving those cattle today," Amy commented to the kids as they paused in their 'reading'. "Your Daddy and Shane will be cold riding the horses."

"Will it snow soon, Mommy? I want to play in the snow," Laura looked up from the book she was holding.

"I imagine it will, but I hope not too soon. Did you put your dirty clothes in the laundry hamper? I am going to wash today."

"Oops. I forgot." Laura jumped up and ran to the stairs, "Don't let Abe take my book," she ordered Amy; "He always chews on them."

"Never mind. Just get your clothes into the hamper, and then bring the hamper down, okay?"

"Okay," Laura answered and continued up the stairs.

Amy turned to Abe, but he had dropped the book and headed to the window to look outside. "'Now, 'now?" He repeated as he put his face against the window.

"No snow . . . . yet. Do not stick your tongue on the glass. Mommy just cleaned that. Come; let's have a snack while we wait for Daddy to come for lunch. Would you like an apple?"

At the mention of an apple, Abe quickly headed for his chair. Amy laughed. Abe was so easy to bribe. Just mention something to eat. Just like his dad, she thought. *I sure hope Ivan is dressed warm enough for today. That wind looks nasty.*

Turning to the fridge, Amy took out two apples and washed them. She was coring them when Laura returned with the laundry hamper.

Chapter 20

Regina, Saskatchewan

Dr. Klein frowned and muttered as he studied the test results in front of him "Now how can that be possible? Someone is not telling the truth here." He set the file aside and buzzed his secretary. "Get me Dave Knight on the line. Try him at his office."

"Yes, Dr. Klein. Right away."

It only took a few minutes and his secretary buzzed back, "Mr. Knight is on the line, Dr."

Picking up the phone, Dr. Klein spoke, "Dave, I wonder if you could come into the office today or tomorrow. I have the results of your tests back."

"Is there a problem, Dr.? I am rather busy here today and don't think I can get away."

"It can wait until tomorrow. However, since you asked me to do some blood tests to see if you could be a match for Sarah, I thought you would like to know the results. In addition, I also have all the tests back on you. I do think you should try to get in tomorrow if possible."

"I can get away tomorrow, I think. Is there something wrong?"

"Actually, you do have some medical problems we need to discuss, among other things."

"Okay, what time do you want me there?"

"I will put you back to my secretary and she will book you in. See you tomorrow."

"Right. See you then."

Dr. Klein buzzed his secretary, and then settled back in his chair. He rubbed his face as he pondered the situation. Dave definitely had an ulcer, which needed looking after right away. He had let it go way too long. No wonder he was having stomach pain and didn't feel well. Dr. Klein had known Dave for years and he was a very likely candidate for a heart attack if he didn't try to relax. His cholesterol was high and his blood pressure was on the high side too. He needed to be on medication as soon as possible, as well as get that ulcer taken care of. However, the other test had him buffaloed. How was that possible? Well, tomorrow would have to be soon enough to find out.

* * *

Dave hung up the phone and tapped his fingers on his desk. Now what was that all about? Surely, his test results weren't that bad? He knew he had not been feeling well, but he was under a lot of stress.

The sting did not work in his department so he was now on edge trying to discover which employee could be responsible for the shortages. He had a strong suspicion, but couldn't prove anything yet. He would have to be patient.

Picking up his coffee cup, he finished it off, and then decided he would work overtime tonight to clear his desk so he could get to his appointment in the morning. Sighing, he reached for the phone to call Alice and tell her not to wait supper.

* * *

Alice heard the phone ringing, but decided to ignore it. She was in the middle of mixing the biscuits for supper and covered in flour. When the answering machine picked up, she heard Dave's voice, telling her not to hold supper; he was working late and would grab something on the way home.

"Yes Dave," she commented aloud, "You will be stopping at one of those greasy spoon places. Just what your arteries need."

She finished mixing the biscuits and washing her hands, called Dave back. "Got your message. How come are you working late again?"

"Well," Dave responded, "I got a call from Dr. Klein today and my test results are back and he wants to see me, so I have to take time off tomorrow."

"Did he say how the tests were?"

"Nope; not even a hint. So I guess I will find out tomorrow."

"Okay, but don't stop on your way home for something. I will make a plate for you here and you can pop it in the microwave when you get home."

"I don't want you to go to the trouble. I can grab something."

"I know what you will grab and it will be full of fat and not good for you."

"Okay," Dave sighed, "I should be home about eight o'clock."

"Good; see you then."

Alice hung up the phone and turned back to the kitchen. Sarah would be home soon and she wanted everything ready. Wondering what Dr. Klein would have to say tomorrow, Alice took the casserole out of the oven and popped the biscuits in. I guess we will find out soon enough, Alice thought as she opened the silverware drawer and started setting the table.

Chapter 21

Regina, Saskatchewan

Dave hated sitting in a crowded doctor's office. There was something about all those people, sitting there waiting, with who knows what kind of contagious medical problem that made him feel uneasy. Shaking his head, he wondered if they thought the same thing about him. He was glad he had booked the morning off from work because it looked like he would have to wait for quite a while. Why do doctors always seem to be over booked, he grumbled to himself.

The day had started out badly with the coffee pot leaking all over the kitchen cupboard and when he went to clean it up, found the carafe was cracked. When Alice rushed into the room, late for her early morning meeting, she was not impressed with how he had cleaned up the mess, complaining that men were all alike. They thought a half-hearted swipe could make everything good. Then heading out to his car, he had slipped on the ice by the garage door and wrenched his back. Now I have another problem to see the doctor about, he sighed as he settled back in his chair to wait.

* * *

By the time Dave was called into the doctor's office, his back was starting to seize up and he could hardly walk.

"What happened to you?" Dr. Klein asked as Dave limped to the chair across from him.

"Slipped on some ice this morning. Just what I needed right now."

"I would agree. Do you want me to have a look?"

"Do you think I might have put my back out?"

"It's unlikely." Dr. Klein motioned for Dave to get on the table where he ran his hand up and down Dave's back, "You probably just pulled some muscles. Try some heat on it and if you need, I can prescribe some muscle relaxants."

"Sounds good. So what about my test results?"

"All the tests are back, and you definitely have an ulcer. I want to get you on medication for that right away. We don't want to see you end up in the hospital with a bleeding ulcer. With medication, it should heal up. Stay away from acidity foods for a while and try to relax."

"So what causes an ulcer to start? Alice said I am not eating properly, says I skip too many meals, mostly breakfast."

"It can have many causes, but stress doesn't help once the ulcer starts. It is actually a form of bacteria and can be cleared up with antibiotics. Are you under a lot of stress at work? I know worrying about Sarah has not been easy for you and Alice, but she is an amazing girl. She is doing very well."

"Yes, things are a bit hectic at my job, but should get better once we solve a couple of things. I can't help worrying about Sarah; she is my little girl."

Dr. Klein smiled, "You have always called her your little princess, but she is also a young, responsible adult who knows what she wants. She is worried about you, and rightfully so."

"You mean there is more for you to tell me?"

"I'm afraid so. You have elevated blood pressure and your cholesterol levels are away up. We need to get you started on blood pressure medication right away. With the cholesterol, we will try diet first and see if that brings the level down. I don't want to put you on medication unless I have to. There are side affects from that. We will have to monitor you very closely for a while. I want you to get your blood pressure checked every week."

"Okay; I have to get back to work so if you can give me a prescription, I can get going." Dave slid off the table and pulled down his shirt.

"Don't you want to know if you are a match for Sarah as a possible donor for a transplant?"

Dave stopped and turned around, "I can't believe I forgot about that. Well, am I?"

"Unfortunately, No. However, there is something else I have to discuss with you. I understand Sarah is adopted?"

"Yes, we got her when she was four years old. She knows she is adopted if that is what you are concerned about."

"Yes, she told me some time ago. But what confuses me is the test we took." After a pause, Dr. Klein continued, "As far as I can see, you and Sarah have the same DNA. She could be your daughter."

Dave stared at the Dr. with his mouth open. When he could speak, he answered, "That is not possible. We adopted her. What are you saying?"

"I am saying that when we get a match as close as you and Sarah, there is a ninety-nine percent chance the people are related. Paternity tests are based on this. That is why I wanted to talk to you alone."

"So you are trying to tell me that, by some freak chance, I managed to adopt a child that is my own?"

"Well, I am sure you know what you did or didn't do as a young man. I am only saying what is obvious. What you do with this information is up to you. It will go no further than my office."

"I can't believe this. There has to be some mistake. As far as I know, I never fathered a child."

"You are absolutely sure?"

Dave stood up. In spite of the pain in his back, he marched smartly to the door, then turned and ordered the doctor, "Redo the test. I need more proof." Then he went out and closed the door.

Dr. Klein laid Dave's file on his desk and leaned back in his chair. He didn't need to redo the test. He was positive Sarah was Dave's daughter. He also knew what a struggle Dave was now going through. If he admits that Sarah is his child, what will that do to his relationship with Alice and with Sarah? Had he been hiding the fact from Alice that he adopted his own daughter? Dr. Klein doubted that. Dave seemed genuinely shocked at the news. Just the same, it would be a bit of a mess if it comes out.

Picking up the intercom, Dr. Klein called for his next patient.

Chapter 22

Regina, Saskatchewan

By the time Dave got to his car, his back was killing him and he could hardly get the door open. Sliding into the seat, he just sat there. The day was just going from bad to worse. Maybe he should just go home and try to rest his back. The pain was intense and he didn't think he would be very productive at work anyway. Starting the car, he headed out of the parking lot and down to the drugstore on the corner to get his prescriptions filled. After that, he would head home. If he felt better in the afternoon, he would go in to work.

* * *

The house was quiet with everyone gone. Dave took his medication, settled into his recliner and closed his eyes.

For the first time in ages, Dave thought back to his school days in Medicine Hat. Is it possible that Sarah could be his daughter? If that is true, then the young man that phoned him had been mislead. What kind of game was Amy playing? But if she thinks that man is her son, where does Sarah fit in? Dave was so confused. Now what do I do, he reflected? How do I find out the truth? When he thought of Sarah, he knew he would never feel any different about her. Blood or no blood, she was his daughter and nothing would change that. However, if she really were Amy's daughter too, maybe there would be a chance that Amy could donate a kidney, being as he wasn't a match. Did he really want to take that chance and have Amy back in his life? He imagined she would not be too receptive to hearing from him or helping him in any way. If she believes Shane is her son, where does Sarah fit in? He was starting to get another headache. *Probably caused by my blood pressure and now all this added stress.*

Dave knew he did some wild and crazy things in his teen years, but he couldn't remember getting close to any other girl. Other than Amy, that is. Though he had to admit, he was drinking a lot back then. That was one thing he was grateful to Alice for. After he met her, he quit with the parties and drinking. They had an instant connection. It was the same when he saw Sarah. *Maybe my subconscious knew that we were related.* Dave moaned aloud, "If this is true, what on earth am I going to tell Alice and Sarah? Alice will never forgive me. Am I being fair to Sarah? If there is someone out there that can help her, wouldn't I be the selfish one if I didn't let her know."

Turning on the TV to the news channel, Dave closed his eyes and tried to rest. Enough time to think on all this another day. Right now, he needed to get rid of his painful back.

* * *

"You did very well on your tests, Sarah. I don't know how you manage to get all your assignments in when you have to be in dialysis once a week," Betty Ames, the instructor informed Sarah.

"I have good support which I am grateful for," replied Sarah as she gathered up her books, "I should let you know, it sounds like I might be starting to have dialysis twice a week. It seems once a week isn't quite enough. I have been feeling tired again lately and the test results show that my kidneys are failing."

"Don't worry. You are doing great. I understand Jesse has been helping you. He is an excellent student so I am sure you will be able to keep up. Is there any hope of a transplant soon?"

"I haven't heard anything. Because of Dr. Klein's persistence, I have my name on the list for a donor. So far, nothing, but I am sure it is a long, long list. There are probably people out there more in need than myself."

"You know, I think we should be letting some of your classmates know about your need. Maybe some of them will be tested and willing to donate."

"I couldn't ask that of anyone. In addition, I know Jesse can't as he already donated a kidney to his sister. No, I am doing okay with dialysis so I will continue for now. Thank you for your concern."

"Okay, but if you need anything, let me know, okay?"

"I will. Now I must get going or Mom will be sending out a search party for me. She worries about me way too much."

"That is what mother's are for, didn't you know?" Betty laughed, "Take care and see you tomorrow."

As Sarah headed out the door, Betty turned to the chalkboard and started erasing the information written there. As she cleaned the board, she could not help but think of Sarah. She admired the way she was determined to finish her schooling in spite of her problems. She is one strong young woman, Betty thought.

Then an idea came to her. Why don't I go and get tested? I don't have to agree to anything. Just find out if I could be a match. I have no family to be concerned about or that I have to report my decision. Yes, I think I will do that tomorrow. If I am not a match, then I don't have to make any decision.

With a final flourish, Betty wiped the board clean, gathered up her papers from the desk and with a final glance around, left the room, closing the door softly behind her.

Chapter 23

Southern Alberta

The weather was cold for late October. Shane was hoping that he wouldn't have to start feeding the cattle too soon, but the pasture below the corrals was starting to get chewed down and the cows were coming up to the gate every day expecting to be fed. Breaking the ice on the creek every morning for watering the cattle was a cold job, but better than having to water at the barns, Shane decided. He was grateful for the two-day rain that had helped bring the creek levels up. He was hoping that November would be a warmer month. Sometimes they lucked out and didn't have to feed until December, but that wasn't going to happen this year. The lack of moisture in the summer had set the pastures back. He was just glad they would have enough hay and straw to see them through the winter. By selling the calves, he would make it through.

He was also glad he managed to get the bank loan paid with the proceeds from the sale of the calves with enough left over to tide them through until next fall. Being careful, he and April would be able to even fix up the house a little and purchase a new lawn tractor. With the grain left to sell, they would do okay.

Ranching is a bit of a gamble, Shane realized, but he loved it. Sometimes he missed the sheep, but he did not miss the intensive labor through lambing season. Thinking of the sheep made him think of his adopted Mom, Laura. He still missed her though she had been gone for quite a few years. He missed Abe too, but he was younger when he passed away. Shutting the gate and starting down to the barn, Shane thought about all the things that had happened in the last few years. With Amy, his real mother coming into his life, Laura passing, his mission with the church to Italy, April coming into his life and their sealing in the temple in Cardston, and finally the joy of his life, his son Michael was born this year. I am a very fortunate man, Shane decided. Now I will try once more to make contact with my real father. Then my life will be complete.

Lad and Sampson saw Shane coming and tried to be the first to reach his side. Laughing, he reached down and ruffled the ears of each dog. "Hey, you two. Ready to head to the creek?" Opening the barn door, he picked up the bridle and headed to Bud's stall. "Might as well get our chores done, eh boys? I have to help Ivan later."

With that, he opened Bud's stall and taking him by the halter, led him into the alleyway.

* * *

April watched as Shane sauntered down the path past the garage and then paused as if deep in thought. "I wonder what has him so engrossed. He looks like he has a lot on his mind," April hugged Michael as she let the curtain drop and headed to the kitchen. "I imagine he is thinking about the ranch as usual. I just hope he isn't still planning to head to Regina."

April had agreed to him going, but was still hoping he would change his mind, since his father didn't seem interested in pursuing any kind of a relationship. April was scared to broach the subject to him in case it would upset him. "He knows I am here for him, whatever he chooses, but I really hope he decides to just stay here and forget about it," April spoke to Michael, though she knew he wouldn't understand a word of it. Michael waved his arm and gave April a big smile. Smiling back, she laid him into his bassinet and covered him lightly with a blanket. "Now you be a good boy and let Mommy get some work done," she admonished him as she headed to the sink to do the breakfast dishes.

* * *

"Drink your milk, Abe. You want to grow big and strong like Daddy, don't you?" Amy settled her son back on his chair and set his glass of milk in front of him, "You can't go outside until you finish your breakfast."

Abe pouted and pushed his milk away. "Okay, if that's the way you feel, you can go to your room," Amy replied as she turned to take the kettle off the stove. When she turned back, Abe was drinking his milk. Amy smiled to herself. There was nothing like sending a kid to their room to change their attitude.

"All done," Abe said as he set his glass down. It wasn't quite empty, but good enough, so Amy nodded, "Okay, you can go outside, but get Laura to help you put your mitts on. And be sure to zip up your coat and wear your toque. Do you need help with your boots?"

Abe shook his head as he ran out to the entry. Amy watched as he got up on the stool to get his coat down. At three and a half, he was growing like a weed, but still not tall enough to reach his coat. Laura had just finished putting her boots, coat on, and was waiting patiently to help Abe. Amy was proud of her. She was always looking out for her little brother. I wonder how much longer that will last, Amy chuckled to herself.

Seeing that the kids were both dressed warmly, Amy shooed them out the door, with a warning to stay in the house yard and away from the corrals. Ivan had a few men over and they were planning to do some work with the cattle. Ivan said something about injections for the calves. Shane was expected over later and Amy was hoping April and Michael would come with him for a visit. Things had been so busy during harvest and after, they didn't get to visit as much as Amy would like. I think I will just give her a call and invite them all for lunch, Amy mused as she headed for the phone.

Chapter 24

Regina, Saskatchewan

It snowed during the night. The temperature was below freezing, making the streets a mess with the heavy rush hour traffic. Alice was glad she had left home a little early so she would not be late for her first appointment. She was expecting a young couple who were trying to get their two children returned to them permanently. Alice couldn't see any problem with it as long as the husband kept his job and the wife was at home to take care of the twins. It was a sad case because the father had left the mother and the twins the year before. He tried to take the little girls with him, but the mother won custody. Then she made it difficult for him to see the kids. Therefore, he didn't have any idea that she had been neglecting the girls until a neighbor reported it. So subsequently, the children were placed into a foster home.

Over the last year, the parents had reconciled and now wanted their girls back. Alice had done a lot of legwork on this case and she truly believed they were capable of taking care of the kids at this time. Both had taken counseling and seemed very much in love. There was more paperwork that had to be completed, and then the girls would be returned on a trial basis. The mother seemed truly sorry about everything. Alice knew it was depression that had caused the neglect, as the woman loved her girls.

It was results like this one that made Alice glad she worked for Social Services. A successful conclusion is always the best story. I sure hope Sarah's story has a happy ending too, Alice thought, as she drove into the parking lot, after maneuvering through the early morning traffic. "Just in case, I think I will go and get tested to see if I am a match for Sarah," Alice spoke to herself as she locked the car and headed into the office. Dave had told her that he was tested and he wasn't a match. Maybe a donor will be found before she really needs it, but Alice knew that donors were rare with the right match. Being as Sarah was adopted, there were no siblings that could be tested. Trying to find her parents at this time would be very difficult, even for health reasons. Alice figured when the time came and it seemed imperative to find her biological parents, she would be in the right position to start looking. She had many resources readily available.

She hurried into her office to find the young couple waiting for her. Putting her purse away and hanging up her coat, she buzzed her secretary and started her day.

* * *

He found the culprit. It was thoroughly by accident that Dave stumbled on his dedicated and reliable assistant, he thought, going through his personal files. When confronted, he broke down and admitted to the skimming. Dave was shocked and angry to find that Allan had been gambling to the point that he was going to lose his house. His wife had left him and taken the kids back to Winnipeg. He told Dave that it all started as a bit of harmless fun, then he found he really liked it. He won a bit on and off, just enough to keep him thinking he would win big. So when his funds ran out, he decided to borrow some and when he won the big one, he would be able to pay all the money back.

Dave just shook his head. Why did people get caught up in these things? Very few people ever win much.

Not knowing how to deal with the situation, he called the Mayor. Let her decide what to do, he contended. He liked Allan and really didn't want to see him prosecuted. The man has a problem and he needed help.

Now that Dave had time to get his office back in shape, he spent the afternoon answering phone messages and signing orders. By five o'clock, he had things shipshape and was heading out the door when Alice phoned.

"Want to meet me somewhere for supper? Sarah has a date so she won't be home until later."

"Sarah has a date?"

"That's what I said. So how about it?"

"Who is the date with?"

"You sound more interested in who she has a date with than having supper with your wife."

"I'm sorry. It is just she never dates, so you caught me off guard. Where do you want to go for supper?"

"Let's try that new place on Broadway. Everyone says it is very good."

"Sounds good. I'm leaving now so should be there in twenty minutes if the traffic isn't too bad."

"Great. See you soon. Love you."

Dave set the phone down and picked up his gloves. He was pleased that Alice wanted to go out to eat. They hardly ever went out, being as Alice preferred to cook at home. She was an excellent cook and Dave really appreciated that, but sometimes going out was nice too. Dave figured he had something to celebrate too, with finding the source of the shortages in his office. He just hoped the Mayor would decide not to press charges against Allan and get him some help.

With that, Dave locked his office and headed out the door, waving to his secretary so she would know he was gone.

Chapter 25

Southern Alberta

April had never been this sick before. Through her childhood and adolescent years, she had avoided even a bad cold. Thinking she was just tired with nursing the baby and not getting a full night's sleep, she had shrugged everything off. Now she felt like she was burning up with fever. She shook Shane to get up when she heard the baby crying and mumbled for him to bring Michael to her so she could feed him.

Shane was shocked at how hot she was and immediately phoned Amy to ask what he should do. In no time, Amy was there and took charge. She took April's temperature and put a cool cloth on her forehead. "If your fever doesn't break in the next couple of hours, it is off to the doctor you go," she informed April as she stripped off her nightgown and found her a dry one. She gave her a couple of Tylenol to help bring the fever down.

"I'll be okay," April croaked, "I think I just have a bug."

"Bug or no bug, fever is nothing to fool with. Don't worry about Michael. He is old enough to drink from a bottle. You shouldn't tire your self out. Try to get some rest. I will take Michael home with me until you feel better. Shane is just out doing up the chores so he will be with you in case you need something." Amy didn't mention that she wanted him to keep a close eye on April. She really didn't look good. Some of the people at church had been talking about a bad flu going around and April seemed to have managed to catch it. When Shane returned, Amy told him to check on April's temperature often and try to get her to take lots of fluids. Bundling Michael up, she left, urging Shane to get hold of her if he needed anything.

April fretted and worried about Michael, but soon settled into a troubled sleep. Shane headed to the kitchen to dig out some broth and heat it up. When April woke up, he planned to make sure she consumed it. He was concerned because April had never been sick since he had known her. He thought about calling April's mom, and then thought better of it. April's Mom was a 'take charge' kind of woman and Shane was not sure he or April needed that now. Michael was safe with Ivan and Amy until April was on the mend. He was capable of taking care of April. Turning the heat off, he dug a mug out of the cupboard and went to check on his patient.

* * *

Though she was very concerned about April, Amy was thoroughly enjoying having a baby in the house again. Abe and Laura were excited that Michael would be staying for a day or two. He was just getting old enough to be aware of everything around him. At two months, he was a chubby baby with a quick smile. Laura found if she tickled his fingers, he would try to giggle and wave his arms and feet. Abe thought it was hilarious. Amy had to watch he didn't become too excited and unintentionally hurt the baby.

Ivan had gone out to do chores after Amy arrived home with Michael. He was going to head over to the Collins' ranch after he was finished to see if Shane needed anything done. Ivan was like that, Amy acknowledged. If anyone needed help, he was always there. One of their neighbors had fallen from his barn loft the winter before and broken his ankle rather badly. Ivan had gone every day for six weeks to feed his cattle and check on things. Being as the neighbor didn't have a wife, at Ivan's suggestion Amy had sent meals over to him. Though this same neighbor used to be a bit crusty and kept to himself, since then he had become quite neighborly, coming over for visits when time would allow. The kids had taken to calling him Uncle Pete, and he seemed very pleased about that. Yes, Ivan definitely had a way with him.

Michael wasn't too crazy about accepting the bottle, but was hungry, so soon decided to accept it. Abe and Laura watched closely while Amy fed him. When he fell asleep, Laura put her finger to her lips and said to Abe in a whisper, "Shhhh. Baby is sleeping; we have to be very, very quiet."

Abe nodded and repeated, "Very, very quiet."

Amy smiled as she got up from the recliner and took Michael into her bedroom. Laying him in the middle of the bed, she propped pillows on both sides of him so he couldn't accidentally roll off. Gazing at him, she felt a lump in her throat. "Nothing is more beautiful as a sleeping baby. I am so fortunate to have this baby in my life," Amy murmured as she silently left the room, closing the door softly behind her.

* * *

Shane gazed at April as she slept fitfully, tossing the covers off and mumbling in her sleep. He had taken her temperature and it was coming down. She managed to drink a bit of broth and enquire about Michael. Shane had assured her that Michael was fine and safe. She just had to concentrate on getting better. He reached over, tucked the quilt back over April, and tiptoed out of the room.

As he cleaned up the lunch dishes in the kitchen, Shane realized his planned trip to Regina was going to have to wait a while. Well, I have waited this long; another few weeks isn't going to make much difference, he thought. His father would still be there when he was ready to make the trip. Knowing that his father wasn't anxious to get to know him made Shane wonder why he was even bothering. Maybe it is the stubborn streak I have, Shane laughed to himself. I just can't let some things go. One thing is for sure; he is going to have to tell me to my face that he doesn't want to know me. Then maybe I will accept that.

Shane settled back in his chair and picked up his scriptures. He found that reading the scriptures helped him to come to terms with many things in his life. Both he and April enjoyed reading them together. Many times, they found the answers to their questions within the pages of their Book of Mormon. It is too bad the whole world doesn't know about this book, he mused as he opened the book to continue reading where he left off.

Chapter 26

Regina, Saskatchewan

Sarah was glad that term papers were in and she could get a break from schooling for a week. She was finding that trying to keep up her studies and be at the hospital for her dialysis twice a week was very tiring. So far, she had managed to drive herself and save her parents. Her dad seemed to be feeling a lot better, too. Dr. Klein had him on medication for his blood pressure and on a diet to lower his cholesterol. Sarah knew her dad was not happy about the diet, as he was very fond of burgers and fries. Her mom had been trying for years to get him away from that sort of thing, but it took Dr. Klein's warning to make him see the light. The medication was bringing down his pressure and he was getting a lot less headaches. Only time would tell if the diet was working. Sarah knew her dad cheated on his diet at times, but at least he was following the rules at home.

Sarah also knew that both her adopted parents had been tested to be a kidney donor, but neither one qualified. In a way, Sarah was relieved about that. She really didn't want either one of them to go through the surgery. Dr. Klein also told her that one of her instructors at school, Betty Ames had been tested, but wasn't a match either. She was grateful to Miss Ames for her thoughtfulness. She was such a great teacher and so compassionate. I will have to remember to thank her in private sometime, Sarah thought as she pulled into her driveway. Gathering her books, she slid off the seat, locked the door and headed into the house. First thing she had on her agenda was a nice long shower and then maybe a short nap before her parents got home.

* * *

"What do you mean; you don't have to redo the test?" Dave stared at the doctor as he sat upright in the chair provided. "I thought I told you there had to be a mistake. I want another test done."

"Dave, it would be a waste of my time and the facilities to redo the test. There is no mistake. Sarah has your DNA. The PCR test is very accurate. As you know, we took a swab from the lining of your mouth. From that, we extracted DNA from the cells and then made copies. Those copies were compared to those of Sarah's DNA. With this comparison, we can safely say that there is a 99.9% chance that Sarah is your child. Now, I don't know your history so I can't comment on anything more than that. I think you had better do some soul searching and come up with a decision that will satisfy you and your family. As I said before, this will not leave my office. Even if some of the lab workers notice the match, they are not familiar with the fact that Sarah is adopted."

Dave sat back and sighed, "I am just in shock. How am I going to explain to Alice that we adopted my own daughter? She will never believe me if I say I didn't know she was my flesh and blood, and I wouldn't blame her."

"Well, that is a bit of a problem. How about the biological mother? Do you think she would be tested to see if she is a match?"

"I don't know. How am I supposed to even know where she is?"

Dr. Klein placed Dave's file on the desk and smiled, "I think you would know more than I would at this point. Maybe you should think about trying to contact her. Sarah is going to need a kidney in the future. Maybe she has siblings and one might be a match." Dave stood up and picked up his gloves. Looking at Dr. Klein he answered, "I don't think that the mother would be all that happy hearing from me. You see, I was eighteen years old when she came to me and I turned her away. I figured she wasn't telling me the truth. Within the next year, I met Alice. I never knew if she had a child or not. I guess she must have. I certainly didn't know she had given the child up. Man, is this ever a mess!" With that, Dave headed out the door.

* * *

Dave got into his car and slammed the door. Just what I need now, he groused. I am finally feeling a bit better and now the Dr. drops this bombshell on me. I was so hoping a mistake had been made in the testing. So now what do I do? Alice will never believe I didn't know Sarah was my biological daughter. Moreover, what about the young man that called me? He thinks he is my son. How can that be, if Sarah is my daughter? Unless . . . Oh, no! It can't be! Would it be possible that there are twins? Maybe that young man is Sarah's twin. The boy must have gone looking and found his mother.

So many thoughts were making Dave's head hurt but he couldn't stop them. So if it is true that that young man is my son, then he and Sarah have to be twins. In addition, if there are twins, they will probably be a blood match. However, how do I approach the family with this? I could save Sarah, but lose Alice. I certainly don't know if this young man, who says he is my son, would be willing to donate a kidney. I am sure he only contacted me to know who his father is. I wonder if he is married and has a family. I don't even know how to contact him. Maybe he will contact me again.

Dave's headache was getting worse. I have to think on all this, Dave lamented, but for now, I am going to let it go and see what happens in the next while. So far, Sarah is doing okay. She is still getting her courses done and the dialysis is working, so that is good.

Starting his car, Dave backed out of the parking spot and headed to the street. Traffic was starting to pick up, as rush hour was imminent. "Maybe I will get home before it really gets busy," Dave voiced aloud, as he signaled a left turn and headed down the ramp to the freeway. Putting all his thoughts on the back burner, so to speak, Dave turned the radio on and settled for the drive home.

* * *

Alice had just put in a very stressful day. Dealing with child neglect was one of the hardest aspects of her job. This case had been especially hard. Not only did she have to remove the children from the home, but also she had to press charges against the mother for assault. Alice had been in many conflicts with different families, but never had one of the parents hit her. She was just lucky she saw the cup coming and got her hand up in time or it would have hit her in the face. It shook her up pretty badly and her arm was bruised and aching where the missile hit her.

She had always prided herself on being able to handle every situation. To date, she had never had this kind of reaction. Upon checking the file after returning to the office, she found that the mother did have a history of violence and arrested as a teenager for hitting a police officer. Many teens do have some temper issues but this one seemed to carry through to adulthood. Then she was abusive in her first marriage, which caused the breakup. She doubted that she was actually married to the man now living with her. Alice felt she was fortunate to get the children out of that home before they were not only neglected but injured as well. The man definitely wouldn't be any help, as he seemed scared of her. He probably had hard evidence of her temper, Alice decided. He also did not seem overly upset about the kids being taken out of their home, which made convinced that he wasn't the father.

Alice looked at the time. Seeing it was nearly 5:00 PM, she gave a sigh of relief and started to clear off her desk. Maybe Dave will have supper started, she thought. He had a doctor appointment this afternoon, so would be home early unless he was tied up there. I sure hope he gets a good report. Now, if I can just keep him on his diet, things will be looking up in that department. Alice knew Dave found it hard to resist all the foods he craved, but he had been trying hard.

Grabbing her coat and gloves, Alice locked the door on her office and headed to her car. Shivering against the cold wind, Alice could see it was beginning to snow. "Just what I need to finish off my day," she lamented as she unlocked her car and slid behind the wheel.

Chapter 27

Southern Alberta

April was feeling better. It had taken the better part of a week before she was starting to enjoy her meals and feel like getting out of bed and dressed. Amy had brought Michael over a few times, but she was concerned about the baby catching the flu. April was still nursing Michael when the flu hit. Because they were keeping the baby away from her, April had been expressing her milk in order to be able to continue when she was feeling better. April missed her son and couldn't wait to have him home. Her mother had called several times, wanting to come and look after her, but April put her off. With Amy looking after Michael, she was able to rest and have peace and quiet. April knew if her mother were there, she would be fussing and puttering around all day, keeping her awake. It was better this way. Amy sent meals over and Shane was managing just fine.

So far, Shane had missed catching the bug. He kept busy, repairing things around the ranch and doing the chores. April knew he wanted to head off to Regina on his quest for his father, but had put it off because of her being sick. Maybe he will be able to go this coming week, Alice contended. I will be fine.

Amy was bringing Michael home. She could hardly wait.

* * *

Shane hammered the last rail onto the corral fence and slid the hammer back into his pouch. He was glad to see the last of the repairs to the calf corral. There was a cold wind blowing and little particles of icy snow were pelting down against his already cold cheeks. So far, November had been very cold. "I sure hope this isn't an omen of the winter to come," Shane voiced aloud as his wiped the snow from his face with his glove. Sampson wiggled his tail in reply and nuzzled Shane's hand. "What do you think there, boy? Is it going to start snowing?" Sampson wiggled his tail harder and whined. Shane laughed and patted the dog. He picked up the remaining rail and headed to the cattle shed. Knowing that Michael was coming home today, he decided he had better call it quits and get up to the house to help April with lunch.

Shane was very grateful that April was finally feeling better. He had taken her into the doctor, but he said it was just one of those things that would have to run its course. So far, he was feeling okay, so maybe he would be lucky and not catch it. Both he and April really missed their son. Shane was able to see him most days when he made a quick trip to Amy and Ivan's, but because they were concerned that April might be spreading the germ, they had kept Michael away as much as possible. Now he was coming home.

Heading into the barn, Shane checked out the sick calf and could see he had cleaned up his rations so that was a good sign. Knowing that this crazy weather was not a good time to put him back outside, Shane filled his water bucket, forked him some hay and left him in the stall. If the weather straightened up, he would turn the calf out tomorrow.

As Shane headed to the house, he thought about his planned trip to Regina. If April stayed well and everything was fine, he hoped to head off in the coming week. He decided he would let Ivan know what his plans were so he could come and check on things for him. He didn't want April to have to worry about anything. Until he knew what kind of reception he was going to receive, he would delay telling Amy. No sense in getting her upset any sooner than he had to. Yes, he would talk to Ivan first thing in the morning and leave on the Monday. He wanted to catch his father at his job rather than his home. He was sure his father's family knew nothing about him and he did not want to cause any problems by just dropping in. Telling them was his father's responsibility.

Chapter 28

Southern Alberta

"I can't believe this weather," Ivan complained, as he kicked a frozen lump with his boot, "This is more like January than November."

"I know," Shane answered, "It sure started early enough this year. I hope we will have enough feed for the winter, being as we are feeding already. I was hoping to be able to hold off for another few weeks."

"I think we will be okay," Ivan rubbed the back of his neck, "Maybe we will get a break in February." Picking up his fork, Ivan continued to fork hay into the calf feeder.

He was wondering what brought Shane over so early this morning but was biding his time, waiting for him to say something. He figured it was probably something to do with his father and all this small talk was just leading up to the real reason.

Shane grabbed a fork and started forking hay into the feeder too while he continued, "It has been a while since we had a good warm spell in the middle of the winter. Maybe we are due for one. It would be something to look forward to."

Finishing the last of the hay, the two men stuck their forks into the next bale and took a break, Ivan leaning on the fence rail and Shane slouching against the bale. Finally, Shane spoke up, "Ivan, I was hoping you could do me a favor?"

"I was wondering when you would get around to the real reason you are here," Ivan said, as he took off his gloves and wiped the frost from his face.

"I am heading off to Regina on Monday morning. April has decided not to go this first time, so if I'm not back by Monday night, could you check on her and Michael Tuesday morning and check the cows for me? I will be giving them lots of feed so they should be okay. I don't expect to be gone more than the day, but it is a long drive and things can happen. I will have my cell phone with me, so you can call me if you need to."

"I don't see that being a problem. So you really are going through with this? Did you talk to your father yet?"

"I tried to. He hung up on me. Therefore, that is why I have to go there. See him face to face. If he rejects me, then I will let it go."

"Amy isn't going to be happy about this."

"That is why I don't want you to say anything to her right now. You can make some excuse to go over to my place Tuesday morning. If I make a connection with my father, then I will tell her."

"I don't like keeping things from her. It can come back to bite us."

"I know and I wouldn't ask this of you if it wasn't important to me."

"Okay, mum is the word. I hope the weather warms up a bit by Monday. It is no fun traveling in the cold."

"That is one reason I am a bit relieved that April decided to stay home. I would hate to be stranded with her and Michael if the car quit or something. Cell phones are good, but some areas don't have good service."

"Well good luck in your endeavor. We'll see you at church tomorrow. April is feeling well enough to come out now?"

"For sure. She doesn't want to miss any more. She missed her primary kids and the women at church. They have all been so good, offering food and help, but we have been doing fine. Of course, Amy has been seeing to all our wants. She spoils us."

"It is her pleasure, I am sure. Well, I'm off to the neighbors. He has a couple of sick cows which he needs some help with."

"Okay, see you tomorrow."

Chapter 29

Regina, Saskatchewan

Dave was late for work. The traffic has been terrible and the accident at Albert and Ring Road had tied up the vehicles for three blocks. By the time the police got there and cleared some of the traffic, Dave was already late. He expected he wouldn't be the only person delayed.

Hurrying into his office, he set his lunch on his desk and took off his coat and gloves. The temperature said minus eighteen degrees when he checked it that morning. It felt extra cold to Dave, but he always thought that until they had a nice blanket of snow. The snow seemed to be a good insulation for the ground. Dave figured it was going to be a long winter, if this cold snap stayed with them. Well, he thought, a good day to be indoors and get some of this work caught up. Maybe he could get a head start on the month end reports.

By eleven thirty, he had cleared his desk and was thinking about having an early lunch, when his secretary buzzed him.

"Yes?'

"Sorry to bother you, Mr. Knight, but there is a young man here to see you. He says it is important."

The first thing Dave thought of was Sarah. Was there a problem with her? "Okay, send him in," Dave replied and put his lunch bucket on the floor behind the desk.

His secretary ushered in a young man that Dave had never seen. Thanking his secretary, he turned to the young man, "Hello, do I know you?"

"I'm afraid not," the young man replied, "I am Shane Collins. I believe we spoke briefly on the phone."

Dave stared at Shane. This he did not expect. He went from being shocked to nervous to worried, and back to shock. Taking the proffered hand, he said, "This is indeed a shock and I really don't know what to say. You told me on the phone you are my son, right?"

"That is what I was told."

"Who told you that?"

"My mother."

"Your real mother or your adopted mother?"

"Well, actually my real mother. It is a long story, but we got together when I was eighteen years old."

"Who is your mother?"

"I can't believe you have to ask me that!"

Dave motioned for Shane to sit down and he sat behind his desk. He was in over his head here, but he owed this young man some kind of explanation. "It is not what you think. Your mother must be Amy, right?"

"That is right."

"Well, I never knew she had a child. I was young and foolish and when she came to me, I rejected her. Shortly after I graduated, I met my present wife and we were married young. We soon found out that Alice couldn't have children, so a few years later, we adopted a little four year old girl."

Shane interrupted, "That is all fine and good, but where does that put me?"

"If you will let me finish. This past summer, Sarah, our adopted daughter became very sick. We then found out her kidneys are failing. She is on dialysis and will need a kidney transplant. When I was tested to be a kidney donor, I found out that Sarah is actually my daughter. Therefore, you can see why I don't believe you are my son. I don't know what Amy is trying to pull here, but if she had any child, that child is Sarah."

Shane felt that someone had punched him in the stomach. Was Dave telling the truth? He seemed to be genuinely as upset about this as Shane now was. Shane leaned ahead and said, "I need to see proof, and I am willing to take a DNA test to see if we are related. I don't believe Amy would mislead me. If your daughter is her daughter, I am sure she doesn't know it. I think there is some mistake. Are you sure we both couldn't be yours?"

"Only if you are twins," Dave ventured as he watched Shane's face.

"Twins? I never thought of that. Could that be possible?"

"A lot of twins are separated at birth. Sarah was not doing well as an infant. That was why she never was adopted. I think probably her kidneys were the problem back then too.

We got her when she was four and she was healthy then."

"So where does this leave us?"

"First of all, my wife knows nothing about Sarah being my child and nothing about the real reason you were calling me. I want to leave it like that for now. If you agree and you said you were willing, I would like to have a test done to see if you are indeed my son. I have some selfish reasons for this. Because if you are related to Sarah, you could help her."

"Listen, I am not willing to donate a kidney at this point, if that is what you are thinking. I have a young wife and a son, which by the way, would be your grandson if I turn out to be your son. I have a ranch to operate and have to think of all this. Even if I am a sibling, it doesn't mean I would be a match."

Dave sighed, "I know. I wasn't a match either and I am her father. We are just hoping that somehow, we can come up with a donor before things get too bad. My life is that girl."

"I understand. Family is very important to me too. If I am truly your son, someday I will fill you in on my life and how I became a rancher in Alberta. That is not important right now. How do I go about having a test done?"

Dave picked up the phone, "I will call my doctor and get something set up this afternoon. Have you had lunch?" Shane shook his head. "Okay, I will get my secretary to make the appointment and I will take you out for a bite. The test results will take a week or so, but we will keep in touch. I will give you my cell phone number or you can call the office here. Please don't call the house again until we get this all straightened out, okay?"

"Sure. I don't want any trouble. I just want to know my parents. I think I owe it to my children to be able to give them their family history."

"You sound like one of those Mormons. They are always interested in family history."

"As a matter of fact, I am a member of the Church of Jesus Christ of Latter-day Saints, commonly called Mormons. The couple that raised me were members. They gave me a wonderful life."

"I am glad. That isn't always the case. I was adopted myself. Though my adopted parents tried hard, they just couldn't show love. Maybe that is why I am so close to Sarah. I don't want her to go through what I did."

"There was no shortage of love in my home. I am so grateful for that."

"Let's go eat. I am supposed to be on a diet and I am starved all the time. I look forward to getting out to eat and away from the rabbit food in my lunch bucket."

Shane smiled, "I like rabbit food."

Chapter 30

Southern Alberta

Being stuck was the last straw. It seemed that things were worsening for Ivan since Shane had returned from Regina.

"I just am not keeping my mind on the business at hand," Ivan groused aloud, "How stupid to drive into the ditch, thinking I could take a short cut. If I was thinking right, I would know that the ditches are soft after all the moisture in the last week or two."

The cold snap had moderated, but with it came the rain and sleet. It was trying to snow, but the warmer temperature was keeping the white stuff at bay. Ivan was grateful for that. The moisture in the form of rain was very welcome, but made for miserable conditions for the animals. He was doctoring several sick calves since the damp weather and he was fighting off a cold. Ivan was thinking it was miserable conditions for people as well. To top things off, he had to drive into the ditch and be stuck.

Digging out his cell phone, he called Shane. Telling him what happened and giving him directions where to come, Ivan settled back and waited.

Shane had returned from Regina on the Monday night, and reported to Ivan on Tuesday morning when Ivan headed over to check on April and Michael. When Shane explained to Ivan about what happened, Ivan was thoroughly surprised. He couldn't believe that Amy would be wrong about Shane being her son, but they had not seen any solid proof and had never even thought of having DNA testing done. Could it be that Shane was not Amy's son, and she really had a daughter instead?

Shane was still waiting on the results of the test he took in Regina. Ivan was waiting impatiently too. There was no way he was saying anything to

Amy until they knew for sure about the test. It would be a real shock to her and to all of them if Shane wasn't Dave's son, which would mean he was not Amy's son either. If he was Dave's son, then Amy also had a daughter that she never knew about and that daughter was Shane's twin. Even if Shane was not Dave's son, according to Dave, his daughter Sarah had to be Amy's daughter. So many complications. It was hard to take it all in. Ivan was getting a headache just thinking about it. Then there was the fact that the daughter needed a kidney. That was another problem. Ivan shook his head. No way was he dropping this on Amy until they knew all the facts. It was going to be difficult enough to deal with all this when the time came. No matter what way he looked at it, he knew that things were going to change in their lives. Moreover, he hated change.

* * *

Amy was not impressed with her young son. He managed to get into the paint from the cupboard in the porch and had decided to paint his favorite tractor. Amy couldn't believe he got the lid off the can, let alone been able to get it out of the high cupboard. She had been busy in the kitchen when Laura came running in and told her what Abe was up to. It was too late by the time Amy got to the porch to save the floor from getting a good splash of the fire red color. Grabbing the can and brush away from Abe, she was very abrupt with him. "Abe, what on earth are you trying to do? You know you are not to go into that cupboard and certainly not to touch the paint. Mommy is very angry with you. You deserve a good spanking."

Abe started to cry, "Mommy, I sorry. I just wanted to make my tractor pretty. Laura said it was ugly. I sorry, Mommy."

"Green is not ugly. Your tractor is a very pretty green. Laura just doesn't like green, so do not listen to her. Now get over here and we will get you washed up in the sink. Laura, don't step in that paint on the floor. Once I get Abe cleaned up, I want you to take him and go to your rooms. I am annoyed with both of you."

"I didn't do anything," Laura pouted, "And I came and told you what Abe was doing."

"Well, you started the problem by saying his tractor was ugly. You knew that would make him upset. Okay, now you two scoot so I can clean this mess up before your father gets home."

Amy wasn't sure what was taking Ivan so long. He was usually home before now. The last she saw, he was heading out with the truck, going to check the creek, he said. Maybe he was stuck, she thought. She knew he had his cell phone, so he could call if he needed help.

Grabbing some paper towel, she sopped up most of the paint. She was thankful it was water-based paint or she would have a real problem. With a bucket of soapy water, she managed to get the paint off the floor. She looked up when she was done to see Ivan drive into the yard.

"Finished just in time," she said as she put the bucket away and hurried to the kitchen to get the rest of the meal on the table.

Chapter 31

Regina, Saskatchewan

Sarah wasn't feeling well. She just did not seem to have the energy to get out of bed. Today was dialysis day and she needed to get up and to the hospital. She was finding it increasingly difficult to concentrate on her studies. She just couldn't believe that having a problem with kidney function could affect the body and make a person feel just like a limp dishrag. Dr. Klein had tried to warn her to pace herself and not overdo things, but she, like most young people, thought she could handle it. Now she was starting to understand what he was talking about. She had been working hard the last few weeks, determined to keep up with her classmates and be able to graduate with them. Jesse was a tremendous help; he was always prompt with delivering his notes to her for the classes she missed because of her dialysis. He would stay and explain everything to her so she would have no problem following the lesson. Sarah was so grateful for his friendship and help. Staying with her studies would have been impossible without his help.

Swinging her legs over the side of the bed, Sarah sat up. She felt a bit light-headed, but managed to stand up. Her legs felt like rubber, making her grab for the dresser to steady herself. Thinking better of her idea to take a shower, she sat back down. She knew she would never make it all the way to the bathroom. Picking up her cell phone, she called the house number.

"Mom? Can you come to my room? I'm not feeling well."

In a few seconds, Alice was in Sarah's room. "Sarah, what's wrong?"

"I don't know. I can't stand. My legs are like two posts, and I am dizzy. Now I am starting to feel nauseous. What do you think is wrong?"

"I don't know for sure, but I am going to call Dr. Klein. Just sit there and don't move."

"But I have to go to the bathroom."

"Okay, lean on me and I will get you in there."

Carrying most of Sarah's weight, Alice managed to get her to the bathroom, then hurried to the kitchen and called Dr. Klein's number. His answering service promised to call her back. Taking her portable phone to the bathroom, she checked on Sarah. She was sitting with her head down and was starting to sweat. Alice grabbed a facecloth and wiped her brow.

"How are you feeling now?"

"Terrible. I feel like someone stuck a needle into me and pumped me full of air."

"I called Dr. Klein's number. Hopefully, he will get back to us right away."

"Where's Dad?"

"He had to leave for work early this morning. Some kind of crisis there. That reminds me; I had better call my office and tell them I will be late."

"I'm sorry, Mom. I am so much of a bother to you and Dad."

"Cut that out. You are not a bother. We love you very much and want to see you get well. I have a feeling we are going to have to be looking for a donor soon. I think all this is related to your kidneys."

Sarah sighed, "I know. I am not looking forward to having the surgery, but it would be nice not to have to get dialysis anymore. Any idea how long a person has to wait for a transplant?"

"Dr. Klein told me it depends on the need and availability of a match. Whoever is in the most need will get the transplant if it is an anonymous donor. If we find a match on our own, then you would receive that kidney. Both your Dad and I were tested and we are not matches."

"I am glad. I wouldn't want you to give up a kidney for me. In addition, I hate the thought that someone who passed away could be a donor. It means a grieving family had to make that decision."

"Many people feel it is the last good thing they can do on this earth is give to others."

"I know, but it is still sad."

Just then, Alice's phone rang.

"Dr. Klein here. You called?"

"Yes, Doctor. Sarah is not well at all. She is scheduled for dialysis this morning, but is very weak and feels dizzy."

"Can you get her up to the hospital?"

"Yes, I can try. Do I take her to emergency?"

"Yes, I will meet you there."

"Thanks, Doctor."

Alice hung up and turned to Sarah. "Do you think we can get you dressed and into the car?"

"Okay, but hang on to me. I feel like my legs are two rubber balls and will give way any minute."

"Don't worry. I will not let you fall. Let's get going. The sooner we get you to the hospital, the sooner we will know what is going on."

* * *

Dave was just finishing his interview when his phone rang. Irritated that his secretary put the call through when he specifically requested no calls, he picked up the phone and barked into it, "What?"

"Your wife is on the line. She says it is very important."

Dave's heart jumped. Alice would never interrupt a meeting if it wasn't necessary. As soon as he heard her voice, he knew something was wrong.

"Alice, is it Sarah?"

"Yes, I am taking her to the hospital right now. I talked with Dr. Klein. We will be in emergency. Can you come?"

"I will meet you there. What happened?"

"She is very weak. I will explain everything when we see you. Bye."

Dave hung up the phone and grabbed his jacket. "I'm sorry," he said to the job applicant, "I have a family emergency. I will review your application later and call you with my verdict. I am sorry about this."

"No problem," the man answered, "I am a family man and I definitely understand."

"Good." Heading out the door, Dave spoke over his shoulder, "My secretary will see you out."

* * *

When Dave arrived at the hospital, Dr. Klein was already there and was examining Sarah. Alice was waiting for him at the emergency entrance. Seeing Dave, she rushed to him and grabbing his arm, burst into tears. "Oh Dave, things are not good. It looks like her kidneys are shutting down. We have to find a donor quickly. I don't think she has much time."

Dave took her into his arms and tried to calm her down. "Alice, get hold of yourself. We don't need Sarah to get upset. If she sees you like this, she will freak out. You are freaking me out. Have you talked to Dr. Klein?"

Alice wiped her eyes and replied, "Just for a moment. He rushed Sarah right into the examining room."

"Well, let's sit down and wait. He will let us know what is going on as soon as he can, I am sure. Did you find Sarah sick in bed?"

"No. She called me on her cell phone because she needed to go to the bathroom, but her legs wouldn't hold her. She was scared she would fall."

"She has been working entirely too hard. I am afraid she is going to have to stop her classes until things are resolved."

"That will break her heart, but I think you are right. She needs more rest."

Just then, Dr. Klein approached them, carrying Sarah's file. Taking the seat next to them, he said, "I am going to admit Sarah to the hospital for some tests. I think she is just overtired. That is also a sign that her kidneys are getting worse. Have you had any luck finding a donor for her?" he asked as he looked at Dave.

Dave glanced at Alice and then answered, "No; I am still waiting for some results. I will know more when I receive them. There is no donor that matches in the donor bank right now?"

"I haven't checked lately because Sarah was doing so well, but her name is in there, so we should hear if a donor turns up. In the meantime, I think it is imperative that you keep looking for her. I will step up her dialysis to three times per week, but it certainly is not a permanent solution."

"I know. Can we see her?" Alice asked.

"Yes, you can go in and sit with her until we get the paperwork done. Dave, I would like to talk with you for a minute if possible."

"Okay." Turning to Alice, he said, "Tell Sarah I will be in as soon as I can."

As Dave walked away with Dr. Klein, Alice watched them and thought, "Now what is all that about? Why would he want to talk to Dave alone? What is Dave hiding from me? Does he have some health problem he isn't telling me about? Well, I am going to get to the bottom of it, one way or another." Straightening her back, she turned and marched into the emergency room where Sarah was.

* * *

"What did you want to see me about?" Dave asked the doctor when they were in the office.

"I was going to call you this morning, but Sarah's emergency beat me to it. The results of your DNA tests are back."

Dave sat up straighter and stared at the doctor, "And?"

"The young fellow that came to see you is not your son. There is no match found there. So I certainly don't believe he would be willing to donate a kidney when he isn't related, even if he would be a donor match for Sarah."

Dave slumped in the chair again and muttered, "I was so hoping he actually was my son and could be a possibility for a match. Now I am confused. Why would his mother tell him he is my son? It sounds to me like she didn't even see her child when it was born. That would be why she didn't know she had a girl instead of a boy. How on earth am I going to be able to explain all this?"

"Well, if you are sure the only child you have is Sarah; I think you should give some thought to talking to Alice and clearing the air there, and then contacting the mother. She might be a possible donor. If she has other children, they might also be possible donors. Siblings are good possibilities. I think Alice is a very understanding woman and she loves Sarah very much and will want what is best for her. I think you should be able to take a little heat for the benefit of your daughter. All this happened before you and Alice dated, right?"

Dave sighed, "Yes; I didn't even know Alice when I took Amy out that one night. I was drinking and don't even remember much about it. I do know Amy was trying to escape an unhappy home life. I feel bad now that I didn't support her when she told me about the baby, but many of the boys were always bragging about their conquests and she was one they mentioned. Therefore, with that in mind, when she said she was pregnant, I certainly wasn't going to accept responsibility when there were all those other guys. I guess I was wrong. They were probably just blowing off steam. Now I have to contact her and that is going to be very hard, but not as hard as telling Alice about all this."

"I know, but I think you have to, and soon for Sarah's sake. Do you want a copy of the report?"

"I guess I had better have it as I am sure Shane is going to want a copy. I feel sorry for him, as he really seemed a nice kid and looking for his father. I hope he finds him."

Dave put the report into his pocket and thanking Dr. Klein, headed out the door and over to emergency. He knew today was going to be the day things in his life changed and he was not looking forward to that.

Chapter 32

Southern Alberta

Shane and Ivan had just finished tagging the last heifer when Shane's cell phone rang. He was tempted to ignore it, but thinking it might be April, he snapped it open and answered, "Hello."

"Is this Shane Collins?"

"Yes. Who is this?"

"This is Dave Knight. I was hoping I had the right number. Do you have a minute?"

Shane signed to Ivan that the call was important and answered, "Sure. I have been waiting for your call."

"I knew you would be anxious to hear the results, though I don't think you will be happy with them."

Shane's heart sank, "What are you saying?"

'The tests show that there is no possibility that you are my son. I have the report and will send you a copy. I am disappointed, too. I was hoping you were."

"There is no hope that there is a mistake?"

"Not likely. Our lab is very thorough. We could have the test redone if you want, but I think it would be a waste of time."

"I appreciate you letting me know. I am sorry I bothered you with all this."

"I'm not. You seem like a fine young man and I hope you find your father. Good luck to you."

"Thank you," Shane voiced as he snapped his phone shut.

Ivan came over to stand beside Shane. Noticing the look on Shane's face, he asked, "Bad news?"

Taking a minute, Shane finally answered, "Not the news I expected, that is for sure. Right now, I am a little upset. I think your wife has a lot of explaining to do and it is going to be right now," and with that, Shane headed out the gate and up the path to the house.

"Hey, wait a minute," Ivan hollered as he hurried to catch up, "Tell me what is going on?"

Shane stopped in mid-stride and glared over at Ivan, "Your wife, and my, oh I don't know what to call her . . . . lied to me. Dave Knight is not my father. Absolutely positively NOT my father. So how do you like those apples? What is Amy trying to pull?"

Ivan stared at Shane, and then replied, "Amy would not lie about something like that. If she said Dave is your father, then she definitely believes that. I don't think you should go barging in there and accuse her of something like that, when she doesn't even know you have contacted Dave."

"I don't care. The air is going to get cleared, right now," and Shane stomped off up the path.

Ivan had a sinking feeling he was going to be in big trouble. No matter which way the wind blew, he would get the brunt of it. Sighing, he followed Shane to the house.

* * *

Slamming through the kitchen door, Shane marched into Amy's kitchen. Startled, she dropped the dish she was washing into the sudsy water and swung around. "Oh Shane, you surprised me. I didn't expect you guys to be done for a bit yet. Lunch isn't quite ready."

"Forget lunch. Why have you lied to me all these years? Didn't I deserve better than that? I can't believe you would do this to our family!"

Amy stared at Shane, "What on earth are you talking about?"

"My father. How long have you known that Dave Knight was not my father?"

"Not your father . . . Who told you that? Oh, I get it. You have been in touch with him and he denied it. Well, I told you he would. He never wanted to take responsibility for having a child."

"He did not deny it. The DNA test did. We were both suckered in. Why would you do this?"

"What do you mean? What test?" By this time, Ivan was in the kitchen, "Ivan, what do you know about all this? What have you guys been keeping from me?"

Shane sneered, "You are a great one to talk. You, with all your secrets. Who is my real father, and do not try to tell me it is Dave. The tests prove otherwise."

"Everyone calm down," Ivan spoke for the first time. "Accusing each other is not going to solve our problem. Amy, if Shane says that Dave can't be his father, then we have to accept that."

Amy dropped down into the kitchen chair and started to cry. Ivan put his arm around her and looked up at Shane. Disgusted, Shane sat down in the chair across the table and said, "Dave told me that he has a daughter he adopted at four years of age and just learned recently that she is actually his daughter. If I am not his son, then I might not be your son either, and this girl might be your daughter. Could that be possible? Could you have had a daughter instead? Did you see your baby?"

Amy's face blanched as she stared at Shane, "No . . . . no. That can't be. You are my son."

"Are you sure? We never did do any tests. Maybe I'm not."

Ivan was in shock. Could that be? Could Shane be right? This was getting worse by the minute. Ivan sat down heavily in the other chair and mulled things over in his mind. Amy was crying softly and Shane was staring out the window. Thank goodness Laura and Abe were over at Shane's with April so they wouldn't get upset, Ivan thought.

When Ivan spoke again, he was watching Shane. "I think the first order of the day is to get some blood tests done. That way, we will know for sure what is what. Do you agree, Shane?"

"I don't," Amy spoke up, "I don't need a blood test to know that Shane is my son. The Collins' raised him, knowing he was my son. How can he be anyone different?"

"Mistakes can be made," Ivan answered, "Could it be possible that the babies got switched?"

Shane thought about that and looking at Amy, said, "If that is what happened, then I have two parents out there that I don't know, instead of one."

"Through her tears, Amy confirmed, "You will always be my son, whether biological or not. We love you; all of us do. Please Shane, let this thing drop and let's just enjoy life and our family."

"I can't," Shane stood up and started to the door, "I want to get the blood work done. I expect you to oblige me in this. Then I will decide where I stand in all this. I will be in touch." Shane stomped out the door, leaving Ivan and Amy staring after him.

When the door slammed, Amy jumped up from her chair and raced to the door, calling out to Shane but he was already in his truck and heading out the lane. Turning to Ivan, she glared at him and said, "Okay, buster. Start explaining what you had to do with all this. I am so mad at you, I could throw things."

"Calm down. I had nothing to do with all this. I knew Shane was contacting Dave and he asked me to be quiet about it until he knew for sure how Dave would react to him. That is the only sin I have committed. I shouldn't have agreed to stay quiet, but I didn't want you upset if Dave rejected him. Then you wouldn't need to know he contacted him."

"So it's okay to keep secrets from me now? Thanks a lot."

"I did it for Shane."

"So now I suppose you think I lied to you about Dave? I know he is the father of my child. I don't care what the tests say."

"Are you sure that Shane is that child?"

"Leave me alone. If you want lunch, make it yourself." With that final remark, Amy headed out the door.

Chapter 33

Regina, Saskatchewan

The phone was ringing when Dave walked into the house. Taking off his overshoes, he picked it up just as it quit ringing. "Drat! Why do people never let it ring long enough?" They had caller ID, but the number was blocked. "Well," Dave voiced, "If it is important, I guess they will call back."

Being as Alice's car was not in the driveway; Dave assumed she wasn't home yet. Checking the fridge, he took out the casserole he found there and popped it into the oven. Setting the temperature at three hundred, he shut the oven door and headed to the bathroom to wash up before setting the table. They have an unspoken rule in their home; whoever arrived home first, got supper started. Lately, with so many people in crisis, Alice had been working a lot of overtime. It seemed to happen every year in the months before Christmas. Alice informed Dave that overspending for the holiday was the main reason for so many family conflicts and money problems.

Dave shook his head. Talk about family conflicts. He knew his family was about to enter into the conflict to end all conflicts. With Sarah's health failing, Dave knew he could not wait any longer before having his talk with Alice. He just hoped that she would not be stressed tonight and would listen and understand. Once he cleared the air with Alice, then they could tell Sarah together. Dave was hoping that Shane would talk to Amy and give her a heads up before he contacted her. That was going to be a very hard phone call to make. Nevertheless, it was his responsibility. His daughter's life may depend on it.

* * *

Alice locked the door to her office and waved good-bye to the receptionist. She had hoped to find time to stop at the hospital before heading home, but she was running late. Digging out her cell phone, she dialed Sarah's number. She picked up on the first ring. "Mom? What's up?"

"Nothing, sweetie. I was hoping to get up to see you before I headed home, but I had to work late. Are you doing okay?"

"I'm fine. Just feeling tired. I just woke up when Jesse dropped by a few minutes ago to see how I was doing. He said he would bring me some work tomorrow."

"I don't want you to worry about your lessons. You just get lots of rest so you can get back home. I will pop in at noon tomorrow on my lunch break. Love you."

"Love you too, Mom. Bye."

Alice pocketed her cell phone and headed out to her car. The weather had moderated so the car didn't take long to warm up. Pulling out into the traffic, she headed north. She really hoped Dave got home early and had supper started. She felt drained. Things were so hectic and so many problems to deal with. If only people would learn, she thought. Many don't realize that money doesn't grow on trees. She was so grateful that Dave was careful about money. Together they made a good team. Now if I can just find out what is on his mind these days, things will be even better, Alice mused. She knew he was worried about Sarah, but there seemed to be more to his worry. She knew the sun rose and set on Sarah as far as Dave was concerned, but maybe he is depressed that he can't help her the way he thinks he should. The thought had crossed her mind as well.

Turning onto her street, Alice noticed the kitchen lights were on. Good. Dave was home. As she pulled into the driveway, the outside light came on. Boy, the days are so short anymore, she thought as she grabbed her purse and stepped out of the car. She decided to leave the car in the driveway, just in case they decided to slip up to the hospital and see Sarah after supper.

* * *

"Dave, what is wrong? You hardly said two words all through supper. You seem so pre-occupied. I am feeling left out here."

Dave sighed and picking up his plate, headed to the sink, "Alice, let's get this mess cleaned up and then have a talk. I do have something to discuss with you."

"Oh? I hope it isn't more bad news. I don't think I can take any more right now," Alice also got up and started clearing away the food.

"I guess that depends on what you call bad news. You will have to make that decision."

"Now you really have me mystified. Can you give me a hint? Does it have anything to do with Sarah?"

"It has everything to do with Sarah. No more hints. Let's get this cleaned up and then we talk."

In short order, the kitchen was clean and Dave and Alice migrated to the family room and their favorite chairs. Dave was mulling over where to start and decided that the best would be at the beginning.

"Well?" Alice prompted after they were seated.

Dave turned to her and said, "Okay, here goes. I just hope you will understand what I am about to tell you. We need to stick together on this."

"Haven't we always?" Alice enquired.

"Yes, you are the best. However, this is different. Okay, remember when I went to be tested to see if I was a match for Sarah?"

"I remember."

"Well, I wasn't a match, but something else came out of that test."

"Oh? What else?"

"Dr. Klein said that Sarah's and my DNA is nearly a perfect match."

Alice stared at Dave, "How is that possible? We adopted Sarah."

"I know. That was my first reaction. I told Dr. Klein that there was a mistake. There is no mistake. Sarah is my biological daughter."

Alice's face went white. Then she got angry. "So you are trying to tell me that we went to Calgary and adopted Sarah at four years of age and she is actually your daughter? And now you are telling me you didn't know?"

"That is what I am telling you. I had no idea she was my daughter until the test."

"Why is it that I am finding that hard to believe? You are the one that wanted to adopt an older child. You insisted, actually. You said it was so we didn't have to worry about diapers, and potty training among other things. You know what I think? I think you conned me. You wanted Sarah for your own selfish reasons," Alice was on her feet by this time and pointing a finger at Dave.

"That is not true," Dave protested, "I wanted to adopt Sarah as she seemed a lonely little child that needed the good home that I knew we could give her. To tell you the truth, I didn't know that I had fathered a child."

"And that is another thing. Why have I never heard of this woman in your life?"

"Because she was not in my life. Before I met you, I did a lot of partying and drinking. Sarah's mother was just one of the girl's. We had a one-night fling. I had no idea she had a child."

"The possibility was there, I'm sure you knew. Things happen."

Dave didn't figure this was the time to tell Alice that Amy had contacted him, saying she was pregnant. She would be more convinced than ever that Dave wasn't being honest with her about Sarah.

"I am sorry if this all upsets you, Alice, but I felt I had to come forth and tell you this now. Sarah needs help and maybe her biological mother or some other siblings can help her."

"Why have you kept this from me for so long? It has been months since you found out."

"For exactly this reason. I knew you would be upset and would accuse me of keeping Sarah's parentage from you. As God is my witness, I did not know when we adopted her."

Alice sat back down in her chair and voiced, "So are you going to contact this woman?"

"I am going to try. I might as well tell you the rest of the story. Do you remember the young man that phoned here a couple of times?"

"Yes."

"Well, he came to see me at work. His mother told him that I was his father."

"Oh, for heaven's sake, Dave. How many women are we talking about here?"

"Let me finish, please. He came to see me and we had DNA tests done. I was hoping that he was my son so he could help Sarah. I thought maybe he and Sarah could be twins. They do resemble each other a bit. The DNA tests proved we are not related. He found his mother a few years ago, and she believes I am his father. So that tells me she never saw her baby or she would know if she had a boy or girl or how many. She believes Shane is her son. I wonder what she will think when she finds out Sarah is actually her daughter."

"So we are only talking about one woman here? What is her name?"

"When we were in school, her name was Amy Stern. I don't know what her name is now. I know she is married and living on a ranch in southern Alberta. She has two other children."

"So . . . you are telling me all this now, because you think she can help Sarah?"

"That is my hope. I knew you would understand."

"I understand that Sarah needs help and I understand why you want to contact this person. What I don't understand is why you felt the need to keep this from me all this time. That is a breach of confidence I am not going to find it easy to get past. We have always been open and honest with each other. Now I am wondering what else you have been keeping from me."

"Oh, Alice. Please understand. I did not want to hurt you. Even though I had this relationship before we even met, I knew it would hurt you. I love you too much to see you hurt. But I also love Sarah and I know you do too, so we have to get past this in order to help her."

Alice had tears in her eyes; tears of sorrow and of anger, but she knew Dave was right. She had to get past what she thought of as a betrayal, for Sarah's sake and for her own.

"I have to have some time to myself to digest all this. I don't want to talk anymore." With that, Alice got up and headed to the bedroom.

Dave just sat in his chair and heaved a huge sigh of relief. It was finally out in the open. It actually went better than he had hoped. At least Alice didn't storm out of the room. He was hoping, given a little time she would come around and then they could talk to Sarah together. The next challenge would be calling Amy.

Chapter 34

Southern Alberta

There was a cool wind blowing from the west, and though the temperature had moderated in the last few days, it felt colder than it was. Amy turned up the collar on her parka and snuggled deeper into the warmth of the jacket. Looking out over the landscape, she could see a couple of mule deer grazing in the coulee, unaware of her approach.

It had been over two hours since she had left the house, informing Ivan to make his own lunch. She knew she had to go back and face up to the problem that was looming, but she was reluctant to do that. She had no idea where to start. She just would not accept that Shane was not her son. Didn't her father adopt him, knowing he was his grandson? Didn't her mother make sure relatives raised him? How could he not be who they said he was? Could there be a possibility that the babies were switched? Amy didn't want to go there, because that would mean she did have a child out there somewhere. What did Shane say . . . something about Dave's adopted daughter being his real daughter? Could that child actually be her child? Amy's heart started thumping. That cannot be. That was just too much coincidence. No, there had to be some other explanation.

Amy stopped walking and stared off to the west. Clouds were starting to build, making the sky darken. Noting the change in weather, she decided now was the time to turn around and start heading back. No sense being caught in a snowstorm. She knew Ivan would be starting to worry and she had to go to April's and pick up the kids.

Shoving her hands into her pockets, Amy headed back the way she came. Before she arrived at the lower pasture gate, she could see Ivan coming toward her. Her walk had cooled her animosity toward him, and she was actually glad to see him. He waved and she waved back. When he got close enough, he said, "I could see the clouds building and didn't want you caught up in a storm. I wasn't sure that you had noticed."

"Thanks for caring. I had noticed and started back. Looks like we are going to get a dump of snow. At least we will have a white Christmas."

"A lot can happen between now and then. Depends if we get a thaw or not. I, for one would like it to stay below freezing. Thaws are never good on the livestock. Are you okay?"

"I will be. I just have a lot to mull over in my mind. I am having trouble taking all this in. I'm not mad at you anymore. I know it isn't your fault. I'm not mad at Shane either. He must be so confused. I certainly am."

Ivan put his arm around Amy and gave her a hug, "We will get through this. Shane will cool off and realize that you are a victim too. Who knows what happened when your baby was born? Maybe there was a switch. Do you think your mother knows about this? It would be the ultimate revenge on your father; have him raise a child whom he thought was his flesh and blood, but not?"

Amy stopped and stared at Ivan, "Oh . . . I never thought about that. Do you think she could be that devious? On second thought, don't answer that. Of course she could be. She has lied to me before. That could be why she never seems to want anything to do with Shane. She knows he isn't her grandson."

"We have no proof she planned this, but it is a thought. Do not jump to that conclusion until you talk with her. Do you think she would admit it at this late date?"

"I will make her talk about it. If she did this, she has a lot to answer for. And her professing to be such a good Christian."

"Even church going people are not always on the up and up. You know that and I know that. Years of experience for us both, right?" and Ivan gave Amy a squeeze.

"I agree. Let's get home and make some plans. I guess the first order of the day is for me to get some blood tests. I need to know if Shane is my son before I confront my mother. And I need to talk with Shane."

* * *

Shane had never been so angry. He just could not believe that Amy could be capable of lying to him all these years. He realized he shouldn't have confronted her so abruptly, but at least this way, she didn't have a chance to make up some story. Well, the truth was out now. He really was an orphan. He didn't have a clue who his father. If Amy was insisting that Dave was his father, then she didn't know whom his father was, so that didn't say much about her character, did it? Maybe her mother had a right to be so controlling when she was a teenager. It couldn't have been easy for her, raising a daughter by herself, one that wasn't trustworthy. Shane shook his head. He was beginning to see a very different picture of Amy, one he didn't like.

Kicking at a lump of snow, Shane turned from the corral and started heading to the house. He had no idea what to tell April. Right at this moment, he was wishing he had listened to her and let this father search go. Now everyone was upset and he had no idea how to solve it. He would have to start from scratch if he wanted to start another search for his real father. Amy certainly wasn't going to be any help. He didn't want her help anyway. He just didn't trust her anymore.

Entering the house, he removed his boots and headed to the bathroom to wash up. It was then he heard the children's voices. "Oh no," he moaned aloud, "I forgot the kids were here. Now what am I going to do?"

"Shane, is that you? I didn't expect you back until after lunch. Did you get done early?"

Shane answered, "Yes, we did. Don't worry about lunch for me. I'm not hungry."

April appeared in the doorway, "Are you sick? You never turn down lunch."

"I guess you could say I am. Can you take the kids home? I need to talk to you . . . privately."

"Okay. Is there something wrong?"

"Everything is wrong. Don't stop at Ivans. Just take the kids home and drop them off, okay? I really don't want to see the kids right now."

"I will be right back. It will take me a minute or two to get them dressed and out the door. Can you watch Michael?"

"Sure."

"Thanks. I will get back as soon as I can."

"Thanks," and as April turned away, "I love you. You will never know how much."

April turned back, "I love you too, Shane."

* * *

"Okay, now are you going to tell me what's up? I am dying of curiosity," April said, as she slid into the chair across the table from Shane, "I dropped the kids off like you said. Amy waved from the kitchen window, but I just waved back and left. She will probably think I was being rude."

"I don't think you have to worry about that. She will know why you didn't stop."

"Oh? So what is going on? Is there a problem with you and your Mom?"

"Right now, I am so angry, I could spit. I hate being lied to and that is just what Amy did. She lied to me. She has been lying all along."

"What on earth are you talking about? Your Mom wouldn't lie to you. She loves you and would never hurt you by doing that."

"Well, maybe you can explain to me why she has insisted all these years that Dave Knight is my father, when DNA proves that he isn't?"

April stared at Shane and then stammered, "What do you mean? You got the results?"

"I got a phone call from Dave. He is sending me the report. It states positively that he is not my father. So now what do you think of the chances that Amy is lying to me?"

April got up and went to the fridge. She took out the orange juice and poured a glass for them both. Sitting back down, she assured Shane, "All I know is if Amy said Dave is your father that is what she truly believes. Why would she lie about something like that? If he isn't your father, that only makes things appear worse for her. That would mean she doesn't know who your father is."

"Bingo! See what I mean? I have lost a lot of respect for her. I don't know if I can get past that."

"I think you need to have a long talk with her. You need to sit down together and straighten this out. For the sake of our families, if for no other reason."

"I did talk to her; or should I say, shouted at her. I know. I should have approached it a little differently, but I was angry. She was very upset when I left."

"Shane, I think you need to pray about this, then go and see your mother."

"Am I even sure she is my mother? If what Dave says is true and the daughter he raised is really his daughter and if what Amy says is true, then Dave's daughter Sarah is actually Amy's daughter. So where does that leave me?"

"Oh Shane, don't even think that way. You will always be Amy's son, even if it turns out you are not blood related. You have to get this settled, one way or another. For yourself, and for Michael and our future children."

Shane sighed, "I know. I just don't know where to start. I guess with Amy as you said. I hope she will agree to some blood tests. We have to prove one way or another if I am her son. Then go from there."

April got up and putting the glasses in the sink, walked over and put her arms around Shane. Giving him a big hug, she said, "You will feel better once you do that. Remember, we all love you, Ivan and Amy included."

"I know. I love you with all my heart. I do love Ivan and Amy, but I am very disappointed in Amy right now. I will get over it, but it will take time. Once I feel I can talk to her without being upset, I will. Right now, I am going to go hug my son."

April laughed, "That is a good idea. Cuddling a baby can chase away all the blues."

Chapter 35

Regina, Saskatchewan

Being as it was less than three weeks until Christmas, Alice decided it was time to get the tree up and the lights on the house. She was hoping Sarah would be feeling well enough to be able to help with the decorating, as she did every year. They brought her home from the hospital the week before but she was struggling. Jesse had been to see her every day and brought his notes for her to study, but she was very depressed. Not being able to attend her classes was really upsetting her. Dave and Alice were trying their best to keep her spirits up but it was not easy. Because of her health situation, they had not spoken to her about her parental issue. Alice was in no hurry and she was sure Dave wasn't either.

   Things had been strained between her and Dave since he had told her about Sarah. Alice knew it was mainly her fault, but she just couldn't get past the fact that he had not told her as soon as he found out Sarah was his child. It was almost as if he had something to hide. More and more, she was thinking he didn't tell her the whole story. Was there more to the relationship than he was telling her, she mused as she headed to the basement to get the decorations. Was this woman actually someone special in his life? Was Dave on the rebound from another relationship when they got together? The girl must have been pregnant when she and Dave got married. Why had she never heard of Amy Stern? Did Dave know she was pregnant? That was the big question. Alice didn't know if she could ever forgive and forget if that was the case. What kind of man leaves a woman pregnant without taking responsibility? She only hoped Dave was being truthful when he said he didn't know he had fathered a child. If that was true, then she had a chance to get past this. No matter what the outcome, their lives were changed permanently. They had to tell Sarah soon and that was going to be hard.

Alice rummaged through the boxes in the storage room and found the one she was looking for. So many memories in this box, she thought as she headed up the stairs with it. Every year, a new Christmas ball had been added, marking Sarah's Christmases with them. Alice had already purchased the new one for this year. It was a praying angel. "We need all the prayers we can get," Alice muttered as she set the box on the coffee table next to the tree, "I particularly need some prayers to forget the past and concentrate on the future."

* * *

Sarah could hear her mother down in the living room. Sitting up in bed, she rubbed her forehead and yawned. She felt quite rested for a change. That was a good sign, she thought. Maybe things were starting to get better. She was due for dialysis in a day or so, but had today free. Checking her calendar, she realized it was only a few weeks until Christmas. She knew her fellow students were writing exams, but she just didn't have the strength to handle a 2-hour session. Sarah sighed. She had so wanted to graduate with her class, but she knew that wasn't going to happen. Even though Jesse had kept her up to date the best he could with his notes, she didn't have enough classroom time to qualify.

Swinging her legs over the side of the bed, Sarah reached for her robe and headed to the bathroom. Because she felt better, she was going to ask her Mom to take her to the Mall. She wanted to do a bit of Christmas shopping before the stores got crazy closer to the Christmas holiday. She had a few people she needed to shop for. Jesse was at the top of her list. Without him and his dedication in bringing the updates to her, she wouldn't even be in the position she was. Because of that, Sarah felt she had a good chance of being able to complete her courses later. She would not be graduating with her class, but hopefully, the next year. Everything depended on her getting a kidney transplant.

As Sarah stepped into the shower, she thought about her chances of a transplant. So far, there had been no matches showing up in the registry. Dr. Klein was hoping for a match soon. Sarah realized that things were not going well for her but as long as she responded to the dialysis, she could hang on. Being adopted, she didn't have any idea where to start looking for relatives. "Maybe I should ask Mom and Dad to do some research into the adoption. Mom works with those agencies all the time. She should be able to get the information if anyone can," Sarah pondered, "I will check with Mom today."

Finishing her shower, she grabbed her robe and toweling her hair dry, headed to the kitchen to grab a juice.

* * *

Alice had just finished setting out the decorations when she heard Sarah in the kitchen.

"Good Morning, Sarah! How are you feeling today?"

"Great, Mom," Sarah responded as she came to the door, "What are you up to?"

"Just getting some of the Christmas stuff out. I want to get the tree decorated this weekend, before things start piling up. Are you going to feel up to helping me decorate the tree this year?"

"Of course. I wouldn't miss that for the world. As long as I can remember, I always helped decorate. The last thing I always put on the tree was my decoration. I was so anxious to see what it was every year."

"I'm glad you are feeling some better. I hope things will continue to improve."

"That's not going to happen, Mom. You know that and I know that. I need a transplant and soon. I was wondering, do you think you could do some research into my adoption and try to find out whom my biological parents were? Maybe I have some siblings out there that can help me, or even my parents. It doesn't look like a match is forthcoming from the registry."

Alice had her back to Sarah as she spoke and she hesitated before turning around. "I will see what I can find, but don't get your hopes up just yet. There is a lot of paperwork involved in getting permission for medical reasons to open the files."

"I think the sooner we get started on this, the better. I am trying to be upbeat about this, but it is getter harder every day."

"I will talk to your Dad today and see what we can do."

"That's good. Things seem to be tense between you two these days. I hope I am not the problem?"

"Don't you worry about us. We are doing okay. Of course, we are worried about you and we will do everything we can to see you get the help you need."

"Thanks, Mom. I love you to bits. Now I have a favor to ask. Do you think you could run me to the Mall? I want to do a bit of Christmas shopping before the stores get crazy. Do you have time?"

"I will make time. Maybe we will have lunch there, too. Okay?"

"Sounds good. I'll go and get dressed."

Alice watched Sarah head upstairs. Then she sat down heavily on the sofa and put her head in her hands. Well, that cinched it, she moaned. They had to talk to Sarah tonight. Things were coming to a head.

Picking up the phone, Alice dialed Dave's cell.

Chapter 36

Southern Alberta

Amy stared at the document her Doctor handed to her. Then she looked up and said, "Explain to me in layman terms, please? I can't make heads or tails out of this thing."

"I know this is not what you want to hear, Amy, but to make a long story short, Shane could not be your son. On his DNA, there are no matches to yours. I am sorry to have to be the one to tell you this. I know how much you and Ivan think of Shane and his family."

Amy's heart dropped. Tears came to her eyes as she looked at the paper and then the doctor. She couldn't speak over the lump in her throat.

"Amy, are you all right? Can I get you something? A glass of water, perhaps?"

Amy shook her head and got up. Clearing her throat, she responded, "Thank you, but I'm okay. I am just having a hard time dealing with all this. How could this have happened? My father, Abe Collins adopted Shane, believing he was his grandson. So naturally, I assumed he was my son. I cannot believe this."

"I understand why you are upset, but nothing has really changed. You accepted Shane as your son. He is still the same person, whether blood related or not. Do not discard the relationship you have with him and his wife and son. I know mistakes do happen when people are adopted occasionally, but it is not common. Is there any way you can check with someone who was there? A nurse perhaps?"

Amy sat back down. "You know, there is someone who might know something. Whether she will tell me anything is another story. My mother was there and she is the one that told my father about the baby. I can't believe she would deliberately hoodwink my father into adopting a child that wasn't related to him, but then again, she was a master at keeping things hidden. Don't worry. She will be getting a visit from me to see what she knows. I expect she will lie about it, but now I am armed with more information. She lied to me about my father, so why not my son?"

The Doctor smiled, "There; that is the fighting spirit I know. Just remember what I said about Shane. He will be just as upset as you are by this news, but together you will get through this. Don't let this information destroy what you have."

"Thank you, Doctor. A lot of this will depend on Shane. He was so angry with me as he thinks I withheld information from him. I have to make him understand that I truly believed Dave Knight was his father. Now it appears that I am not his mother either. That will not be easy for him to take. Now I know I have a child out there somewhere that I have never met. That is not easy for me to accept."

The doctor closed the file and replied, "Let me know if there is anything else I can do. How are Abe and Laura?"

"Just fine. I hope none of this will upset them too much. Thank God they are young enough and probably won't understand." With that, Amy got up and headed to the door. "See you next month."

* * *

Ivan was anxious for Amy to get home. Much as he liked spending time with his kids, her trip to the doctor was reason for Ivan to worry. When they received the call this morning for Amy to come in, Ivan knew something was up. They had been waiting anxious ever since Amy and Shane had supplied the DNA samples. Shane seemed relieved that Amy agreed to the testing and though he hadn't really been the same, he was now coming around and trying to make the best of the situation. This test would be the telling as to what the future would bring. Ivan sure hoped it was good news.

"Daddy, when is Mommy coming back? I want to show her what I made," Laura asked as she patted Ivan on the arm.

"Soon I hope, honey. She had an appointment in town. I think she might be getting some groceries, too. Have to keep our little munchkins fed."

"Oh, Daddy, I'm not a munchkin. I am a little girl. You are so funny!"

"What about Abe? Maybe he is a munchkin."

Laura giggled, "No, Daddy! He is a little boy. But he is really messy. Are munchkins messy?"

"Really, really messy," Ivan answered and grabbing Laura, tried to give her a whisker rub. Giggling and squirming, she managed to avoid it and took off up the stairs. Abe came in from the porch where he was playing with his trucks to see what all the ruckus was about.

"Come here, Abe. I want to give you a whisker rub," Ivan growled at him. Abe screamed and headed to the stairs. Ivan pretended to try to catch him, but giggling, Abe made his getaway. Laughing to himself, Ivan sat back down in his easy chair and opened his bible to where he was reading.

Because he couldn't concentrate, Ivan bowed his head and offered a prayer. He prayed that no matter what the report was today, they would manage to get through it as a family. He prayed for understanding on Amy and Shane's behalf so they could accept whatever came out of this conflict. Then he prayed for his little family and told God how grateful he was for his two children and Amy. He also prayed for guidance on how to deal with any fallout. Ivan was really determined to keep things calm and secure for his children. With them being so young, they really had no idea about the upheaval going on in the family. "Please, God, let's keep things that way," Ivan voiced aloud as he ended his prayer.

* * *

Shane heaved the last of the bale over the fence to his horse, and stepped back. Rubbing his hands together, he then brushed the hay from the front of his parka. The chores were completed and now he had some time on his hands. He knew Amy had gone into the doctor's office that morning, so he was anxious, wondering what the test would reveal.

He was trying not to worry April too much, but it was hard to keep his feelings to himself. He had no idea what he would do, no matter what the report said. If Amy was really his mother, then she wasn't telling him the truth about his father. If Amy wasn't his mother, then he had no idea who his mother and father were. Which would mean Amy was not lying to him, but had been a victim herself. Shane could not understand how that could happen. It made more sense that Amy was not telling the truth, but then why did she so readily agree to the DNA test. Things were really complicated and confusing.

Checking the gate to be sure it was closed, Shane started up the path to the house. Amy should be home soon and he expected he would be getting a call or a visit. His stomach was in knots, but he didn't want April to know just how scared he was.

As he opened the door into the porch, April called, "Shane, is that you?"

"Yes, what's up?"

"Oh, nothing. I am just feeding Michael, but will start lunch right away. Do you have any preferences? I can make Denver sandwiches if you like."

"Anything is fine. I'm not really that hungry, so don't hurry. Amy didn't call yet?"

April came out of the bedroom carrying Michael. "No; no calls. Do you think she had time to get back from town yet?"

"Probably not. I am just anxious to know what the doctor said. I'm sure she would stop for groceries while in there, too." Shane took Michael from April and stroked his fuzzy hair.

"You're right. I talked with her yesterday and asked her if she would pick up some milk and eggs for us."

"Good. Then we won't have to go in this week. We will make plans to head in shopping next week. Christmas is definitely creeping up on us and I'm sure you will want some time to shop. We could drop Michael at your Mom's while we are in town."

"Oh, Mom would love that! She always says she doesn't get to see Michael enough. Of course, my brother and sisters will spoil him rotten, but that's okay."

"He is pretty young to spoil, so I don't think you have to worry."

April laughed, "I guess you are right. Now that you are holding Michael, I will see to our lunch."

As she headed to the kitchen, Shane headed to his chair in the living room. With any luck, he would have Michael asleep by the time lunch was ready. Snuggling the baby close to him, Shane felt a huge lump coming into his throat. He felt so blessed to have April and Michael in his life. No matter what the doctor says, Shane thought that would never change. Feelings of love so strong washed over him as he gazed at the cherub face staring up at him.

"What's up, guy? Are you wondering what I am all about? Well, I am your daddy and I will love you always. Don't ever forget that."

Michael waved his arms around and attempted a smile. That made Shane smile too, as he wiped away the moisture that for some reason was starting to run down his cheeks. The baby closed his eyes, and clutched Shane's finger in his chubby little hand, and as Shane gazed down at him, he drifted off to sleep.

"Lunch is ready," April called as she placed the cutlery on the table. Putting the baby into his bassinet, Shane headed to the kitchen. April gave him a hug and said, "Michael asleep? Good. Now we can have an undisturbed lunch."

However, that was not to be. Just as they sat down and Shane blessed the food, the phone rang. Both Shane and April looked at the phone and then at each other. April reached over and picked up the phone.

* * *

The first thing Amy did when she arrived home was head straight into Ivan's arms.

Startled, Ivan threw his arms tight around her and quizzed, "Are you okay? What's up?"

"Just hold me for a moment. I need to feel your love. I need to feel that things are still okay and nothing will change. I need things to be the way they were, before all this garbage hit us. Can you relate to that?"

"Can I ever? But one thing will never change. My love for you. I need you and the kids need you. Don't ever forget that."

"I know. Now I have to do the hardest thing I think I have ever done."

"Then I assume the news was not good?"

"Oh, Ivan, the very worst. Not only does Shane not know who his father is, he also doesn't know who his mother is. And I have lost a son." With that, Amy started to cry.

"I am so sorry. Nevertheless, you haven't lost Shane. Just because he isn't of your blood, doesn't mean you can't go on the same. I love Shane like a son and I have always known I wasn't his father. You will, too. What do you want me to do?"

Amy wiped her eyes and looking up at Ivan, asked, "Could you phone Shane and ask him to come over? I think I need to talk to him right away. I also have the groceries I picked up for them."

Ivan gave Amy a squeeze then released her. "I will do that right away. The kids have been asking for you, so you might want to get them settled before Shane comes. I gave them lunch already and I think Abe is ready for a nap."

"Okay. Thanks for doing this for me. I don't think I could talk to him on the phone without breaking down."

"I understand. Go take care of the kids."

As Amy left the room, Ivan picked up the phone. After several rings, April picked up. "Hello?"

"Hi April. This is Ivan. Is Shane there?"

"He's right here. Just a minute."

"No, that's okay. Could you just ask him if he can come over? Amy wants to talk to him."

"We are just having lunch, but he can come over right after."

"Good. And thanks, April."

"No problem. See you soon."

Ivan hung up the phone and headed to the kitchen. Seeing the groceries on the table, he started putting them away. Anything to keep his mind busy until Shane arrived. He was actually grateful he didn't have to talk to Shane on the phone. He was sure Shane would have asked many questions, which he didn't want to answer. That was Amy's privilege.

Chapter 37

Regina, Saskatchewan

Sarah and Alice had a wonderful time at the Mall. Sarah was feeling good and managed to get most of her shopping done. They stopped at the Food Court and enjoyed some Thai food before heading home. Sarah was especially happy as she managed to find the book Jesse had been raving about. She planned to give it to him before Christmas in case he managed to find it and buy it for himself. Now she was feeling tired and planned to have a rest when they got home.

For Alice, it was a relief to see that Sarah seemed so much better. It was a shame that things had to change, but Alice knew they had to talk to her; the sooner the better. She had called Dave and though he wasn't happy about it, agreed. They planned to have the talk after supper. Alice wanted Sarah to have a rest after they got home. Dave should be home by then. He usually didn't work on Saturday, but had a few things to clear off his desk that morning. With Christmas coming, Dave usually tried to have a few extra days off during the season. Maybe he can do some looking for that woman, Alice mused as she glanced over at Sarah and noticed she had nodded off.

* * *

Dave looked out the window and saw that snow was starting to fall. "Just what we need, more snow to contend with," he complained as he headed to the sink with his plate and cup. "I sure hope those two get home here before things get worse. I hope Sarah didn't play herself out."

With his nerves on edge, Dave just could not settle down to do anything constructive. Ever since Alice had called him, he could feel his stomach churning. The sandwich he had for lunch did not help matters any, either. The medication from the doctor had been working very well, but this was something new. Not butterflies of excitement, but of dread. How was Sarah going to take this news? She had so much to deal with already. However, maybe there will be hope too. He knew he would have to stress that even if it tore him apart.

Just the thought of contacting Amy made the pain in his stomach worse. He could just imagine how it was for Alice. He felt bad that he hurt her. She had been rather cool toward him lately, but seemed to be accepting things now. Dave had no idea what he would do if he ever lost her. She was his anchor and best friend. He never had too many male friends. Oh sure, he had drinking buddies when he was young, but as soon as he quit partying and started concentrating on his education, they all dropped him. Then he met Alice. The day he married her was the best day of his life.

They had their struggles financially, as most newlyweds did as they were both furthering their education, but they made it through. Adopting Sarah was the second best day of his life. Now everything was threatened. Dave sat down heavily in the kitchen chair and pondered how he was going to break the news to his little girl.

* * *

The snow was starting to come down heavy by the time Alice turned onto their street. She was glad to be home. Because the weather wasn't too cold, the snow was sticking to the windshield and making the drive a bit more hazardous.

Sarah woke up when Alice slowed for the turn. "Oh, sorry Mom. I guess I fell asleep. I sure wasn't much for company, was I?"

Alice smiled, "Don't give it a thought. It is good you were able to rest. We are almost home. With this snow coming down, I am really happy for that." Turning into the driveway, she commented, "I see your father is home. So he must have finished his work. After you have your rest, maybe we can all work on the tree and get it decorated today."

"Sounds good. I won't need too much of a rest, being as I slept all the way home."

"Just don't get over tired. Your body needs rest to heal."

Sarah opened the door when the car stopped and answered, "I won't, Mom. If I forget, I have you and Dad to remind me." Sarah grinned and dodged the playful slap Alice aimed at her. She jumped out of the car and headed for the door.

Alice shook her head and turning off the motor, slid out of the car and locked the doors. When she entered the house, she could hear Sarah in the kitchen talking to her Dad about her purchases. That was when Alice remembered them in the trunk of the car. She headed back out the door, unlocking the trunk as she went. "I would forget my head if it wasn't fastened on," she commented to herself, "Too much on my mind, I guess."

Grabbing the packages, she again locked the car and headed inside. Dave met her at the door and took the bags. "I wondered why you came in, and then headed back out."

"I guess I'm getting forgetful in my old age. Did Sarah go to lie down?"

"Yes, she said she was a little tired. Where do you want me to put these?"

"Just set them by the stairs. They are all Sarah's. After she has her nap, we are going to work on the tree. Do you have time to help us?"

"Sounds good. I don't have any plans for this afternoon. We are talking to her this evening?"

"I think that would be best. I want her well rested before we dump this on her. I'm not looking forward to this."

Dave sighed, "Me neither. I would do anything to change things, but now all we can hope is something good will come out of this."

"It had better, or I don't know how I will deal with all this. I am still struggling with this whole thing."

"I know," Dave answered as he laid his hand on Alice's arm, "I pray some day you will be able to forgive me."

"I already have done that. It is the forgetting I am having trouble with."

* * *

The tree decorating was a blast. Sarah was having a lot of fun, choosing where to put each ball. When Alice brought out the new decoration for Sarah, there were tears of joy all around. Taking the angel gently, Sarah found the ideal spot and hung it there. "Now I can gaze at her every time I sit in my chair," she announced to her parents. After everything was hung, Dave did the traditional placing of the star on the top of the tree. Alice and Sarah applauded when it was all finished and Dave turned on the lights.

"It looks beautiful," Sarah sighed, "I think every year we do a better job."

"Well," Dave remarked, "Being as some of our former trees had a little kid decorating, I guess things would improve."

"Oh, Daddy!" Sarah laughed as she threw an empty box at her Dad, "I remember some of those trees with great fondness."

"We do, too," Dave answered, "I can't think of anything more fun than having a little kid help decorate. The joy and excitement on their face is worth it all. Who cares if the tree ends up with all the balls on one side?"

"I don't remember that," Sarah questioned, keeping a straight face.

"Just kidding. You did a very good job every year. Of course, you had the expert guidance of your mother."

"I know. Mom, you used to fix the tree after I went to bed. I remember that. I would come down in the morning and there was something different about the tree, but I couldn't figure it out. I think I was seven or eight when I realized some of the balls had been moved."

"Guilty as charged," Alice laughed, "I just couldn't stand to leave things alone. You never said anything, so I figured I got away with it."

Dave and Sarah laughed as Dave commented, "Have to get up before breakfast to put anything over on our little girl. Let's have a hot chocolate to celebrate the decorating of our tree."

"Sounds good," Alice said as she headed to the kitchen, "Anyone want marshmallows on top?"

Chapter 38

Southern Alberta

Amy was grateful to Ivan for making the call to Shane. It was going to be hard enough to see his face when he read the report. She was praying he would be able to understand that she had nothing to do with the whole mess. How was she to know that Shane was not her son? Thinking back on it, she should have insisted on a DNA test, but can't a person take some things on faith? Talking about faith; the situation could really try a person's faith, Amy thought as she tucked Abe in for his afternoon nap. Why would God let this happen? Shane was a good Christian, going to church every Sunday and accepting all his callings in the church. Was this some kind of test for them all? She had read in the Book of Mormon, where tests of a person's faith came in all kinds and shapes. "Well, this is really a test for us," Amy muttered as she headed to Laura's room to see what she was up to. She found her playing with her dollhouse and rearranging the furniture in it.

"Hi, Mommy. See what I made?" Laura said excitedly as she shoved a sheet of paper in Amy's face. Holding it back so she could see it more clearly, she answered, "Wow! That is beautiful. What is it?"

"Oh Mommy! It is a rug for my dollhouse! See, there's the fringe on the edge and that is a horse in the middle. I wanted a rug for the floor of my living room and I couldn't find anything so I made one."

"That is very nice, Laura. If you like, I have some scraps in my sewing bag. Maybe later, we could make you a rug."

"Really?" Laura jumped up and gave Amy a hug, "When can we make it?"

"Later. Right now Shane is coming over and we will be doing some business, so I want you to stay up here in your room, okay?"

"Do I have to? I want to see Shane, too."

"I know, honey, but we have to do our business first. I will call you when we are finished, okay?"

"Okay," Laura agreed, "But don't forget."

"I won't. I hear Shane's truck now. I will call you."

Amy went out and closed Laura's door. If there was going to be any harsh words, she didn't want Laura to hear them.

* * *

Ivan opened the door when Shane knocked. "Come in. Amy will be right down. She is just putting Abe down for his nap."

"No hurry," Shane commented as he headed to the kitchen, "I could use a glass of water, though."

"Help yourself. How's April and Michael?"

"Fit as a fiddle. That boy is getting bigger by the minute. He is only a couple of months old, but he smiles, gurgles, and seems so happy. I am sure he knows who we all are."

"I'm sure he does. It is amazing how fast they learn certain things. I couldn't get over that with our two. They always knew Amy was the one with the food, though. I think they just tolerated me then."

Shane laughed, "I know what you mean."

"Who just tolerated you?" Amy asked as she entered the kitchen, "Hello, Shane."

"Hi," Shane answered, "We were just talking about babies and how fast they learn things. Michael surprises me everyday."

"They certainly are little miracles," Amy said as she opened the cupboard and grabbed a glass for some water, "Anyone else for a drink?"

"Thanks, but I helped myself," Shane voiced as he picked up his glass and took a swallow. "I imagine you asked me over here for a reason, so here I am."

Amy swallowed over the lump in her throat and glanced at Ivan. He was looking down at the floor. She reached into her pocket, produced the report, and handed it to Shane. "I believe this is self explanatory."

Shane scanned the paper, and then looked up at Amy, "I'm not sure I understand this. Explain it to me."

"I had trouble understanding it too, but the short of it is, our DNA does not match. You are not my biological son."

Shane stared at the paper, then threw it away from him and abruptly stood up and started pacing the floor, "So this means someone was not telling the truth way back when. We were both duped. Who would do something like that? Not my adopted parents, surely?"

Amy got up, headed over to Shane, and placed her hand on his arm, "Maybe the babies somehow got mixed up. I don't know. All I know is this was a terrible shock to me, too. I was so sure you were my son. I would have staked my life on it. I just could not believe this when the doctor told me."

Shane turned and gave Amy a hug, "I am so sorry for accusing you of lying to me. I should have known you would not do that. Can you forgive me?"

"Of course and remember; you are still my son. I don't care what the DNA says. Ivan has always considered you his son, and he knew there were no blood ties. Can we just accept this and go on from here?"

"I don't know. I now have a father and a mother out there I have never met."

"Yes, and I have a child I have never found, either."

"That reminds me," Shane looked at Amy, "Dave Knight said the daughter he adopted is his biological daughter. Could she be your daughter?"

"Maybe; and maybe he had more than one child out of wedlock. I will not get my hopes up until some tests are done."

"I think Dave would be only too happy to co-operate, as his daughter is sick and needs a kidney transplant."

Amy stared at Shane, "A kidney transplant? That is not good. If she is my daughter, and I say if, it means Dave is looking for family members to be a donor. I don't think I am prepared to put my family through such a thing. I don't know this girl, even if she proves to be my flesh and blood. Why would I donate a kidney?"

"Because of whom you are," Ivan spoke up for the first time, "But I'm not sure I would want you to do that. Let's not rush things here. Let's find out just what went on back many years ago. I think Amy; you have a source you can head to for some answers."

"My mother. Yes, I think she has a lot of explaining to do. She is still keeping secrets and I am getting tired of all this."

Shane shook his head, "You know, I always wondered why she never seems anxious to get to know me or my family. Maybe she knew all along that I wasn't really her grandson. That really bugs me. Maybe I should come along with you and let her know how much she hurt me."

Amy gave Shane a hug back and replied, "I don't think that would be the best idea. She would just clam up. I think the first thing on the agenda is to contact Dave and set up a DNA test. Would you do that for me, Shane?"

"Sure. I will do that tonight. I think copies of Sarah's DNA could be forwarded to your lab for analysis. That way, there would be no need for contact until we know the truth."

"That sounds good," Ivan commented, "The sooner we get to the bottom of this mess, the better I will like it. If Sarah proves to be your daughter, then we can make some decisions as to what we plan to do about it."

Shane nodded, "Sounds good to me. Once we get this all settled, then I am going to start a search for my parents. Will you help me with that, Amy?"

"Of course. I will get all the information I can from my mother. I think the place to start will be that home in Calgary."

"Okay. I had better get home. April will be wondering what is going on."

"Can you just say hi to Laura before you go? She will be upset if I let you leave before she gets a chance to show you something."

Shane laughed, "Of course. Send the little sweetie down."

Ivan smiled. He was so grateful that Shane seemed to be resigned to the news and accepting things very well. One hurdle jumped. Now on to the next. That one would not be so easy.

Chapter 39

Regina, Saskatchewan

Supper was a fun affair. Sarah seemed relaxed and enjoying bantering with her parents. Alice was thinking how sad it was that they had to spoil the atmosphere by the subject they were about to discuss. Dave seemed reluctant to leave the kitchen table and Alice could understand why. Once they cleared up the supper and dishes, there was no excuse to avoid the topic any longer.

Jumping up from the table, Sarah grabbed her plate and glass and headed to the sink. She announced, "I will help you clear this up, Mom, then I want to call Jesse and see if he can come over so we can study a bit. Is that okay?"

Alice glanced at Dave for his input, but he was looking down at his plate. Well, I can see he isn't going to take the initiative here, Alice groused to herself as she spoke up, "Actually Sarah, your dad and I were hoping we could have a talk with you tonight. It is very important."

"What do you want to discuss?"

Alice got up, picked up the meat platter, and headed to the cupboard, "Let's get this cleaned up first, then we can talk."

"Will it take long, this talk? Maybe I will still have time to meet with Jesse?"

"I think you had better hold off on calling him. If you still want to after we talk, then that will be okay with us."

"Mom, you are being very mysterious. Now you really have me curious. Here, let me put the food away. You load the dishwasher."

Through the conversation, Dave had just sat at the table, drinking the last of his coffee. His stomach was starting to heave again and he was worried he would lose his supper. He had no idea how he was going to start the conversation with Sarah, but one thing was sure, he knew Alice would expect him to take the reins. It was his story, after all. Much as he would like to avoid this confrontation at all costs, he knew it was time. Picking up his cup and plate, he took them to the sink. Alice gave him the look, which he knew meant, 'This is your game; get with it.' He nodded and heading to the living room, said over his shoulder, "I will turn on the tree lights and wait for you two."

"Okay Dad. Just don't go moving any balls around."

Alice starting laughing, "That wasn't your father's trick, only mine. He rarely looked at the tree after we were done. One thing he does not have is a good eye for balance and style."

"I know. I was only kidding. Let's get finished here. I am anxious to know what you two want to talk to me about. Is it something to do with my condition?"

"In a way, yes. Your Dad will fill you in."

Just then, the phone rang. Sarah wiped her hands and picked it up.

"Hello. Knight residence."

"Hello. May I speak to Dave Knight, please."

"May I ask who is calling?"

"Shane Collins"

"Okay," Sarah covered the receiver and called to Dave, "Dad, somebody by the name of Shane Collins is on the phone. Do you want to talk to him?"

Dave's heart gave a lurch. What on earth would Shane want? Why would he call him at his house and not call on his cell? Then Dave remembered his cell had gone dead and he forgot to put it on the charger. Dave answered, "Okay. I will take it in here."

Picking up the living room phone, Dave greeted Shane, "Hello Shane. How are you?"

"Hello. I could be better. I need to talk to you about our situation."

"Okay. What's up?"

"I don't know if this is what you want to hear, but Amy and I had DNA tests done. We are not a match. This means I don't even know who my mother is as well as my father. But that is not why I called. Amy now wants DNA tests done with your daughter to see if they are a match."

Dave's heart started racing, "Does that mean she thinks Sarah may be her daughter?"

"It is the only thing that makes sense. Maybe the babies were switched at the Home, and I was taken in place of her real child. You mentioned that Sarah was sickly as a baby? Maybe they thought she wouldn't make it, but I was healthy so switched us. Amy feels the first thing she has to find out is if Sarah is her child."

"I know Sarah is her child. I only had a relationship with her, no other. I wouldn't even call it a relationship. Just ships passing in the night. Anyway, I am talking to Sarah tonight, so it is a good thing I heard from you now. I will discuss all this with her. How does Amy want to go about getting the testing done?

"We thought maybe your doctor could send the report to her doctor. That way, in her words . . . . in case the DNA is not a match, there will be no contact."

"Does this mean that she would consider being a donor if she is a match?"

"I didn't say that. I am sure she hasn't thought that far ahead. You may be sure Sarah is her daughter, but she is far from sure. She had no idea what kind of lifestyle you lead."

"I understand. What is the name of her doctor and where is he located? I will see what I can do at this end."

"Thank you. You have my cell number. Let me know what happens, okay?"

"Will do. Thank you for calling."

Dave hung up the phone just as Alice and Sarah came into the room.

"Timed that just perfect. All finished in the kitchen?"

"Yes," Alice replied as she sat down on the sofa. She patted the seat next to her and spoke to Sarah, "Come sit here. Your Dad has something he wants to discuss with you. He has been putting it off, but we realize we must talk to you now."

"Okay. Shoot, Dad."

Dave took a deep breath and started, "Do you remember a few months ago when I was tested to see if I was a match for you so I could donate a kidney?"

"Don't tell me you are a match?"

"No, nothing like that. I wish I were, then there would be no problem, but unfortunately, I am not. However, something else came out of that test. I would not believe it when Dr. Klein told me, but I am happy about it."

"Don't keep me in suspense. What else?"

"It seems you and I have matching DNA."

Sarah stared at her Dad, "That's not possible. I am adopted."

"That was my first thought. No way. Your Mom and I adopted you from Calgary. You had been in foster care for the first four years of your life. I understand you were not a well baby so no one could or would adopt you before that."

"I don't understand. Are you saying I am actually your biological daughter, one you didn't know about? I cannot believe that. How could you have a daughter and not know about it?"

Dave sighed, "That is the hardest part. I didn't know I had a child. In my teen years, I did a lot of partying and yes, there was one girl I was intimate with one time. I did not know she had a baby. I graduated and came here to school, met your mother and that was that."

"So you are really my blood kin? This is so hard to take in. Mom, are you okay with this? Did you know all this time too and never told me?"

Alice took Sarah's hand, "Sweetie, I didn't know until this last while. Your Dad wasn't sure how I would react. You see, my first thought was he knew you were his daughter when we adopted you and that hurt. To think he kept that from me. Nevertheless, I realize now that he didn't know and it was just a fluke that we adopted you. We both fell in love with you at the very beginning. That has not changed."

Sarah stood up. "I have to think on this. I am finding this very hard to take in."

"Don't go," Dave urged, "There is more. The phone call I just received? Shane Collins? He came to see me some time ago, thinking he was my son. His mother told him that. Only we had DNA tests done and he was not my son. Then Shane and his mother had tests done and found out they are not related either. Therefore, his mother now wants DNA tests with you. She feels that you may be her biological daughter. If she is your mother, then maybe there will be some help coming from that direction for your transplant. I am really hoping for that."

"Dad, you can't expect a complete stranger to be willing to donate a kidney to a person even if we are blood related. I am a stranger to her and she is to me. I don't want to meet her right now. I just am not prepared for this. You and Mom are my parents. I don't want anything to change that, though it is weird to think that you and I are actually blood related."

"I don't think you will have to meet her. Shane suggested that Dr. Klein could send your DNA samples to her doctor and see if there is a match. If there is, then we can discuss any further considerations."

"I want to think on this. This is way too much to take in all at once. Wow, I sure did not expect this when you said you wanted to talk to me. I thought it was probably something like wanting me to drop out of studying or something like that. Oh, and thanks for suggesting I wait to call Jesse. I am not prepared to study tonight. Do you mind if I go to my room now? I am feeling tired and need to lie down."

"Of course," Alice voiced as she got up and hugged Sarah, "You know we only want the best for you. I am not excited about making contact with this other woman either, but if it can help you in the long run, I will only be too happy to see it done."

Sarah hugged her back, turned to Dave, and gave him a hug, too. "I know this was hard for you Dad, but don't let this cause your ulcer to act up. I'm okay. I can handle this information. Just let me digest it all, and then I will come to a decision, okay?"

"Okay, princess. I love you a lot. Even though I didn't know you were my daughter when we adopted you, I am very happy that you are, though blood or no blood, you will always be my little girl."

Sarah laughed, "I know. See you in the morning." With that, she headed to the stairs.

Dave and Alice watched her go and then turned to each other.

"Well," Dave sighed, "That went better than I expected. She never ceases to amaze me. I thought she would be upset with me, but she seems to roll with all the punches."

"So that was Shane on the phone?" Alice asked.

"Yes, I guess when they found out that Amy is not his mother, Amy decided she wants to find out if Sarah is her daughter. I sure am not looking forward to having that woman in our little girl's life, but if she can help Sarah, we have no choice."

"How do you think I feel? However, I agree, Sarah's health is the most important thing and we have to put our feelings aside and do what is best for her. It is Sarah's decision. I pray she makes the right one."

Chapter 40

Southern Alberta

The wind was blowing from the west, heralding a Chinook coming in. It was only one week until Christmas and Ivan was glad to see the weather moderating a bit. With any luck, the warm temperatures would last through the Christmas holidays. Having a break in the cold was always welcome, for not only the people but the livestock as well. Ivan knew he had lots of feed for the winter, and Shane did too, but it was always nice to be secure in the knowledge that there was a surplus.

Ivan opened the gate on the barnyard and headed in to check on the calf he had in the barn. The heifer had developed a cough and Ivan was taking no chances. He had planned to keep her as a replacement heifer, but decided she would go out on the next shipment. A chronic lung condition was not something he wanted in his foundation herd.

The calf appeared much better, but Ivan decided to keep her inside for a day or two until the wind died down. He cleaned her pen and fed her, then headed out to the corral to check out the feed situation. Seeing all the bunks still had enough hay for a day or two, he decided to leave the tractor in the shed.

With the dog frolicking beside him, Ivan headed to the horse corral. Bell nickered to him as he approached.

"Morning, girl. I suppose you are looking for your usual handout. Don't worry; it's forthcoming as soon as I get this bale open."

Reaching over the fence, Ivan gave Bell a pat, and then headed to the barn to grab a pail of oats. "Spoiled horse," he muttered, smiling, "Expects oats every time she sees me. I better be careful how many I give her or she will be pitching me off with all her added energy."

Ivan figured the last thing he needed was his horse to buck him off. His knee was not improving with the years, and now he could feel some pain in his back. He knew it was just a matter of time before he wouldn't be able to ride anymore. That made him sad, as riding was one of his greatest pleasures. He was only sorry that Amy had not developed a liking to ride. To be fair to her, she really didn't have much of a chance to learn before she become pregnant with Laura. After that, she always seemed to be too busy with the house and the kids. To top it off, after Scamp died, they only had one horse, so there was no way they could ride together.

Ivan was hoping that Laura would continue to enjoy the horse. So far, she always wanted to go riding with Ivan. He was thinking that maybe he should purchase a smaller horse for her. "I'll have to discuss that idea with Amy," Ivan spoke aloud as he headed back to the horse corral and poured some oats into Bell's pail.

Thinking about Amy made him remember she had a birthday coming up. Being as it was on December 24th, they always tried to celebrate it a few days earlier, so it didn't interfere with Christmas Eve. Ivan thought he better get on it and plan. Maybe something quiet this year would be best, he thought. Just invite Shane and the kids and have a cake at home.

There had been no word from Dave Knight and his daughter in Regina, so everything was still up in the air pertaining to the DNA tests. They knew Shane had contacted Dave but there had been no response to date. Amy was being a little stressed about the hold-up, but Ivan knew it was a big decision for the family to make. Life changing for all of them, in fact. Ivan was just grateful that Shane seemed to accept the verdict and was the same with them. As soon as they heard from Regina, Amy planned to do some checking to help Shane in his search for his parents. With Christmas right around the corner, Ivan was hoping to have all this settled first, but maybe it was better not knowing until after.

Closing the gate on the barnyard, Ivan headed back up the path to the house. Feeling the warm breeze on his face, he turned and looked to the west. Soft, billowy clouds hung low over the hills, looking like big doughboys ready for the oven. I wish I were a painter, Ivan thought. It would make a beautiful picture.

* * *

Amy watched Ivan come through the gate and stop and look to the west. She had so much on her mind the past few days; she knew she was neglecting her husband and her kids. Only that morning Laura had wanted her to help her move her doll house in her room and she had put her off. Just getting the meals, doing the laundry and cleaning up was done automatically. Thinking about anything else seems momentous.

"Why don't we hear something?" she complained aloud. "What is the problem with them? I thought Dave and his wife was anxious to find a donor for their daughter. You would think they would send that DNA right away. Well, I'm not going to beg them. I just have to forget about all this and get on with my life. I always thought Shane was my son. Can I forget that there might be another child out there? You would think if Dave knew Sarah was my daughter, he would be in touch. Maybe he isn't being truthful and there could be another child of his out there and that Sarah isn't mine. I wouldn't put it past him."

Turning from the window, she headed to the sink and tackled the dishes there. When Ivan came into the house, she was busy loading the dishwasher.

"Hi, honey," Ivan said, "Do you want anything from town? I will be running in shortly. Shane asked me to pick up some feed for him too. Maybe Laura would like to come for the ride?"

"I'm sure she would. Check with her. Abe will want to go too, but I will keep him here. It is good you have some time with your daughter alone."

"Laura!" Ivan called up the stairs.

"Yes, Daddy?" Laura came to the top and called down.

"Do you want to go to town with your old Daddy? We will be stopping by Shane and April's on the way home."

Laura squealed with delight, "Yes! Yes! Just a minute, I have to find my socks."

Ivan laughed as he turned to Amy, "That girl! She never keeps her socks on. Makes me think of me when I was young."

"Well, she should," Amy laughed, "She is so much like you. I'm glad you can have some time together. It is so important for a father to spend time with his daughter. Abe's time will come."

Ivan gave Amy a hug, "How are you doing? Are you holding up okay?"

Amy hugged him back, "As well as I can, I guess. I'm sorry if I appear distant lately, but I have so much on my mind. I just wish this would all be settled and we could get on with our lives. It is so hard to think I have another child out there somewhere."

"You don't think this Sarah is your child?"

"I really don't know. Who knows how many relationships Dave had back then? I was so stupid to get involved with him. I know I had a child and he was the father, but not necessarily is it Sarah as far as I'm concerned."

"Maybe we will hear shortly. Keep you chin up. Love you."

"I love you, too. Thank you for being you and supporting me through all this. I bet you never dreamed when we became an item what you would have to endure."

Ivan laughed, "I would do it all again in a heartbeat. Makes life interesting."

"Who needs that much interest?" Amy replied, but she laughed and turned to see Laura dashing down the stairs.

"I'm all ready, Daddy. Can I bring Sandy?"

"Who's Sandy?" Ivan quizzed.

"Sandy is my doggie," Laura replied as she held up a stuffed, spotted dog.

"Sure. Let's go. We'll be back for lunch," Ivan said to Amy as he and Laura headed out the door.

"Okay," Amy called, "Have fun!"

* * *

Ivan and Laura had a great time. Laura was jabbering all the time, filling Ivan in on all the doings with her dollhouse. She told him how Abe was always trying to interfere in her play. Ivan listened, smiling to himself. This was something he had missed growing up, as he was an only child. He had no sibling rivalry. Laura, being the oldest, was always trying to boss Abe around, but he was an independent spirit, taking after his Mom, Ivan mused. He was glad they had more than one child. Both him and Amy were from one-child families and had agreed that they wanted at least two children. Ivan would have gladly welcomed more, but Amy convinced him that they were getting to the age where things would be harder for them to deal with. Now they were content with their little family and now looking forward to the grandchildren. Michael was so special in their lives. Ivan didn't know what they would have done if Shane had decided to cut them out of his life. He thanked God every day for Shane and the type of man he was. Not many young people were as caring and compassionate as Shane was. Of course, Ivan realized he had the best teachers in the world. Abe and Laura Collins were wonderful people and neighbors. Ivan remembered the way they took him in when his father was neglecting him, even wanting to adopt him. Yes, Shane was special and so was his little family.

"Daddy, are you listening?" Laura prompted.

"I sure am. You were telling me about Sandy and what he did to your doll house."

"No, Daddy. Not Sandy. Abe. See, you were not listening," Laura pouted.

"Sorry, honey. I guess I was thinking about how special you are and what I plan to get you for Christmas."

"What, Daddy? Tell me, okay? I want to know."

"Can't do. It is a surprise. You want to have a surprise come Christmas morning, don't you?"

"Santa will surprise me. You don't have to. Please, Daddy? What are you getting for me?"

Ivan laughed, "You are a little munchkin, for sure. But you won't get it out of me. I can keep a secret. Besides, your Mommy would be upset with me if I told you. She is so excited about it."

"Okay. Can I buy Mommy a present today? I want to get her something special for Christmas. Mommy has been so sad lately. Why is she sad, Daddy?"

"Mommy isn't really sad. She just has a lot on her mind. No matter what, she still loves you and Abe and wants what is best for you. Don't worry about that. For sure, you can buy Mommy a present. Do you think you can keep it a secret from now until Christmas? It is a week away. This reminds me, your Mommy has a birthday coming up soon. Shall we get a present for her birthday?"

"Yes! Yes! Mommy should have a birthday present. She always gets us one."

"I agree. Okay, we will pick up our feed, and then head to the store. We promised Mommy we would be home for lunch so we have to hurry."

* * *

Amy checked on Abe and found that he was busy in his room, making a track with his blocks for his truck to drive on. He hardly looked up as Amy checked in. It appeared he didn't even realize that Laura had left with Ivan. Amy was glad. Now she would have time to clean the bathrooms without having to console him. She had just enough time to get that done and then start lunch.

The fact that Ivan took Laura to town made Amy relieved that she had the time to herself. Much as she loved her little girl, sometimes she could stretch the patience. Laura was quite demanding and had been ever since Abe arrived on the scene.

"I think it is time she started school," Amy thought. She had kept her home this past September because she seemed very immature for her age, but now Amy was wondering if she had done the right thing. It was a long bus ride, but other kids had done it for years and they made out okay. "Yes, I have to let go and let her grow up. If she is out with other kids, maybe she will become more relaxed, having some playmates from school."

At primary in church, Laura did have some little friends, but Amy noticed Laura seemed to be the one in control. Someday, she would have to have a talk with the primary teacher. Amy didn't want Laura to get the idea that she could always control the situation. "Boy! Shades of my mother coming out! I sure don't like that. I plan to nip that in the bud before it gets to be a problem," Amy commented aloud.

Scrubbing the sink and counter in the kids bathroom, she did not notice Abe until he pulled on her shirt.

"Oh, did you say something, honey?"

"You were talking. What did you say to me?"

Amy reached down and gave him a hug, "I wasn't talking to you, just to myself. Sorry, are you okay?"

"Where's Laura?"

"Honey, Laura went to town with Daddy. They should be home soon."

Abe started to cry, "I wanted to go. Why couldn't I go?"

"Sometimes Daddy wants to spend time with each of you by yourself. Next time he will probably take you and leave Laura. Okay?"

"Okay. I'm hungry. Can I have an apple?'

"Sure. Just let me finish here and I will get you one."

"I can get it myself," Abe declared.

Amy laughed, "Okay; be sure to wash it before you eat it."

"Okay," and with that, Abe took off running for the stairs.

Amy finished the sink and put the cleaning rag into the hamper. She was so glad Abe seemed to be talking better. He was completing his words now and not repeating them twice. He looked so much like his father, but had her independent streak. Smiling, Amy realized just how lucky she was to have two such wonderful kids. Dealing with their different personalities was part of the upbringing. "I should just be grateful for that, and forget about finding out about my other child," Amy admonished herself as she headed downstairs to check on Abe.

She found him sitting at the table, happily munching on his apple. It seemed his disappointment about not getting to go with his Dad was forgotten. Oh, to be a little child again, and not have a care in the world, thought Amy as she ruffled Abe's hair and headed to the fridge to start lunch.

Chapter 41

Regina, Saskatchewan

With Christmas fast approaching, Dave and Alice didn't want to push Sarah into making a decision about her DNA. Since the night of their talk, Sarah had gone on as if it had never happened. She chatted happily about her classes and spent time with Jesse. Though tired when she got home, she never complained. She was still getting dialysis twice a week and seemed to be holding her own. The doctor had her on some drug that was supposed to help the kidneys function better and it seemed to be working, along with the special diet she was on. Dave and Alice thought it would be wonderful if they could find a magic cure for kidney failure, but knew it was a pipe dream. They hoped every day to hear that a donor had been found in the registry, but nothing seemed to be available. Dave especially, was hoping for that so they could forget contacting Amy or getting DNA samples to her. He knew he was being selfish, but knew that once contact was made, he might have to share his little girl. Not only would it upset him, but also it would be very hard on Alice. Alice was an innocent by-stander in all this, and unfortunately, she would be the most hurt. Dave felt bad about that. Therefore, that was why he was hoping every day for good news from the doctor.

Things were quiet at Dave's work, so he was able to take some time off and get some Christmas shopping done. He wanted this Christmas to be extra special for his two girls. In some ways, he was glad Sarah seemed to want to put things off. Maybe they could get through the Christmas holidays before having to deal with any of the problems. Time enough to get things settled in the New Year.

* * *

Sarah closed her books and rubbed her forehead. She was getting a headache from trying to decipher the last lesson. She knew she was studying too hard and her eyes seemed to be bothering her. Jesse had brought over his notes earlier and she couldn't seem to make heads or tails out of them. Lying back on the bed, Sarah closed her eyes and let her mind wander. Of course, as soon as she did that, all she could think about was the talk she had with her mom and dad. She still couldn't believe that her Dad was actually her real Dad. That was a real shock. Then to know that her real Mom was out there somewhere that she could contact any time she wanted to made her a little uneasy. If she did agree to send her DNA and found out this person was really her mother, would she be able to leave things as they were? The last thing she wanted to do was to hurt her Mom. She knew if she did want to communicate with this woman, it would hurt her. She loved her Mom and Dad with all her heart and didn't want anything to spoil that. It was bad enough that they had to go through all the problems with her kidneys, let alone another ordeal. For that reason, Sarah decided to leave things as they were for the time being. So far, things had been good lately with her kidneys. The new medication seemed to be helping so maybe a transplant could hold off for a while. She did tire easily, but was feeling a lot better the last couple of weeks. Dad and Mom seem to be waiting for me to say something to them, so I guess I should tell them my decision, Sarah commented to herself. I will do that tonight.

* * *

Alice had outdone herself. The chicken was delicious and Dave had a second helping, though he knew Alice would frown at him. Just to pacify her, he also took a second helping of vegetables and decided to pass on the dessert. Sarah was chatting away, telling Alice how confused she was by the last lesson and would have to get Jesse over to explain things to her.

"I am glad you have Jesse to help you out. He is such a nice boy," Alice commented as she got up to clear the table, "When is he coming over?"

"I don't know. I have to call him. It might not be tonight. I think he has some meeting to attend tonight. But that is okay, because I wanted to talk to you and Dad tonight."

Dave glanced up from his coffee, "Oh? Is there something wrong?"

"Not at all. I just wanted to let you know that I have decided to wait before sending DNA samples to that other woman. I am feeling a lot better since I have been on the new medication, so I think it will be best all round if we just let things ride for now. Let's get through Christmas and enjoy it before we have to deal with all this."

With tears in her eyes, Alice went over and hugged Sarah, "You are such a special young lady. But I don't want you putting this off because of me . . . . and don't try to tell me that's not true, because I know how your mind works. You want to save me the ordeal of contacting this woman, who probably is your biological mother. I can deal with this. I don't want you to jeopardize your health because of my feelings."

Sarah hugged her back and replied, "Don't worry. Yes, I thought about you when I made my decision, but it is for my peace of mind, too. I want to enjoy the Christmas holiday without the entanglement of trying to deal with this. You know that you will always be my Mom. No one will ever take that place in my heart. Just like Dad is my Dad, whether he is related to me or not. I don't know this woman, so she is a complete stranger to me. Just by giving birth to me does not make her my Mom. Why did she give me up? Was it because I was sick? I have been thinking about that and that doesn't endear her to me."

Dave spoke up for the first time, "If you knew her mother, you would understand why she probably gave you up. It is possible she didn't have a choice. I'm not defending her, but I don't think we should judge her in this until we know all the facts."

"I think I know all the facts I want to," Alice muttered as she turned away and started to load the dishwasher, "But I for one, am only too happy to forget all this for a while and have a great Christmas. If that is what you want, Sarah, then I am behind you."

"That is what I want. I hope you will agree with us, Dad?"

Dave smiled and reached over and gave Sarah's arm a squeeze. "If this is what you want, I agree. But the first sign that you are failing, I want you to promise me you will agree to send that DNA sample to that doctor in southern Alberta."

"Okay. I promise."

"Now get out of here and go phone Jesse," Dave said.

Chapter 42

Southern Alberta

April was putting the final additions on Amy's birthday cake when the phone rang. Washing her hands quickly to remove the frosting, she picked up the receiver.

"Collins Ranch; Good morning."

"Good morning. I have been trying to get Shane on his cell phone but he isn't answering. He wouldn't happen to be there, would he?"

"No; I'm sorry. Shane left here an hour ago to pick up some feed in town. May I ask whose calling?"

"This is Dave Knight. Can you give Shane a message for me?"

"Of course, but I don't understand why Shane isn't answering his cell, unless he left it in the truck while he is in the store. You could try him later."

"I have a meeting in a few minutes and don't know when I can get back to him. Just tell him Sarah has decided to wait on the DNA. Maybe in the New Year, she will be willing to look at this again. I'm sorry, but that is her decision. Shane can let Amy know, okay?"

"Okay. I am sorry to hear that, as Amy was wanting to have this settled, one way or another, but I understand. I just hope she does."

"This is not easy for any of us, but we have to be sensitive to Sarah's feelings."

"How is she doing? Shane told me about her kidney problems."

"She is holding her own. The new medication seems to be helping. That is one reason she has decided to hold off. She is in no hurry for the surgery."

"I understand. I will give Shane the message."

"Thank you. I have to run now. Have a nice day."

"You, too. Good-bye."

April hung up the phone and turned back to her cake. Well, that was not going to be good news for Amy, she thought, as she picked up the bowl and the spatula to finish the cake. Amy was hoping to have this thing settled before Christmas, but that wasn't going to happen. With only 4 days left, even if the DNA were sent, there would not be time to get the results. April had to admit she was happy that things would remain the same through Christmas. She would like to see things remain the same forever, but knew that wasn't going to happen. Even if Sarah didn't turn out to be Amy's daughter, April knew that eventually Amy would start looking for her other child, just as Shane was going to be trying to find his real parents.

With a final swipe on the side of the cake, April took the bowl to the sink and rinsed it out. Putting it in the dishwasher, she then got her cake saver from the pantry and placed the cake in it. Now the only thing she had to do for Amy's birthday was wrap the sweater they bought for her. Amy was easy to buy for. She had very modest tastes and was always happy and grateful for any gift. Shane actually picked this sweater out, saying how the emerald green color brought out the highlights in Amy's auburn hair. April had to agree with him. Amy had beautiful hair, and Abe had the same color, though his was a bit more unruly, just like his Dad's.

April smiled when she thought of Laura and Abe. The two children were so different from each other. Abe was easy going and content just to play by himself with his trucks and cars. Laura on the other hand, was more aggressive, usually wanting to be in charge and liked to boss Abe around. April loved them both for their individuality. I am so glad that family is part of mine; she smiled as she thought about it. Moreover, I'm happy Shane has decided to not let the information that became known in the last while ruin their relationship with the Johnson family.

"At least, if things don't go right with the search for his real family, Shane has Ivan and Amy, and of course, he will always have us," April stated as she headed to the bedroom to check on Michael. Seeing as he was still sleeping, she rummaged in the closet for her wrapping paper and headed to the living room to wrap Amy's gift. "I had better make a note for Shane, in case I forget to tell him about his phone call. With the supper and birthday celebration planned for Amy, I just might forget. I will leave it up to Shane as to when he tells Amy about the call."

* * *

Ivan was up to something. Amy could tell by the way he evaded all her questions that morning. When she asked him what he wanted for supper, he ignored the question, in turn asking her where his black shirt was. He never questioned where his clothes were, just taking what was easiest. Why the question now? She knew she had a birthday in a few days, but no one had mentioned it, so she figured with everything else going on, it had skipped Ivan and Shane's mind. Now, she wasn't so sure.

A couple of times, Laura started to say something, but Ivan cut her off and changed the subject. Yes, Ivan was definitely up to something. Maybe he plans to take the kids and I out for supper, she mused. That would be nice, but I really am not in the mood to celebrate this year. I would be happy just to stay home and watch a movie or something with the kids.

Amy finished loading the dishwasher and headed to the laundry room to start a load of wash. Ivan had left early to check on the neighbor to the west. He was elderly and recently had taken a fall. Ivan was concerned and wanted him to see a doctor, but he refused, said he was fine. Amy had told Ivan to invite him back for supper that night, but Ivan had not responded, which was different for him.

After checking the washer to make sure it was clean, Amy put her first load in, added the soap and started the cycle. She then headed to the stairs and called up, "Laura, do you have all your clothes down for the wash?"

She heard some scuffling and then Laura appeared at the head of the stair, her arms full of clothes.

"Oh Laura! How many times have I told you to make sure your clothes are in the laundry basket in the bathroom? Now I have to re-sort everything."

"I'm sorry, Mommy. I forgot."

Amy sighed, "Okay, but don't forget next time. You know I do laundry Mondays and Thursdays. I think I might just have to leave yours out a few times and soon you will have nothing to wear. Then you might remember."

Laura giggled, "Oh Mommy! It is too cold to have nothing to wear. I might freeze."

"That you might. Now throw those clothes down to me and go check on Abe. If he is still napping, wake him. I don't want him to sleep too long and then want to stay up half the night."

"Okay. Then can I have a snack? I'm hungry."

"Get Abe up and then you can both have a snack. What do you want? Cheese and crackers or fruit?"

"I want fruit. Do we have any grapes? I will get Abe up now," and with that, Laura headed to Abe's room.

"I shouldn't do that," Amy voiced, "I am not helping by giving Laura so much control over her brother. Next time, I had better make her bring the clothes down and I will do the checking."

Taking the clothes to the laundry, she headed to the kitchen to get a snack ready for the kids. It was only 2:30 pm with lots of time before supper, so if they wanted a snack, that was okay with Amy. She just might have one herself.

* * *

"I'm worried about Pete," Ivan remarked when he arrived home at 4:00 pm. "He doesn't look too good. He assured me he is fine, but he seems a bit disorganized. He has always been so fussy about everything in its place, but that wasn't the case today. I will check on him again tomorrow."

"You couldn't persuade him to come for supper?" Amy asked.

"Actually, I didn't ask him. I am taking you and the kids out for supper."

Amy started to laugh.

"What? Did I say something funny?"

"No, but I knew you were up to something this morning."

"How did you know that? I never even gave you a hint. Did Laura say something?"

"No, Laura hasn't said a word. It was the way you avoided my questions. You never could fool me."

"Okay, you smarty. Where are we going for supper?"

"That I don't know, but it will have to be somewhere the kids like, I'm sure."

"Oh yes, they like this place. So get your glad rags on. We are celebrating tonight!"

"And just what are we celebrating?"

"Now you are trying to be funny! It seems to me we have a member of this family that is getting one year older."

Laughing, Amy sighed, "Don't remind me. Okay, I will get ready. Can you check with the kids and wash them up?"

"Sure. We are not going fancy, so jeans are fine if you like. Did you start supper? I had hoped to be home sooner and let you know."

"Isn't that funny? I just had a feeling and decided to wait and see what you were up to, so didn't start anything. So see; I can read you like a book."

"Oh boy, I never could put anything over on you, could I?" Ivan announced as he gave Amy a squeeze and then headed for the stairs.

An hour later, they pulled into Shane's driveway.

"Oh, are Shane and April going with us?" Amy quizzed.

"No, this is our destination," Ivan answered smugly. "You said I never could pull anything over on you. Well, I just did!"

"Okay, okay! I have to concede. What a nice surprise! I always enjoy time with the Collins's. I can hardly wait to hold Michael again. He is growing so fast."

"Happy Birthday, Mommy!" Abe and Laura chorused from the back seat.

"Wow! How did you keep this a secret so long?" Amy asked them.

Ivan laughed, "Do you think I told those two about coming here? No way! They would be so excited, they would have blabbed right away. No, they didn't know until now, either. Did you, kids?"

"A big secret," Abe nodded, "I can keep a secret."

Both Ivan and Amy laughed as they started to get out of the car. This was going to be a fun night, Amy acknowledged as she looked up to see April standing in the kitchen window, waving.

Chapter 43

Southern Alberta

It was a day later when Shane discovered the note on the bulletin board in the kitchen.

"When did you get this message from Dave?" he called to April, who was feeding Michael in the living room.

"Oh Shane! I'm sorry. He phoned yesterday. I completely forgot about it. I wrote the note because I was worried I might forget with the party and all."

Shane answered, "Now I don't know what to do. Do I tell Amy now this close to Christmas or wait until after? She isn't going to be happy about this, no matter when I tell her. What do you think?"

"It is up to you, but I wonder if you should keep anything from her. She is bound to be upset if she finds out you knew and didn't tell her."

"I think you are right. It is best to keep things out in the open. I will go over there this morning. Do you want to come?"

"No, I think it is best if you do this on your own. Amy does not need an audience. If she needs to talk later, I am always here."

"Okay. I won't be long. When I get back and finish the chores, do you want help to get the tree decorated? I will have time."

"That would be great. I want Michael's first Christmas to be very special."

"I don't think he is old enough to remember this one," Shane laughed, "but we will, I guess."

Walking over, he gave April a kiss and caressed Michael's baldhead before heading for the door.

"Good luck," April called as he walked out the door.

* * *

Amy was surprised to see Shane's truck pull into the yard. Ivan was already out doing chores and she expected to see Shane head to the corrals but instead, he came to the house. Knocking and then stepping into the porch, he called, "Anyone home?"

"In the kitchen," Amy answered as she wiped her hands on the towel and turned from the sink. "Ivan is out doing chores if you are looking for him."

Shane removed his cap and boots and headed to the kitchen, "No; actually I am looking for you. Where are the kids?"

"Upstairs. Why?"

"Because we need to talk and I don't think you want them listening."

Amy's heart thumped in her chest as she stared at Shane. "Is it bad news?"

"Well, I guess that depends on how you take it. I had a call from Dave Knight yesterday, but April forgot to give me the message until this morning."

"So what excuse does Dave have for not sending the samples?"

"I guess Sarah has decided she doesn't want to pursue this right now. She thinks that it is best all round to let things go for now. I imagine this is very difficult for her, too. She needs a kidney, but contacting her real mother is probably upsetting to her."

"She doesn't know if I am her mother. Not until we have the tests done."

"Dave has probably told her that you are. It will be very hard for her to make a decision of this magnitude I'm sure. Especially as she does need a kidney."

"Well, I for one am not sure she is my daughter. How do I know how many other children he fathered in his youth? When I knew him, he was a party animal. He ran with a bad crowd, drinking and carrying on. I guess I was no better, so I shouldn't criticize but I learned my lesson fast. Maybe he didn't."

"I know you have a grudge against Dave, but he really is a very nice man. He has treated me very well. I imagine it has been exceptionally hard for him too, having to inform his wife and daughter about all this."

Amy sighed, "I know I shouldn't hold grudges. I should be Christian about this and forgive Dave because I know this wasn't his entire fault. To be honest, maybe he really didn't remember being with me and when I approached him about being pregnant, maybe he thought I was trying to pull a fast one. Who knows? All I know is I really; really hate having our family in this turmoil now."

"Don't worry about me. April and I have come to terms with everything. After Christmas is over and things settle down, we plan to put a search out for my real parents. I know they probably are not together, but I do need to know my parentage. I hope you understand."

"Not only do I understand, but I will help you all I can. I know you will always be my son, no matter what. First, I am going to contact my mother. I won't be seeing her over Christmas, but plan a trip there right after the New Year. I am going to try to find out what happened at that Home. I think that is where we have to start."

"Okay. Sounds good to me. So you are able to deal with the delay on the tests?"

"I don't have much choice, do I? If Sarah does not want the tests, then we have to wait. Even if we are mother and daughter, it doesn't mean I would be a donor match. If I was, I am not sure I would be willing to donate a kidney to her. I don't know her."

"Let's just pray the registry comes up with a match. According to the message I got, she is doing well right now on dialysis and the medication and diet the doctor has her on. I hope it stays that way, for everyone's sake."

"Me too," Amy agreed.

The outside door opened just at that moment and Ivan entered. "Noticed your truck, Shane. Is everything okay?"

"I think so. I just brought Amy some news. Now I have to get home and get my chores done. I promised to help April with the tree this afternoon. I suppose you have all your chores done?"

"Not quite. I was nosey and wanted to see what was up."

Amy laughed, "No more nosey than I would be. Do you two want a glass of juice or something?"

"I had better get home," Shane answered, "But thanks anyway. See you Christmas day."

"For sure," Ivan agreed as he took the glass Amy handed him.

With a final wave, Shane headed out the door.

"Okay, what was all that about?" Ivan asked Amy as he downed about half of the juice.

"Sarah doesn't want to do the DNA right now. She wants to wait until into the New Year. So here we go, on the waiting list again. Everything is up in the air. Will this ever end?"

"I guess it is her prerogative. Did she say why?"

"Oh, something about getting through the holidays. I would think it would be easier to know one way or another, but maybe not for her. I just wish we could get on with this and get things settled. I hate this hanging over my head."

"I know," Ivan rose and took Amy into his arms. "I was hoping we could put this behind us too, but try to not let it spoil the Christmas time for you. Let's just enjoy our kids and have a good time."

"I will try, but now you are smothering me. I think you must have been wrestling with a calf or something. You smell very much like the barnyard."

"Oops. Sorry. I did have to doctor that heifer again this morning. I will go finish chores, and then change my jeans. I think I might have some manure on them."

"And you are sitting on my kitchen chairs?" Amy shooed him away and went to check the chair.

Ivan laughed, "Don't be so fussy. You know you live on a ranch. Just think; the manure smell is the smell of money."

"Go finish your chores so I can clean my kitchen." Amy threw her dishcloth at him.

Dodging the wet cloth, Ivan chuckled and headed out the door. It was good to see Amy kidding around. Maybe things would straighten out eventually and life would get back to normal. As normal as life can ever be on a ranch, he thought.

Chapter 44

Regina, Saskatchewan

Christmas came and went in Regina and the New Year started out with a blizzard. Peering out the window early New Year's morning, Dave found he couldn't even see across the street. As he checked the thermometer, he saw that the temperature had also dropped to minus 25.

"A nasty day out there," he commented to Alice as he entered the kitchen. "I don't think our company will be showing up unless it quits snowing soon."

Alice turned from the stove and answered, "I think you are right. I will give Bob and Eileen a quick call and see what they think. I sure don't want them on the roads when it is like this. It would be different if they lived in Regina, but coming from White City could be treacherous."

"I agree. I can barely see across the street. I sure wouldn't want to be on the highway."

Alice nodded and headed for the phone to call their friends. Dave grabbed a cup of coffee and sat down at the kitchen table. He really wasn't disappointed about the weather. Although he always enjoyed company and the Elliot's were good friends, he was just as happy putting his feet up in his easy chair and checking out some of the games on TV. Lately, there never seemed to be much time just to relax and enjoy life a little. He was grateful that Sarah's health had stayed good throughout the holidays and she seemed to be okay with everything. She had even brought up the tests the other day and said she was still deciding what to do about that. Dave was enjoying the lull and was in no hurry to push for the tests. He was amazed that Amy had not called, insisting the DNA tests be done, but then, he thought maybe she was in no hurry to find out the answer. He realized it was probably not easy for her right now, thinking Shane was her son all those years and finding out he wasn't.

Alice finished her call and turned to Dave. "They had decided to wait and see what this afternoon brings, but according to Bob, the forecast is for snow and wind all day today and tomorrow. I sure am glad I don't have to go back to work until Monday, so that gives me a couple of days before I have to brave the cold. How about you?"

Dave took a drink of his coffee before answering, "I'm off until Monday too, but don't forget, Sarah needs dialysis tomorrow. I sure hope it lets up before then."

"Me too. She must be sleeping in this morning. I haven't heard a peep from her room yet. I hope she is okay."

"I'm sure she is, but if you will feel better about it, I will go check on her, while you finish making breakfast, or do you want me to finish?"

"No, you go check. I have everything under control here. Do you want waffles or pancakes?"

"What? You mean you really will let me have those?"

Alice smiled and flipped her dishcloth at him, "Well, being as its New Year's morning, I thought it would be nice to have a little something extra. However, you can only have two. Your blood pressure has been staying good, so don't rock the boat."

Dave kissed Alice on the cheek and then patted her butt. "You are the best; you know that, don't you?"

"Hey, keep your hands to yourself, Dave Knight!" Alice said as she playfully punched him on the arm, "Go away and let me get things cooking."

Laughing, Dave headed for the stairs. Yes, he thought, Alice was the best. How many wives would accept all that had gone down in the last few months and still keep her priorities on the family and what was important? I don't deserve her.

Alice watched Dave out of the corner of her eye as he headed for the stairs. She was glad he seemed to be feeling well and able to joke around with her. She knew that the whole mess of things that was going down was very hard on him. It was hard on her too, but she didn't have the health issues that he did. She sometimes just wanted to scream, but what good would that do any of them? She had managed to hide most of her feelings about the other woman issue from Sarah and Dave, but sometimes it was very hard not to feel angry and betrayed. Oh, if Dave really knew how I really felt about everything, he wouldn't be so jovial, Alice grumbled to herself. She only knew she would never let on, mainly because of Sarah. A strong, stable family was what she needed right now. With the decisions she had to make in the near future, it would not be easy for her at the best of times.

Alice was cooking the waffles when Dave returned to the kitchen.

"Sarah said she would be down in a couple of minutes. She wants to have a quick shower first."

"Okay. You might as well start, as it takes a while to cook waffles. Do you want syrup or jam on them?"

"Syrup, please." Dave helped himself to two rashers of bacon and one egg. "Wow! A breakfast fit for a king. You are the best, for sure."

Alice chuckled as she answered, "You are starting to sound like a broken record. You already told me that once this morning."

Just then, there was a huge crash upstairs. Dave jumped out of his chair and headed for the stairs. Alice, waffles forgotten, was right behind him.

Chapter 45

Southern Alberta

Ivan and Amy welcomed the New Year in all by themselves. New Year's Eve was their wedding anniversary and Shane and April had kept the kids so they could go out for supper and a movie. April had insisted the kids stay over night as it would be late when they returned. It would be a shame to take the kids out in the cold she said. Amy knew Shane and April just wanted them to have some time together without the kids. Actually, it was very nice. When they got back from town, Ivan had lit the fireplace and they had enjoyed that for the first time for ages. When the kids were around, they were always worried they would fall into the flames.

Cuddling together on the sofa, they had chatted over their plans for the coming year. Not once was DNA, Dave Knight, Sarah or any of the problems looming over them discussed. It was wonderful.

"You know what this reminds me of?" Ivan said as he stroked the nape of Amy's neck.

"No, what?"

"When we were dating. Do you remember how we used to snuggle up together and sometimes things got a little hot? You were so scared of commitment."

"Yes, I was. And you knew why. I don't know if I ever would have overcome that without your help. You knew just when to push and when to back off."

"There were a few times I thought I had gone too far. You were one skittish filly."

"And you were one persistent cowboy, but I'm glad you were."

Amy reached up and pulled Ivan's head down so she could kiss him. Ivan responded immediately by pulling her into his arms and kissing her back with anticipation.

"Oh Amy! You still know how to get to me. Do you think that will ever change?"

"I sure hope not. Our special times together mean the world to me. It was nice of Shane and April to take our kids for the night. That way, we won't have any interruptions. I am glad to have you all to myself tonight."

"Me too. Do you think we should go up or do you want to stay here by the fire for a while?"

Amy started to giggle, "You know what I would like? I know this is silly when we have a perfectly good bed upstairs, but I would like to get the sleeping bags and snuggle here on the floor in front of the fire. We can't do that when the kids are around and I have always wanted to."

Ivan moaned, "Oh, my poor aching back! You are going to be the death of me, woman!"

"I forgot about your back. Forget that plan. Let's go to bed."

"Oh, no! You aren't getting off that easy. I think that is a perfectly splendid idea. I have never made love to a lady on the floor."

With that, Ivan jumped up and headed to the storage closet to grab the sleeping bags. "Here, zip the two together while I stoke up the fire."

Laughing, Amy grabbed the bags and started getting them ready. Once she laid them on the rug in front of the fire, she turned to Ivan and started removing her blouse.

Making sure the drapes were closed, Ivan moved to her and started to help.

* * *

Shane lay in bed, listening to April's steady breathing. For some reason, he was finding it hard to sleep. His mind was going over and over everything that had happened in the last year. Here it was, the start of a New Year and he still had no idea who his parents were. Going from thinking Amy was his mother, to Dave Knight being his dad, to now knowing neither one were related to him was a bit hard to digest. Somewhere out there, he had two parents. He wondered if they ever thought about him or had tried to find him. Maybe there was a registry somewhere that recorded people looking for their children they had given up for adoption. He would have to check that out.

April sighed and moved onto her side and threw her arm over his chest. Shane looked at the time. In one hour, she would be getting up to feed Michael. So far, the baby still woke up around two or three o'clock for his night feeding. April said he would probably do that until he started on solid food. Shane wished he could do that feeding for her so she could get a good night's sleep. Being as she was nursing the baby, he knew it wasn't possible.

Shane planned to be up early and make breakfast for everyone. Having Laura and Abe here was a lot of fun. Laura loved mothering Michael, even wanting to help with his bath and dressing him. Abe was more interested in playing with Michael's toys, but did enjoy watching Michael have his bath. They were good kids.

Turning on his side, Shane thought of Ivan and Amy. Letting them have a night alone without the kids had been April's idea and it was a good one. Right now, he figured they needed some time for each other without interference. I bet this is the first time they have been alone since Laura was born, Shane mused. It was time. Maybe I will end up with another brother or sister; he chuckled to himself as he closed his eyes and tried to sleep. Seven o'clock would come early and he knew the kids would be hungry.

Chapter 46

Regina, Saskatchewan

Dave and Alice arrived upstairs at the same time, to find Sarah on the bathroom floor, moaning and holding her head. Dave quickly knelt down and exclaimed, "What happened? Are you okay? Did you slip on something?"

"Of course she slipped! Why else would she be lying on the floor?" Alice retorted. "Sarah honey; answer us. Where are you hurting?"

Sarah opened her eyes and tried to focus. Everything was blurry. "I can't tell. I hurt all over. I think I hit my head when I tripped on the bath mat. My head really hurts and my leg."

Dave reached over and checked Sarah's head. "I would say you hit your head for sure. You have a goose egg coming."

Alice grabbed a facecloth and running it under the cold water, handed it to Dave, who then applied it to the bump. He then checked Sarah's leg. It did not take him long to make an assessment.

"Alice, call 911. We need to get Sarah to the hospital."

"Oh no! What's wrong?"

"Well, besides maybe a concussion, probably a broken leg. Just call, will you?"

Alice scurried out of the room to make the call while Dave kept pressure on the bump. Sarah seemed to be going into shock, which scared the dickens out of him.

"Sarah honey, stay with me. Keep talking."

Sarah tried to open her eyes, but it made her dizzy every time she did and she felt nauseous. "Dad," she moaned, "I think I am going to throw up."

Dave managed to get the basin in time. Getting a new facecloth, he wiped Sarah's face. "Feel better?"

Sarah nodded and closed her eyes. Just then, Alice returned, carrying a blanket and pillow. Placing the pillow under Sarah's head and covering her, she stated, "The ambulance will be here as soon as they can. The roads are terrible and the plows are out, so hopefully, within the half hour. How are you doing, honey?"

Sarah didn't answer, but Dave replied, "She was nauseous and threw up, but that is probably from hitting her head."

"Try to keep her awake. That is what they told us in emergency training."

"I know. Sarah! Sarah, come on. Stay with us. Can you hear me?"

Sarah opened her eyes, "Don't yell. It hurts my head. I'm awake. What is that smell? Is there something burning?"

"Oh, no! My waffles!" Alice wailed as she made a dash for the door.

Dave was still holding the cold rag to the bump on Sarah's head. "You always did have a good nose. I didn't smell a thing. Thank goodness you did, or we would have the fire trucks here along with the ambulance."

"I'm sorry to cause all this trouble. I just wanted a quick shower before breakfast. I can't believe I was so clumsy. Do you really think my leg is broken?"

"I'm pretty sure. I'm no doctor, but it looks like it. The medics will know when they arrive. Until then, we can't move you."

"I know. I'll be okay."

Alice returned carrying the phone. "Well, thanks to Sarah, I didn't burn the kitchen down. However, we have two very black waffles. How are you feeling now, Sarah?"

"Like someone ran over me with a truck. Don't worry, Mom. I'll be okay."

Just then, the phone rang. It was the ambulance, letting them know they were on their way and expected to be there in about ten to fifteen minutes. Dave let Alice take over and headed downstairs to put on his outer clothes. He needed to get his driveway clear so the ambulance didn't get stuck. He wasn't looking forward to going out in the storm, but Sarah was the most important now. Checking out the window, he could see the wind had let up a bit, so grabbing his gloves, headed out. The cold astounded him. He turned his back for a moment, then grabbed the shovel and started clearing snow.

* * *

Four hours later, Sarah was sitting up in her hospital bed. Her head was wrapped with a gauze and her right eye was starting to blacken. She also had a full-length leg cast. It was discovered she had indeed broken her femur bone in her right leg. It was a clean break, so the doctors were able to set the bone rather quickly.

Dave and Alice had followed the ambulance back to the hospital and waited impatiently for the results. Though Sarah had banged her head, the doctors didn't think she had a concussion, though they planned to keep a close eye on her. Her vision had cleared up and the pain was just a dull ache. What hurt the most was the leg, but Sarah was determined not to complain. It was bad enough her parents had to come out on a nasty day.

While Dave and Alice had waited for the doctors to set Sarah's leg, they had phoned their friends to be sure they were not still planning on coming in. Bob informed them that the police were still urging people to stay off highway #1, because of poor visibility, so they weren't planning to come in. Alice told them she would call later that night to let them know about Sarah.

Now, Sarah was sitting up and looking alert.

"Mom, Dad; I want you to go home. I am fine here and the doctors will let you know how I am. I don't want you traveling when it gets dark. Please go home."

"Are you sure?" Alice quizzed, "We have a couple of hours before it gets totally dark."

"But it is still snowing and the roads will not be getting any better. I will feel a lot better if you go home now. Call me to let me know you made it home okay."

"All right," Dave replied, "I am a bit concerned about the roads. Well, at least there is something good about this. You will be here for your dialysis tomorrow."

Sarah laughed, "I guess if we have to look for 'the glad's', that is one of them."

"I'm not making light of your accident; just if it had to happen, at least you are where you can get your treatment."

"I know, Dad. I was just joking. I will be fine. Don't try to come tomorrow if the roads are still bad. You can call me."

Alice reached over and gave Sarah a hug, "You are such a brave, young woman. I am so proud of you. I am sorry that this had to happen and believe me; I am going to make some changes in that bathroom. You take care and we will talk later."

"See you, princess," Dave kissed Sarah on the cheek and squeezed her hand. "Be good until we see you."

Sarah watched them leave with a sigh of relief. It was so hard to keep up the pretense of being good. As soon as she was sure they were gone, she rang the bell for the nurse. She definitely needed something for the pain.

Chapter 47

Southern Alberta

They woke up to a blizzard. It was the first thing Ivan noticed when he rolled out of the sleeping bag. The wind was howling around the house and the floor was ice cold. The fireplace had gone out during the night. They hadn't noticed, as they were snug in the sleeping bags, curled up together.

"Wake up, sleepyhead!" Ivan patted Amy on the leg, "Can't sleep all day. Happy New Year and welcome to our first blizzard of the year!"

Amy rolled over and threw the sleeping bag off. Having second thoughts, she threw it back over her. "It's cold out there! How about turning up the thermostat before I have to get out?"

"Chicken! Just stay there and I will get the fireplace going. That should warm you up in a hurry. I don't know if we are going to be able to pick up the kids this morning. I will have to check out the roads."

"Do you think it is that bad out there?"

Ivan pulled on his pants and headed to the window. Pulling open the drapes, he replied, "I would say so. I can't see the barn or even the house yard fence. It is going to be tricky even to do the feeding. I think we had better phone the kids."

This time, Amy did throw off the sleeping bag and stood up. Grabbing her shirt and pants, she headed to the stairs. "I will get dressed, and then phone them. I'll turn up the heat on my way."

Ivan watched her as she headed to the stairs and smiled to himself. Talk about turning up the heat, he reminisced as he remembered their night. Amy never ceased to surprise him and he was grateful they had a night to themselves to just be husband and wife. Now it looked like they might have more than one night due to the blizzard.

* * *

Shane woke up to the sounds of little feet pattering down the stairs. He jumped out of bed, realizing he had slept in. It was then he noticed how the wind was howling. Glancing out the window, he moaned, "Oh no! Not a blizzard! That is going to make things difficult for doing chores." He quickly pulled on his pants and grabbing a shirt, headed for the stairs. He wanted to be sure that the kids didn't try to start breakfast without him.

April rolled over and sat up. "It is really cold in here. Did the furnace go out?" She struggled out of bed and hurried over to the crib. "I hope Michael is okay." She checked to see if he was covered, but he was warm and sleeping peacefully. It was then she remembered Laura and Abe. "Are you going to check on the kids?"

Shane nodded, "They are already down stairs. That is what woke me. I have to get there before they start making their own breakfast or something. I'll take care of it. You can get organized."

"Okay. I do need to head to the bathroom."

Shane bounded down the stairs, only to find Laura and Abe standing at the window, looking outside. Laura turned and said, "Shane, I can't see anything out there! Is this a blizzard? How will Mommy and Daddy come for us if they can't see?"

"Shane reached down and hugged the two kids and answered, "I am going to call them and tell them to wait and see what the storm does. You two are safe with us here. We don't want to take any chances and head out in a snow storm."

Abe started to cry, "I miss Mommy and Daddy. I want to go home."

"I know, Abe. You don't want Mommy and Daddy to try to come for you when it is storming. They might get lost and not find their way."

"Daddy never gets lost. He is very smart," Laura answered as she stared out the window.

"I know your Daddy is very smart. That is the reason he will stay home because he knows you two are safe with us. Come on. I'm making breakfast. What would you like?"

"Cereal," Abe answered, the storm forgotten for the moment. "Do you have cereal?"

"I have whatever you want. Just name it," Shane replied as he shooed the two into the kitchen and away from the window with the storm raging outside. Heading to the sink to wash his hands, he reminded himself he would have to keep the kids busy so they wouldn't get too homesick.

April appeared in the doorway and smiled at the kids. "Hey, you two. Do you want to talk to Mommy and Daddy?"

"Me first; me first!" Abe yelled as he scrambled to beat his sister to the phone. Handing it to him, April headed to the fridge to get some juice. It wasn't long before Laura decided it was her turn to talk and she took the phone from her brother. A bit of a spat started and Shane had to intervene. Taking the phone from the kids, he spoke to Amy, "Don't worry about the kids. They are fine here. They miss you guys, but as long as it is storming, they are safer here than trying to bring them home. Enjoy your freedom for another day."

"It is such an imposition to ask you guys to keep the kids for so long."

"We don't mind. We aren't going anywhere and April and I love having the kids."

"But they do fight and can be annoying at times."

"I can handle it. I never had a sibling so it is interesting to watch the interaction between the two."

"Too much interaction can drive you crazy," Amy laughed, "But I guess you are stuck for the time being. As soon as the storm lets up, Ivan will come for the kids with the four by four. He should be able to get through with that. I am going to hang up now. I won't talk to the kids again as it will only upset them. Take care and Shane . . . . Thank you for this and thank April for me."

"No problem. Enjoy your quiet day."

"Ha-ha. Will try. Bye for now."

Chapter 48

Regina, Saskatchewan

Sarah spent three days in the hospital, mainly because the road conditions were not good. The blizzard that arrived on New Year's Day lasted well into January. The police were warning people to stay off the highways unless an emergency. In the city, traffic had slowed to a crawl. The plows had been working day and night to clear the main arteries, but the side streets didn't see any snow removal until January 4. Many businesses had closed their doors until things improved. Sarah talked every day to her parents to assure them that she was doing fine. Her leg was just a dull ache and the goose egg on her head had gone down, though she still had her black eye. Sarah was glad no one could come to visit her, as she looked like she had been in a fight. A fight with the bathtub, she thought ruefully. How stupid to not watch what I was doing when half asleep. However, it could be worse, she acknowledged. She was lucky she didn't have a concussion or something worse. Her Mom and Dad had enough to worry about.

Thinking about her parents made her remember the DNA tests. Dr. Klein had stopped in to see her the day after her fall, but he didn't mention anything. Sarah knew it was only a matter of time before he would insist that she make a decision. She was sure this Amy person wasn't going to let things just die either, not if she thought Sarah was her daughter. Sarah did not know how to deal with all this. If Amy really was her mother, why did she give me up, Sarah reasoned with herself. Did it mean she didn't want me because I was sickly? What kind of mother would just throw her baby away because it wasn't what they expected? What was it Dad said? Something about; if you knew her mother, you would understand. Sarah smiled to herself. Amy's mother would be her grandmother, but maybe she would be better off not knowing her by the sounds of things. She had never met any grandparents. She knew her Dad's parents both died in a car crash when she was first adopted. Her Mother's parents lived in Ontario. Although her mother told her she met them when she was little, she had no recollection of them. They were both gone now, too. She wondered if Amy's mother was still alive. Shaking her head, she settled back on her pillow and closed her eyes. She would worry about all this another day. With the bad roads and cold weather, nothing could be done anyway.

* * *

Dave was like a caged lion, pacing back and forth and every so often, looking out the window to see if the plows were anywhere in sight. He was anxious to get to his office and up to the hospital to see Sarah.

"Dave, for heaven's sake, would you please settle down? You are giving me a headache with your pacing up and down," Alice grumbled as she set her book aside and got up to refill her coffee.

"I'm sorry. I just cannot seem to put my mind to anything else. I should be at work. Things have a tendency to go all haywire when I'm not there."

"How many others do you think will be there? Everyone is in the same boat as we are. The city is at a standstill. I called my office and got the answering machine, so I know there is no one there. I bet there are very few at your office, either."

"I called there this morning and checked with maintenance. They said no one was in the office, but I still feel I should be there in case of problems."

"They know your home phone number. I'm sure they will call if they need you. There is no way you can get there unless they come for you by snowmobile or helicopter, so quit fretting."

Dave sighed and sat down at the table and picked up his already cold coffee. "You're right. Nevertheless, I really would like to get up to the hospital and see Sarah. I know she says she is fine, but I want to see for myself."

"She phones every day and I talked with her doctor yesterday and he said she was doing okay. She is tolerating the pain with the help of medication. As soon as the roads are clear, she can come home. He said it is best that she stays there until then because of her treatments. I have to agree."

"I know, but I miss my little girl."

"Dave, you have to learn to let go. I know you are concerned about the DNA tests and I am too. However, we have to remember; Sarah is a young woman with a strong mind and knows what she wants. I know she will do the right thing when the time comes."

"I just hope she makes up her mind soon. I know Amy isn't going to let this slide for too long. If she thinks Sarah is her daughter, I am sure she will be making contact. I am not looking forward to that."

"How do you think I feel? The last thing I want is contact with your old flame, but I will do what I have to for Sarah."

"She was not an old flame; just one of the crowd. You don't have to be concerned about the contact with her for my sake. I have absolutely no feelings, one way or another, for Amy Stern though I am a little apprehensive about seeing her again. She was so angry with me the last time I saw her."

Alice stood up and headed to the sink with her cup. "I am really praying that you have no feelings for her, Dave. Because if you are lying to me, I will never forgive you." With that, Alice headed to the laundry room to start her day.

Chapter 49

Southern Alberta

The Johnson's family planned trip to Medicine Hat didn't happen around January 1 because of the blizzard that hit all of southern Alberta and Saskatchewan on New Year's Eve. It was January 3 before the wind let up enough for Ivan to take the 4 by 4 truck and tackle the roads over to Shane and April to pick up the kids. Much as Ivan and

Amy enjoyed their time by themselves, but they really missed Laura and Abe. Though they talked to the kids every day, it just wasn't the same as being with them. They knew their children were safe at the other ranch, but Abe was very homesick and cried himself to sleep every night. Ivan knew he had to try to bring them home.

Amy had talked to her mother at New Year's, telling her they would be coming to Medicine Hat as soon as the storm settled and things were brought up to date at the ranch. With all the snow, Ivan knew he would have lots to remove from the pens and roadways. Shane would be over to check on things while they were gone. Amy planned to book a room at the Holiday Inn for one night so they wouldn't have to hurry back. Now they just had to decide when they were going.

* * *

Two days after the storm ended, a Chinook started blowing, bringing warmer weather from the west into the valley. It was a relief after the minus twenty during the storm, though the wind chills at times were more like minus thirty. Getting the tractor started, Ivan was able to get the snow removed and get feed into place in anticipation of their trip.

There was no word from Regina and Amy was trying to forget about Dave Knight and his daughter for the time being. She was having enough trouble dealing with the idea that her mother might have been involved with switching babies when hers was born. For that reason, she was anxious to get the trip to Medicine Hat over with. After she confronted her mother, maybe she would have some news for Shane to help him in his search for his parents. Amy was trying very hard not to be angry with her mother until she found out the truth, but it was not easy. She didn't feel very charitable at times, though she knew she had to try to forgive whatever happened back then. During their family prayers every morning, Ivan asked for patience and charity toward all those that offended or betrayed them. She knew the prayer was directed at her in Ivan's quiet way. Because he cared and was concerned for her, she didn't say anything. Amy knew he was right. Holding grudges did not help any situation. Her mother was never going to change and Amy had to accept that. She just hoped she would be honest with her when she confronted her. Then maybe they could finally get to the bottom of things.

* * *

Shane had enough of waiting. It had been weeks since Dave had talked to him and he was anxious to know just what the plan was with Sarah. Picking up the phone, he dialed Dave's office. When his secretary answered, Shane asked, "May I speak with Dave, please?"

"I'm sorry. Dave isn't in his office right now. May I take a message?"

"When do you expect him?"

"That is hard to say. His daughter is in the hospital so he is up there. Who is calling, please?

"Sarah's not well?"

"Are you family?"

"No. Listen; just tell Dave that Shane called when he comes in."

"Certainly."

Shane hung up the phone just as April came into the room, carrying Michael.

"Any luck?"

"No. It appears Dave is up at the hospital because Sarah is in there. I wonder if she is worse. I think I will call him on his cell."

"Are you sure you want to find out? Anything you find will have to be reported to Amy. Maybe it is best to let sleeping dogs lie, as the old saying goes."

"Somehow, I feel a connection to that family. I really need to call."

"Okay. I'm going to put Michael down for his nap."

Shane dug Dave's business card out of his pocket and dialed his cell number. It rang several times, and then Dave finally picked up.

"Hello. Dave Knight here."

"Dave? This is Shane. I called your office and they said you were up at the hospital visiting your daughter. Is Sarah worse?"

"Hang on. I have to get to a secure area."

"Okay."

Half a minute later, Dave came back on the line, "Shane? Okay, now we can talk. I was in Sarah's room and didn't want to talk in front of her. Sarah broke her leg on New Year's Day. We had a terrible time getting her to the hospital because of the blizzard and once we got her here, it was decided to keep her at the hospital until the roads and everything were clear because of her treatments. She is doing okay. She hit her head when she fell and that was a concern, but other than a black eye, she is coming along. Thank you for calling. I imagine you are wondering what is going on with the tests?"

"Yes, I was concerned about Sarah's health and wondering if she had decided to have the tests done. I know Amy is anxious to know the results."

"I imagine she is. Sarah hasn't said anything to us lately, but with all this going on, we just let it ride. I will quiz her again today and see what she says. Dr. Klein is hoping for a match as soon as possible before her kidneys fail completely. We are, too."

"I am praying every day that a match turns up for her. I am actually thinking of being tested, too. I know I am not related, but I feel an attachment to your family."

"Shane, you don't have to do that. You have a young family and a great future. Look after your own."

"I know I don't have to, but I want to. Anyway, take care and I hope to hear from you shortly."

"Thanks for calling. Talk soon."

As Shane hung up the phone, April spoke from behind him. "How could you? How could you decide something like that without consulting me? I will not let you donate a kidney to an unknown person and jeopardize our family that way! What on earth are you thinking, Shane Collins?!" With that, April slammed her book down on the counter and stormed out of the room.

Shane stared after her in shock. He had never seen April that angry. "What did I do?" he spoke aloud, "I haven't promised a kidney to anyone. April! What is up with you? Come back here so we can talk."

But April was gone into the bedroom, slamming the door behind her. Shane thought it was probably smart to let her cool off before confronting her. Grabbing his coat and cap, he headed out to the porch to put on his boots. Maybe by the time I return from doing chores, she will be ready to talk, Shane thought. Let us hope so.

Chapter 50

Regina, Saskatchewan

Dave and Alice brought Sarah home five days after she was admitted to the hospital. Because of her broken leg, they moved Sarah to the spare bedroom on the main floor for the time being. They didn't want to take any chances of her falling down the stairs while trying to negotiate them with her cast.

"Don't fuss over me," Sarah admonished as Alice got her into the recliner in the living room and tucked a blanket around her. "I'm okay. Just be sure my crutches are close so I can get up if I need to."

"Don't try to get up on your own. I will help you. We don't want you to fall again."

"Oh Mom. I am not an invalid! I was walking on my own at the hospital with my crutches. Quit fussing."

"Okay, okay. But if you fall and do more damage, I will never forgive myself."

"Mom, you have to let go of the guilt. It is not your fault I fell. I was just clumsy and tripped. That rug has been there forever."

"I still feel responsible. I can't help it."

"Don't." Sarah reached up and gave her Mom a hug. Alice hugged her back and headed to the kitchen to start lunch. Calling over her shoulder she asked, "Grilled cheese okay for lunch?"

"Sounds yummy," Sarah answered and settled back in the chair. She felt bad that her mother was blaming herself for the accident. *How can I convince her that it wasn't her fault,* Sarah wondered. *Maybe Dad can make her see the light.* Thinking of her Dad, she remembered the conversation they had at the hospital. Her Dad was asking about the tests. At that time, Sarah told him she was going to wait until she got home. Well, now she was home, so would have to make a decision. First, she knew she would have to be sure her mother was okay with it. It really affected everyone in the family, but especially her mother. Though her mother wanted her to believe that she was okay with contacting this other woman, Sarah knew it had to hurt. Am I willing to hurt the only mother I have known, on the off chance that this other person is a match and is willing to help, Sarah thought. I just don't know if I am prepared to go that route. I just hate the thought of disrupting families, hers and ours. I don't know her, but I am sure she probably has the same misgivings as I do. Sarah sighed and closed her eyes. I will make a decision tomorrow. Right now, I just want to forget all the bad things and concentrate on getting better. She picked up the TV remote and started surfing to find something decent to watch.

* * *

Dave headed back to the office after he deposited Alice and Sarah at home. He was very glad to have his little girl back under his roof. She seemed okay and was cracking jokes about being a cripple so I hope she is okay, Dave mentally prayed. He knew she was good at hiding things, but did seem to be happy to be home. A few of her friends had showed up at the hospital after the weather cleared and that seemed to boost her moral. Now Alice had taken a few days off from work to be at home with her. She was getting around quite well on her crutches, but Dave was glad they had moved her downstairs for the time being. Climbing the stairs while on crutches was a recipe for disaster as far as Dave was concerned. Much better that Sarah be on one level.

Pulling into his parking spot at work, Dave turned off the engine, grabbed his brief case, and headed into the building. He had a lot of work to catch up on and was hoping to have a quiet afternoon to succeed in that.

As he walked in the door, his secretary handed him his messages and informed him he had a visitor in his office. Dave groaned. He just knew it was not going to be a quiet day. Opening his office door, he saw the mayor sitting in his chair behind his desk, going through the messages there. Clearing his throat, Dave greeted her. "Good Morning, Mayor. May I ask what brings you over so early to see us?"

Chapter 51

Southern Alberta

It was the middle of January and because of the recent Chinooks, most of the snow had melted. With temperatures hovering around the freezing mark, the cattle were consuming less feed, which gave the ranchers a bit of a break.

Ivan kept busy with getting the barn ready for calving starting in February, while Amy was preparing for their anticipated trip to Medicine Hat. They had a couple of reasons for wanting to make the trip as soon as possible. One was the weather. It was so much nicer to travel when road conditions were good and it wasn't too cold. The second reason was to make the trip and be back before calving started. The third and most important reason for the trip was to find out what happened all those years ago at the Home for unwed mothers in Calgary. Ivan knew that Amy would not be satisfied until she found out the truth. He also knew that Shane would not let things rest until he found his parents. With all this in mind, Ivan knew the time had come for their trip to the Hat.

Amy had checked the calendar that morning and agreed that if Shane was available, they could leave the next morning. She quickly phoned and rebooked their hotel room, which was available and got busy packing for them and the kids. Amy had thought about leaving the kids at home while she confronted her mother, but knew they would not be happy about being left behind, especially after being forced to stay at Shane's just recently due to the storm. Any way, she mused, her mother should see the kids again. Ivan could take them out for ice cream or something while she talked with her mother. It would work out. She just hoped she would come away with information to help Shane in his search.

* * *

April and Shane had come to an understanding. Shane agreed not to be tested for a match to Sarah and April agreed that she would not interfere in his search for his real parents. Though Shane believed he would be doing the right thing by being tested, he didn't want to upset April again so he let it slide. She had already agreed earlier that he could look for his parents, so Shane figured he was getting the worst of the deal, but he let it be. Nothing was as important as his marriage. He loved April with all his heart. The last thing he wanted was a rift between them. In a way, he could understand why she didn't want him tested. She was concerned for the family. However, being a good Christian, Shane really felt it was his duty to try to help Sarah. As he thought about the whole situation, he decided he would let it ride for the time being, but if a donor wasn't found shortly, he would have another talk with April.

Shane tossed the bale over the fence into the horses and climbing over the gate, took the strings off the bale and spread the hay around. Patting his big gelding on the neck, he spoke aloud, "Well Bud, old boy; I bet you are glad the weather warmed up. Sure wish I had your nice warm coat when that old wind blows. Now, don't be bossy. Let the other two have some breakfast, too." As the gelding made an aggressive move toward the two mares, Shane groused at him, "Hey, you old grouch! Quit being a pig!" Bud shook his head and went back to consuming his hay.

Shane had to laugh. It seems there is always a pecking order in the animal world. He noticed it with the cattle and horses, but not so much with the sheep. Usually with them, there would be one lead ewe but the rest would all feed together. Sometimes a bit of head bunting, jostling for space at the feeder, but nothing as aggressive as cattle or horses. This made him think about humans and what pecking order they were in. In so many families, the father seemed to be in charge and then there were others where the wife called all the shots. Shane was beginning to wonder which category his family was in. "I guess I will find out if I push this testing issue," He spoke ruefully. "Maybe I will find out quicker than I plan to."

* * *

April had just finished sewing up the hem on her new skirt when the phone rang. Running to pick it up before it woke the baby; she answered breathlessly, "Hello. Collins Ranch."

"April? Is that you?"

Realizing it was Amy, April responded, "Oh, hi Mom. Yes, it's me. I just hurried to get the phone so I'm a bit out of breath."

"Sorry for phoning now, but I wanted to talk to Shane when he is in for lunch."

"He's not in yet, but I expect him within the half hour. I can get him to call you."

"Actually, you can just tell him; we plan to go to Medicine Hat in the morning. We want to go while the weather is good and before calving starts. Shane had said he would check on things here while we were gone. It would be good if he came over later and talked to Ivan about what needs to be done."

"Oh, sure. I will tell him. I know he will be happy to do that. I am so glad the weather smartened up. I really don't like blizzards. I think it is because a person feels so isolated when you can't see anything."

"I know what you mean. When I lived in the city, it never seemed so bad because you knew there were people all around you. But out here on the ranch, neighbors are not that close and no way can you see their lights and especially not during a blizzard. You will get used to it, but it takes time."

"I know. As least we are warm and comfortable inside the house. But I still am glad to see the sun shining again."

"Me too. Well, I had better go. Is there anything you would like for us to bring back for you guys from the city?"

"Not really. Unless you see a good buy on diapers. It seems like we go through a lot these days."

"I will check. Bye for now, and thanks."

"You're welcome. Give Laura and Abe a hug from me."

"Will do, and a big hug to you and Michael."

April hung up the phone just as Shane walked in the door. "You just missed Amy. She wanted to ask you to come over and talk to Ivan about doing chores while they are away."

"They are finally getting away?"

"Yes, leaving in the morning."

"Good. I will run over there this afternoon. What's for lunch?"

Chapter 52

Regina, Saskatchewan

"So, what are you trying to tell me?" Dave stared at Sarah, "Are you saying that you never want to compare your test results with your biological mother?"

"Yes, that is what I am saying. I have given a lot of thought to this, and I just don't think it is in the best interests of our families to proceed with this. I am sure her family doesn't need the upset and I know we don't. I am confident another donor will show up. Right now, I am doing okay, so why rock the boat. I want you to get hold of this Shane person and let him know my decision. Will you, Dad?"

"Sarah, are you sure this is really what you want? Your biological mother might be the only one that can help you. The most important thing to me is getting you well. We can deal with the fallout."

"But can Mom? I know she is only going along with this because of me. I know underneath she is not happy about it. The fact that she knew nothing about my real mother being in your life certainly was a surprise. Mom is brave, but it is tearing her up inside."

"Did she say anything to you?"

"No. She wouldn't. That is why I know she is hurting."

"I will have a talk with her. She assured me she was okay with this, so I took her at her word. Maybe I have been missing something."

"Oh Dad, women are just more sensitive to another woman's feelings. Men are inclined to believe what is actually said instead of reading between the lines."

"So how did you get so smart, my girl? It certainly isn't years of experience."

"Well, the last time I looked, I am a woman. That explains it," Sarah laughed. "Don't feel bad, Dad. This is best all round. If things change in the future, I will reconsider, but for now, let's leave things alone."

Dave stood up and walked over to Sarah. Leaning down, he gave her a hug. "I love you a lot. I would die if anything happened to you, and I would die twice if it were my fault for not pursuing this further. But I will concede and let it go for now."

"Thank you, Dad. I know you love me. I love you, too, but this is best for now. Can you hand me my textbooks? Jesse is coming over later and I want to study up on our assignment before he arrives."

Picking up her books, Dave replied, "Don't overdo it. Be sure to get your rest." Dave handed Sarah her books, and patting her on the shoulder, headed to the kitchen to grab a cup of coffee before heading out to work.

* * *

Alice stood at the head of the stairs with tears running down her face. She had been coming down the upstairs hallway, when she heard Dave and Sarah talking. She knew she shouldn't eavesdrop, but when she realized what they were talking about, she couldn't help herself. Now she wished she had just gone back to the bedroom. She had heard the saying, "Don't listen in on conversations or you might hear something you don't want to hear." Well, now she knew what that meant.

Backing away from the stairs, Alice did head back to the bedroom. Sitting on the edge of the bed, she let the tears flow. She had no idea that Sarah was so attuned to her thoughts that she discovered how she really felt. She had tried so hard to hide it from Dave and Sarah, but she should have known that Sarah would catch on. She was always very sensitive to other people's feelings.

Wiping away her tears, Alice mumbled aloud, "How am I going to convince Sarah to agree to the testing? I can't fool her into thinking I had a change of heart. She would see right through that. What am I going to do?"

"Do about what?" Dave spoke from the doorway.

Alice quickly turned her face away and blew her nose, "I thought you left for work."

"Well, I was leaving, but when you didn't come downstairs, I thought I had better check and see what was up." As Dave moved closer, he said, "You've been crying? What's wrong?"

"Nothing. Just go to work, okay?"

"I don't believe that. You never cry." Sitting on the bed, Dave took Alice's hand, "Tell me."

Alice started crying all over again, and through her tears, answered, "I heard you and Sarah talking. I'm sorry; I know I shouldn't listen in, but I couldn't help myself."

Taking Alice into his arms, Dave consoled her, "So what Sarah said is true. You really are upset about contacting Amy. Why didn't you tell me?"

"Because you would think I was being selfish. I was thinking that about myself. How could I worry about that when Sarah's health is at stake? Does that make me a bad person?"

"Oh honey, that just makes you human. I should have understood that. Like Sarah said, I am a man and I guess we just do not understand how a woman feels about many things, but I am trying. I want you to talk to me about these things. If I don't understand, make me."

Alice turned and hugged Dave back. "You are such a good man. Why is it that things from the past have to jump up and bite us in later life? I guess there must be a reason."

"I guess so. But this is my fault and I feel bad hurting you. Can you forgive me?"

"Yes, I already have. Now I have to go talk with that girl of ours. She mustn't put off this test because of me."

"Okay, I'm off to work. Are you going to be okay?"

"Yes; I will wash my face so Sarah doesn't know I've been crying. Did you have breakfast?"

"Sarah and I had some toast. I'm fine." Kissing Alice, Dave stood up and headed to the door, "See you tonight."

Chapter 53

Southern Alberta

Ivan jerked awake. Staring around the room, he was trying to figure out what woke him when he realized the phone was ringing. Grabbing the bedside portable, he pushed the button and mumbled, "Hello?"

Within a few seconds, he sat upright and swung his legs over the bed. Listening intently, he answered, "Okay, we will be there as soon as we can."

Amy spoke sleepily from her side of the bed, "What was all that about? What time is it anyway?"

Ivan stood up and reached for his pants, "You had better get up. That was the hospital in Medicine Hat. Your mother had a stroke and she was just admitted to the hospital. It doesn't look good."

"Oh no; What happened?"

"The hospital didn't say. Nevertheless, we had better get going. It is five o'clock now. By the time we get there, it will be a while. I think we should leave the kids with April and Shane."

Amy jumped out of bed and headed to the bathroom, "I agree. Can you call them, tell them what's up, and see if it is okay? I'm going to have a quick shower. Will Shane do your chores for you?"

"I'm sure he will. Actually, maybe it would be a good thing if Shane was the one to go with you, unless you want me there."

Amy paused in the doorway. "I always want you there, but maybe you are right. Shane might want to be there. After all, she is the only grandmother he has known. I will be okay. There is a good chance she will come out of this and live for another twenty years; who knows?"

"It didn't sound like that. However, I will quiz Shane and see what he wants to do. Go have your shower."

* * *

As it turned out, Shane made the trip to Medicine Hat with Amy while April looked after the children and Ivan did the chores on both ranches. It was eight o'clock before they were able to get away. Amy had called the hospital and her mother was holding her own. Her friend was at the hospital and Amy was able to talk with Edith. She urged her to hurry, as things did not look good.

Amy was glad Shane was driving as she found herself to be too distracted. So many thoughts were tumbling through her mind; thoughts of the past and problems she and her mother had over the years. Now it may be too late to get the records set straight. As she glanced over at Shane, she was sure he was thinking much the same thing.

"Thank you for coming with me, Shane. I know this isn't easy for you. My mother has never been very open with you over the years, but I think we both know why now. I really hope she will be able to communicate with us, so we can find out more information as to your birth."

Shane sighed, "I know it seems selfish of me, but I am really hoping for information. I said some prayers for her, but I know that my heart isn't really in it. Does that make me a bad person?"

"No. I have said prayers for my mother since the day I joined the church and I knew I had to forgive her for my own salvation. I know God will be listening and I hope He will give us the time we need with her to find some answers. My mother has always been a very tough woman. She will probably survive this and continue living for years yet."

"I am finding it hard to understand why she did what she did, if she did. I shouldn't complain as some wonderful parents raised me, but I still don't understand. Why would someone want to do that?"

"We don't know for sure if my mother had anything to do with that. We are only guessing. I do believe she knew because of the differences in sex. She couldn't mistake a girl for a boy and she was there when I gave birth."

"Well, I am sorry we didn't make an effort to get to Medicine Hat before. Maybe this would have been all settled before now."

"I know. Maybe if we had approached her earlier, she might have had the stroke then. Let's just hope we can communicate with her. Edith said she seemed to be unable to speak. That is not good news."

"I guess we will find out soon enough. We are only an hour away now. Why don't you try to rest? It will probably be a very long day."

* * *

Ivan was very glad that Shane went with Amy. He was very happy to stay at home with the kids and look after the chores. He woke Laura and Abe at eight and after giving them a quick breakfast and explaining the best he could about Grandma and why their mommy had to head to Medicine Hat so early, he bundled them up and took them over to April. While he was there, he did Shane's chores and then had lunch with April and the kids. Now he was on his way back to his ranch to get his chores done. April had asked him to come back and have supper with them so he was relieved he wouldn't have to cook. He would bring the kids home to sleep.

Amy had phoned when they arrived in Medicine Hat, but they had not seen Gladys yet. Ivan was really praying that she would be able to talk with Amy and Shane. There was so much that needed to be said. Ivan knew if Gladys died without things settled between her and her daughter, Amy would find it very hard. Losing a parent was not easy, even if you didn't always get along over the years, Ivan thought. Through his own experiences, Ivan knew that once someone is gone, there is no way to make amends. He had experienced that with his own father. He didn't really remember his mother that much, but he and his father were not close. Ivan wondered many times over the years if he had been fair to his father. He had blamed him for his lack of love and caring for him, but failed to understand what his father went through after losing his wife. Ivan knew if he ever lost Amy, he wouldn't be sure how good a father he would be to his own kids. He didn't even want to think about it.

Parking the truck by the corrals, Ivan climbed out and headed to the tractor shed. Getting the chores done was the first order of the day. He wanted to be finished in time to have supper with April and the family. He was sure she would have heard from Medicine Hat by then, too.

* * *

Amy paused in the doorway to the ICU and gazed at her mother. She didn't recognize her. She looked so frail and pale with oxygen in her nose, an IV in her arm and hooked up to all kinds of monitors. The nurse on duty glanced up and then came over to Amy.

"You are her daughter?"

"Yes. How is she?"

"She is stable right now. Did you talk to her doctor?"

"No; we just got in. When did she have the stroke?"

"They are not sure but they think sometime in the night. The staff at the Home heard her fall and rushed to her room. They found her on the floor of the bedroom. The phone was on the floor, so they think she was trying to call someone for help."

"Can she talk at all?"

"She hasn't since she came here. You should talk to her doctor. I think she is still in the hospital. Do you want me to page her for you?"

"Yes, please. Can I sit with her?"

"Certainly. Are you by yourself?"

"No, my son is here, too."

"He can come in too, if he likes. I will go page the doctor."

As the nurse left, Amy sat down in the chair by the bed and took her mother's hand. Gladys opened her eyes and stared up at the ceiling.

"Mom? Mom, can you hear me?"

Slowly, Gladys turned her eyes, but not her head. Recognition seemed to flare in her eyes, but she didn't respond. Amy squeezed her hand, "Mom, we are here. Shane is here with me. Can you talk?"

Amy could see her mother was trying to move her arm, but only a small movement in one finger. As Amy watched, Gladys' lips tried to move, but no sound came out. With a lump in her throat, Amy soothed, "It's okay, Mom. Don't try to talk; just relax and let your body heal. I will do the talking for now."

Gladys seemed to be relieved and closed her eyes. Then Amy said, "Mom, if you can understand what I say, can you blink your eyes?"

Her mother opened her eyes and slowly closed and opened them again.

"Wonderful, Mom. Now I know you can hear and understand me. Shane and I drove up this morning as soon as we heard. As you know, Ivan, I, and the kids were planning to come to see you today. We were coming right after New Years, but with the blizzard, all our plans were delayed. The kids all send their love. Ivan kept them at home. Between him and April, they will do chores and keep the kids, so everything is looked after. I see Edith is out in the lounge. She brought me up to date on things. She is a good friend to you."

Amy knew she was babbling, but she couldn't seem to help herself. As long as her mother could understand, maybe there was hope she would be able to communicate eventually.

The nurse had returned and had Shane with her. He took the other chair, reached out, and held Amy's hand. "Hello, Grandmother. April and Michael send their love and best wishes. We pray you will soon be up and about again."

There was no response from Gladys and Shane turned to Amy with a question in his eyes. Amy just shook her head and squeezed his hand.

"The doctor will see you now," the nurse commented as she checked the monitors. "She is waiting for you in her office. Just ask at the front desk."

Amy stood up, "Okay. We will be back as soon as we are finished with him."

"Actually, it's a her. Dr. Mitchell. She is very good."

"Thank you." With that, Shane and Amy left the room. As they did, Gladys opened her eyes and tried to follow their departure.

"Don't worry, Mrs. Stern. They will be back shortly," the nurse said as she patted Gladys' arm.

* * *

"What are you trying to tell us?" Amy questioned Dr. Mitchell.

"Your mother has had a very massive stroke. She is completely paralyzed on her left side and partially on the right. We are not sure how much she understands of what we say, but we are monitoring her very closely."

"I think she does understand. I asked her to blink her eyes if she knew what I said and she did blink."

"Are you sure it was because she understood what you said, or just a coincidence?"

"Well, I'm not sure, but she appeared to know what I said."

"It is good to maintain hope, but I am not too optimistic about her chances of recovery. I'm sorry."

Amy sighed, "Thank you, doctor. I know you will be doing your best. How long do you think she has?"

"It is hard to say. She could suffer another stroke and be gone today, or last for days. I wish I could give you better news. Now I have to complete my rounds. Take your time. You can stay here if you would like some privacy for a spell."

With that, the doctor left. Amy and Shane continued sitting in their chairs, each in their own thoughts. Finally, Shane spoke, "Well, I guess that is that. She will never be able to tell me what happened. All that is left for me to do is pray for her and ask the Lord for guidance in finding my real parents."

Reaching over and patting Shane's arm, Amy answered, "Don't give up hope yet. The Lord works in mysterious ways, and things may improve for Mom. I know she knew who we were and I know she responded to my question. Let's go to the chapel and say some prayers for her."

"Do you think she would be upset if I called some of the elders at the church here and asked them to come and give her a blessing?"

"Oh, I don't think that would be a good idea just yet. She really is against our church and we don't want to upset her."

"Okay. Then let us go check on her, and then have some breakfast. It is nearly lunchtime and I am feeling famished. Then go to the chapel."

"That sounds like a good idea. I think we should call her minister too, just in case he doesn't know."

"Sounds good. I'm sure she would appreciate a visit."

Chapter 54

Southern Alberta

Amy was sitting by her mother's bedside when James Wiggins walked in. He was Gladys' lawyer and Amy was a little surprised to see him. Shane had gone for a bit of a break and to grab something to drink for both of them. Because Amy was expecting to see the minister from her mother's church, she was a little startled to see James.

"Hello, Amy," James spoke softly, "I am so glad to see that you are here. Edith phoned me a couple of hours ago but I had to rearrange some appointments to come up here, or I would have been here sooner."

"There was no need for you to hurry. Mom is stable at the moment and hasn't responded. She can't seem to talk and movement is very slight."

"I am sorry to hear that. Is she sleeping right now?"

"I'm not sure. She does open her eyes every once in a while."

"Do you mind if I try to talk with her?"

"Not at all, if it is okay with the nurse."

"She's the one that let me in here. You see, your mother has some requests and the hospital knows that I have her will." With that, James took Gladys by the hand and spoke to her, "Gladys, can you hear me and understand what I am saying?"

Very slowly, Gladys opened her eyes. James squeezed her hand and said, "Can you understand me?"

Gladys closed and opened her eyes. James glanced at Amy who answered, "That means yes, she can understand you."

James nodded and went on, "That's good. I am here to see that your wishes are carried out, Gladys. As long as you are sure. Blink if you are sure."

Gladys blinked. "Wonderful. I will see that everything is done exactly to your request. Now, I won't tire you out. Rest and God bless you, Gladys."

When James stood up, Amy did, too. "Thank you for coming. I know my Mom depended on you for years to look after things for her."

"I would like a word with you, if I may. I will get the nurse back in here so we can talk in the lounge."

"Okay, if you think that is necessary."

"It is," James responded as he patted Gladys' hand and headed out to the hallway to get the nurse.

"I will be right back, Mom," Amy assured her mother as she followed James out.

* * *

"I don't understand. What are you saying?" Amy's voice rose as she stared at James.

"What don't you understand? It is pretty straightforward. Your mother signed her donor card and she wants her organs to be used to save other lives. It is a very unselfish thing she is doing. More people should be like her and sign those cards. I don't know why she didn't tell you that she did this."

"I understand that, but the other part is what I am having trouble understanding."

"Oh, you mean about her kidneys going to her granddaughter? She only had one child which is you, so the granddaughter has to be your daughter."

Amy felt lightheaded. What was James saying? Did her mother know about Dave's daughter? Could it really be true and Sarah was her daughter? Then Amy started to get angry.

"Well, this really takes the cake! I am so mad, I could spit. Therefore, she did know all along that Shane was not my son. How could she keep that away from me? How could she be involved in something so despicable as to steal my child and replace it? I don't know if I can ever forgive that."

"Calm down, Amy. I know your mother was not always perfect and probably did some things in her life that she is not proud of. That is probably why I have a letter in my possession that I am ordered to give to you upon her passing. I also have her will. The reason I am here at the hospital today is to insure her wishes are carried out and that her organs be used to help others."

"I suppose she thinks by doing something like this, it will compensate for all the other hateful things."

"I don't know the workings of her mind, but I will carry out my instructions to the best of my ability. You have to let go of your anger, Amy. Your mother is dying, and you must make peace with her while you can."

"I don't know if I can. I have to find Shane. Please excuse me; I'm sorry if I appear rude to you, but this is a bit of a shock to me, though I did expect she was involved with the switch. You see, things have cropped up and I did find out that Shane was not my son. I was hoping to have a talk with my mother and find out just what happened but now I won't have the chance."

"Maybe the letter she left for you will explain everything. I can't give it to you until after, but I wish I could so you could settle things."

"If the letter explains things, why don't you ask her if I can have it now, being as she can't talk to us?"

"I don't know if a blink of the eye could be called consent, but I will ask her and see what happens; with her doctor's permission, of course. I don't want to upset her."

"I understand. Thank you. You will get in touch with me?" When James nodded, Amy headed out the door of the lounge hoping to find Shane.

* * *

Shane was sitting by Gladys' bed when Amy found him. She signaled him to come out.

"What's up?" Shane enquired.

"We need to talk," Amy remarked. "Let's go to the cafeteria and have a break."

"Okay."

Leading the way, Amy stomped along, deep in her thoughts. Shane hurried to keep up. "Where's the fire? What did the lawyer say to you to get you so riled up?"

Amy stopped short and glared at Shane, "He just confirmed what we thought all along, and he really didn't have to tell me anything."

"What do you mean?"

"Just that Mom knew about Sarah. She wants her kidneys to be donated to her."

Shane took Amy by the arm and guided her to a table in the cafeteria. "Sit here. I will get us a drink, and then you can tell me everything."

When Shane returned, Amy continued, "James didn't have to tell me too much, but I could read between the lines. If she is donating a kidney to her granddaughter, it has to be Sarah. Laura is not in need of a kidney so that is how I know she knew all along about the switch."

"Do you think she has been in touch with the Knight family?"

"I don't think so or Dave would have said something to you, don't you think?"

"That's true. Would they even consider a kidney donor that is older, like your mother, for a young girl like Sarah?"

"I don't know. I suppose if there is no one else and the recipient is in need, it could be done."

"How long does your mother have?"

"We don't know. She is still responding a bit, but I don't dare confront her about this now. It would probably kill her and I don't want that on my conscience. James said he had a letter that is to be given to me when she passes on. I assume it will explain everything. I asked James to get Mom's consent to give me the letter now."

"That would be good. It is my only chance to find my parents."

"I know. I am praying for that, too. Now I have to make some decisions. What do I do about my daughter? It is so hard to believe I really do have another daughter. You know, my head hurts just thinking about all this. I have to phone Ivan. I talked with him a couple of hours ago, but I need to hear his voice again."

"You do that. I will head back to the ICU. Love you." Shane reached over and gave Amy a hug.

Chapter 55

Southern Alberta

Ivan had just finished the chores when his cell phone rang again. He answered without checking to see whom it was and was surprised to hear Amy's voice.

"What's happened? Are you all right? You sound a bit stressed."

"You bet I am stressed and I'm upset and mad, all at the same time!"

"Calm down, honey. Did you find out something that upset you?"

"You might say that."

"But I thought your mother couldn't talk."

"She can't. Her lawyer was here and relayed some information to me that was very upsetting. Mom has signed her donor card and she has requested that her kidneys go to her granddaughter. So you know what that means."

"Well, it certainly isn't Laura she is thinking about, so it has to be . . . Oh, I see. This means she knew about your first child being a girl, right?"

"Right on. In addition, by the sounds of things, she has kept up with her and knows about her problem. I also wonder if she was instrumental in Dave adopting his own daughter. I would not put it past her. A form of revenge on him for deserting me and ultimately her with his denial. Oh, Ivan! I am so mixed up and upset over this whole thing."

"Does the doctor have any idea of a prognosis?"

"She really didn't give us much hope. It is a very massive stroke. The nurse thinks it is a miracle that she can still seem to understand a bit."

"I'm so sorry, Amy. Do you want me to come there?"

"No. It is best if you look after things there. I will be okay. I just wanted to hear your voice again. Oh, and James is going to check and see if he can give me a letter that Mom has for me. He had orders to give it to me when she passes, but due to the circumstances now, he thought I should have it. Mom seems to understand by blinking yes, so he is going to check with her."

"She wrote you a letter?"

"I guess so."

"And you are hoping it will explain everything."

"That is the hope. James seems to think that."

"Okay. Let me know if there is anything I can do from this end."

"You are doing enough by looking after the kids and the chores. Give the kids my love and a hug from me."

"Will do. How about one for me, too?"

"Always. I don't know what I would do without you. You are my anchor."

"The feeling is mutual."

"Bye for now. I have to get back to the ICU. I will call later tonight and talk to the kids."

"Love you and pray all goes well. I am glad Shane is there with you. Talk soon."

Closing his cell phone, Ivan slid it back into his pocket and headed for the tractor. He just had time to put it back into the shed and head over to April's for supper. He hoped the kids were having a good time and not causing too much work for April. He would be glad when things were back to normal, but by the sound of things, that wouldn't be for a while.

* * *

April had just set the kids down to supper when Ivan walked in. Immediately, Laura and Abe had a barrage of questions for him.

"Daddy, did you remember to feed the kitty? Did you get your cows fed? When is Mommy coming home?"

Laughing, Ivan sat down at the table and answered, "One question at a time, please. Yes, I fed kitty and I fed the cows. Mommy phoned and she will phone and talk to you tonight. We don't know when Mommy can come home, as Grandma Stern needs her right now. We must pray for her and to keep Mommy and Shane safe. Can we do that?"

Abe spoke up, "I will. I get to say the blessing tonight." Bowing his head, he blessed the food, and then went on, "Please God, bless Mommy and Shane so they can come home, and please bless Grandma. If you want to take her home, God, we will understand. You will look after her. Thank you, God. Amen."

Ivan felt a lump in his throat. From the mouths of babes, he thought. Abe managed to say what everyone was thinking. Ivan knew he was hoping for the same thing. If Gladys would be unable to move or talk, it definitely was in her best interests to pass away. He hoped that Amy had time to settle things with her mother first.

"Okay, everyone; let's dig in. Supper is getting cold." April reached over and passed the mashed potatoes to Ivan.

"Do I have to eat potatoes?" Laura whined, "Daddy, you know I don't like potatoes unless they are French fries."

"Now, Laura; you know Mommy always makes you take a small spoonful, so that is the same here. You must try everything. You don't want to offend April, do you?"

"No; I just don't like potatoes. I will eat twice as much carrots, okay?"

"Not okay." Putting a small spoonful on her plate, Ivan replied, "No dessert for anyone who doesn't clean their plate."

With a big sigh, Laura took a small mouthful of potatoes, made a face and then swallowed. April and Ivan glanced at each other, both trying not to smile.

Just as they finished supper and Ivan washed Abe's hands and face, the phone rang. When April picked it up, she discovered it was Shane.

"Hi, honey. How are you doing?"

"We are doing fine, Shane. Abe and Laura have been a big help. Laura is going to be a great baby-sitter and Abe has been running lots of errands for me. How is Grandma Stern?"

"Not good. Between you and me, I don't think she will make it through the night. The doctor was in just a few minutes ago and didn't give us much hope. She seems to have slipped into a coma."

"I'm so sorry, Shane. So you weren't able to talk with her?"

"No, but we have discovered some things, which I will tell you about when I get home. Amy is here now and would like to talk to the kids."

"Okay. Love you and take care of yourself."

"I will, and April . . . thank you for all you are doing. I love you and miss you."

"Me, too. Talk to you tomorrow."

April turned to Laura and handed the phone to her, "Here, your Mommy wants to talk to you."

Laura eagerly took the phone and headed into the living room. Abe started crying, "I want to talk to Mommy, too."

Ivan hushed him, "Hey, you will. Laura gets to talk first this time. Just be patient."

"Have you talked to Amy today?" April asked Ivan.

"Yes, she phoned twice today on my cell. She was upset the last time. It seems she found out from her mother's lawyer that Gladys definitely knew that Shane was not her son and she knew that Sarah was her daughter. So that didn't sit well with Amy."

"I bet not. Why would her mother do something like that? Do you think she was involved in the baby switch?"

"We don't know, but according to Amy, the lawyer told her that her mother left a letter with him to be given to Amy upon her death. It might tell the whole story."

"Well, that would be good. Maybe it will have some clues as to who Shane's parents are. I don't think Shane is going to be content until he finds out whom they are. I can't imagine not knowing who your parents are. I guess I am very fortunate, even if my Mom can be controlling at times," April laughed.

"I like your parents. Your Mom is a very capable woman and she loves you and Michael unconditionally. I know she would do anything for you."

"I know that, too. I do love her, but I wish she would realize that I am capable of looking after my family. She always wants to come out and help me. I need to have my independence. But you are right. I should accept her help once in a while."

"That's my girl. Now, I am going to take my kids out of your hair and head home. See you in the morning."

"Okay. Let me get their coats."

Chapter 56

Southern Alberta

As it turned out, Gladys' lawyer, James Wiggins never got a chance to ask Amy's mother about the letter.

Amy was sitting with her mother at two in the morning, when monitors started beeping and Amy was escorted from the room. As she paced the floor in the corridor, Shane arrived. He had been resting in the lounge.

"What's up?" he asked Amy.

"I'm not sure, but her monitors started beeping and nurses rushed in and chased me out. It doesn't look good."

"Maybe she quit breathing?"

"I believe so. We should know soon."

"I'm sorry. I know this is hard for you."

"You know, Shane, I never thought it would upset me that much when my mother passed on but I feel there was a lot that remained unsaid between us. Now I will never have a chance to tell her some things I have been meaning to. Like I do appreciate the fact that she cared enough to try to keep me from making mistakes in my life. At the time, I thought she was interfering and controlling, but now that I have children, I understand a lot better. What will I be like when my kids get to be teenagers?"

"I'm sure you will be great. You know how you felt about your mother and you won't want your kids to feel like that about you. I am finding out that having the responsibility of children can be a bit intimidating."

Amy sighed, "I was just hoping for one more chance to talk with Mom. I guess God in His wisdom, didn't want me to have that opportunity. There must be a reason."

"There always is. Oh, here comes the doctor. Now we should know something."

Amy looked up to see the doctor and nurse coming down the hall. They were conferring together as they approached.

"Mrs. Johnson?"

"Yes?"

"We are very sorry to inform you that your mother passed away. We tried our best to resuscitate her but there was no response. We are very sorry."

Shane took Amy's hand, guided her to a chair, and spoke for her, "Thank you for trying. Did she say anything before she passed?"

"No. As you know, she has been in a coma and her passing was eminent. I'm sorry. Is there anyone I can call for you or anything we can do?"

Amy found her voice and spoke up, "Yes, you should call James Wiggins. Mom had signed her donor card so there are things that need to be taken care of."

"Yes, we know. We are preparing for that right now. Do you want to go in and say good-bye?"

Amy nodded. As she and Shane made their way to Gladys' room, Amy's cell phone rang. It was an unknown number so she didn't answer.

* * *

The phone ringing finally registered to Ivan. Grabbing the portable, he mumbled, "Hello?"

"Hi honey. Sorry to wake you. I know it is only three in the morning, but thought you would want to know. Mom passed away at two o'clock."

Ivan sat up on the side of the bed, "Are you okay? Do you want me to come?"

"I'm okay right now. Maybe it hasn't sunk in yet. Shane is here with me. We are both exhausted and are on our way to the hotel for a rest. We will have to make some arrangements tomorrow. I will call you when things are settled. Shane isn't going to call April right now as she needs her sleep and he doesn't want to wake Michael. Can you let her know in the morning? Shane will call her later, but he needs some sleep right now."

"Sure; I can do that. The kids are really missing you, not mentioning your husband."

"I am missing all of you, too. When we have the details settled for the funeral, I will let you know. Do you think the kids should come to it?"

"That is up to you. If it were my decision, I would say yes. They are old enough to understand about death, don't you think?"

"I don't know. I will think about it. Thanks for being my strong shoulder. I don't know what I would do without you."

"I will always be here. Be strong and call me if you want me to come right away."

"That is a promise. Love you."

"Love you, too. Bye for now and get some rest."

"I will. Bye."

Ivan hung up the phone and sat on the side of the bed thinking. He knew that Amy was still in a bit of shock and he was very concerned about the next few hours. It was a sure thing that she didn't get to settle things with her mother. That wasn't good. Old scores were not laid to rest and would haunt her in the days to come. Ivan knew this. He had spent many days and weeks, fighting through his emotions when his own father passed away without anything being settled between them. Amy was tough, but this was her mother and no one can take the place of a parent.

Standing up, Ivan decided to have a shower and get dressed. He would talk things over with April, and check with his neighbor about chores, but he really felt he should head to Medicine Hat. Even if she didn't realize it, Ivan knew she was going to need some support. That way, Shane could come home and look after things. Having made his decision, Ivan headed to the shower.

Chapter 57

Regina, Saskatchewan

Dave woke up from a sound sleep to the phone ringing. When he was able to focus his eyes, he could see it was the hospital calling. His heart gave a lurch. Why would they be calling this early? Glancing at the clock, he could see it was only five in the morning. Picking up the phone, he croaked, "Hello?"

"Mr. Knight?"

"Yes?"

"This is Dr. Olsen at the hospital. Sorry for calling so early in the morning, but we have a match."

"A match? For what?"

"A donor match for Sarah. A kidney has become available. We will need her in here as soon as possible."

"What? A match? Is this a live donor?" Dave was sitting on the side of the bed already and Alice was staring at him.

"No, it's not a live donor. That is why we need Sarah here as soon as possible."

"Okay, we will get there as soon as we can."

Alice was out of bed and heading to the bathroom before Dave hung up the phone. "Wake Sarah while I get through the bathroom."

"So you know what is going on?" Dave questioned her.

"I assume we have a match for Sarah. Let's not dawdle. We don't want to miss the opportunity."

Dave grabbed his housecoat and headed to Sarah's room. Pushing her door open, he could see she was already awake.

"What's up, Dad? I could hear you and Mom talking. Was that the phone I heard?"

"Yes. It was the hospital. They have found a match for you. They want you at the hospital as soon as possible."

"A match? I can't believe it. I hope no one died."

"It is not a live donor. Some one did pass away. I am sorry for someone else's loss, but this could help you. I am very grateful that this person signed their donor card."

"Yes, I guess I am too. Okay, I'm up. I will grab a quick wash and be ready to go."

"Be careful. No tripping on the rug. We don't need another broken leg."

"Don't worry, Dad. I will be careful. Now scoot."

* * *

It was several hours later by the time Sarah had all the tests done and prepared for surgery. Dave and Alice were by her side the whole time. Sarah was very happy about that because she was petrified at the thought of the surgery. It wasn't even so much the actual surgery, but the thought of whether the kidney would function for her. She didn't want to go through the surgery, only to find her body rejected the kidney and she still had to have dialysis. Whoever the unknown donor was, Sarah was sad that person had died. She just could not get past that feeling. Even knowing that person had no further use of the kidney didn't help. The one reason she didn't want anyone she knew donating a kidney to her was the feeling of guilt if something happened to his or her other kidney. She would feel like a thief. Having a kidney from a deceased person was a bit like robbing the grave. In her heart, she knew these thoughts were crazy, but she couldn't help herself. Closing her eyes, Sarah tried to relax.

Alice reached over and took her hand, "Are you okay, honey?"

"Yes and no. Yes; I am feeling okay but I am scared. I feel so bad for the family of the person that passed away. Will we ever know who it is?"

"I don't think so. It is not a good idea to have communication between the two parties involved, I am told. I can understand that."

"I guess you are right. But it would be nice to thank them."

"I know." Alice glanced over at Dave. He was trying not to worry Sarah, but he looked more upset than she was, Alice mused.

"Dave, why don't you go and get us some coffee? I could sure use a cup."

"Okay. Sarah, can I get you something?"

"Oh Dad! You know I can't have anything until after the surgery."

Dave shook his head, "I am such a dunce. Sorry. I will be right back."

As he left the room, Sarah leaned over to her Mom and whispered, "I think you will have your hands full with Dad when I go into surgery. Maybe we should ask the doctor to knock him out too."

Alice laughed. Leave it to Sarah to think of something like that. "Do you think that would help? He is such a worrywart. I know you will do fine. You are in fine condition right now and once you get this kidney, things will improve a lot. I am counting on that."

"But you know Dad. He worries about everything. I will try not to stress him."

"We are supposed to be comforting you, not the other way around. Would it be easier for you if your Dad wasn't here?"

"Oh Mom; you can't chase him away. He wouldn't like that."

"Well, you are the most important right now."

"I'm fine. I just have some issues with receiving a kidney, but I will get over it. Dad will be fine. I'd like you both here."

"Okay. Try to get some rest while you can. I will go and see what is keeping your father."

Dave was just heading back to the room when Alice met him in the hall.

"We have to talk," she said to him as she took her coffee and motioned him to the chairs by the wall.

"What's up? Is Sarah okay?"

"She will be, but you have to settle down. You are not doing her any good by being so antsy. I am scared for her, too but she doesn't need any more stress by you being so uptight."

"I'm sorry. I can't help myself. She is my little girl and if anything would happen to her, I couldn't take it."

"She's my daughter too, even if not biologically. I love her with all my heart. However, for her sake, I am trying to put up a good front. You have to try harder."

"You're right. I will try." Dave took a sip of his coffee. "Maybe this will help calm me down."

"Sarah suggested maybe the doctor should give you a sedative," Alice laughed, "Maybe she is right."

"She said that? I guess I had better shape up. Let's head back in there. I will put on my happy face."

"Okay." Alice squeezed Dave's arm. "I love you and I know you love Sarah. Let's be strong for her."

* * *

It was four o'clock by the time Sarah was back in ICU from the kidney transplant. She was hooked up to all kinds of monitors, but she was doing well. Alice and Dave were allowed to sit with her for ten minutes every hour. Dr. Olsen, the surgeon had come and talked to them as soon as she was out of the operating room. He told them everything went well and Sarah was doing great. Now it was just a matter of time to see if the kidney would take over and function properly.

Dave and Alice were very relieved that things appeared to be doing well. Dave didn't know how much more stress he would be able to take. He could feel his insides tied up in knots. He knew he should lay off the coffee as it irritated his stomach, but he couldn't help himself. Maybe he should have asked the doctor for a sedative, he thought. He wished he were more like Alice. She dealt with stress at work every day, but could shed it all as soon as she walked in the door at home. It was a real talent to be able to do that.

They were sitting in the lounge, waiting for their next ten minutes with Sarah. The last time they were in, she was awake and smiled at them. She looked so frail and helpless, lying in her hospital bed. It was hard to believe that she was actually a very strong, determined young woman. Dave was hoping this time she would be able to talk with them if they had removed some of the hoses.

Alice had closed her eyes and appeared to be resting, so Dave decided to do the same thing if he could. "I do need to try to relax," he mumbled to himself. Leaning back in the chair, Dave rubbed his eyes and tried to sleep.

Chapter 58

Southern Alberta

Ivan and Amy were sitting in James Wiggins' office, listening to the contents of Gladys' will. Ivan had arrived in Medicine Hat the day before, and Shane had headed home to look after things on both ranches. Amy was overjoyed to see Ivan as she was finding it hard to make any decisions. As they heard Gladys' will, Amy found that they didn't have to make many decisions at all. Gladys had written out everything she wanted. She was to be cremated and her ashes buried in the Medicine Hat cemetery, in a plot she had already purchased. She wanted her minister from her church to perform the service. She had listed the pallbearers and ushers. James had already contacted the parties concerned. Amy was very grateful for his diligence in seeing everything was done. Between him and the funeral home, there wasn't much left for Amy to do.

James paused in his reading of the will and looked up at Amy and Ivan, "This last part pertains to her assets and the distribution of such. Do you want me to continue?"

Amy nodded and James proceeded to read: "To my daughter Amy, I leave all my personal possessions, the monies in my chequing account in the Bank of Nova Scotia, and my Canada Savings Bonds. The monies in my savings account at the Canadian Imperial Bank of Commerce are to be set up as a trust fund for the education of Amy's children." James quit reading. "Do you want me to go on? That is really the gist of what she says."

"No," Amy responded, "That's okay. I can read the rest myself. How much money are we talking here for the trust fund?"

"The last time I checked, with the interest accumulated, we are looking at around $50,000.00."

Ivan and Amy stared at James. Ivan spoke up first, "Where on earth did she get that kind of money? She was always living hand to mouth, never spending much money. We thought she was having trouble paying her bills. We even offered to lend her some money and she turned us down. Now we know why."

James smiled, "Because she was so frugal, she was able to amass this sum. Of course, she did have some money from the sale of her condominium, even though her husband ran off with a large portion of her house sale. Gladys didn't believe in frivolous things and hardly ever went out for entertainment. She did tell me that she wanted her grandchildren to be educated and not have to struggle like she did."

Ivan looked over at Amy, but she was looking down at her hands. When she looked up, she had tears in her eyes. Wiping them away, she spoke softly, "I had no idea that she had that kind of money. I feel so bad that she did not spend more on herself, but it is comforting to know that she wants her grandchildren to benefit. I thought she didn't really care about them. She never showed any emotion to them."

"Gladys was a very unemotional woman," James replied. "I have known her for many years and never once found that she let her guard down. Something from her past, I'm sure. Anyway, I think we have covered all the bases here. Do you want me to do anything else for you?"

"Thank you for all your time and patience, James. You have gone above and beyond the call. I will get hold of the minister and make the final arrangements." Amy rose and held out her hand.

"Just one more thing. Here is the letter I was to give to you. I'm sure you will want to read it in private."

"Thank you."

* * *

It was much later that day that Amy pulled the envelope from her purse. Ivan had gone out to fill the car with gas and bring them back something for supper. Sitting in a restaurant was the last thing that Amy wanted to do at this point. She was just so tired, mentally and physically. Listening to her mother's will had been hard and had many surprises. She also knew dealing with her mother's personal effects was going to be hard.

Fingering the envelope, Amy knew reading the contents of the letter were also going to be very hard. She was almost tempted to leave it sealed for a while, but she knew Shane was going to want to know what was said about him. So taking a deep breathe, Amy opened the envelope. Taking the letter out, she spread it out on the table and started to read:

To my daughter Amy,

I am not very good at sharing my thoughts and emotions, so I will just tell you what has to be said. As I write this, I am not apologizing for anything that I have done, but I do want you to understand why I did what I did. I have given instructions to James Wiggins to give this letter to you after I am gone.

First, as you already know, I lied to you about your father. I was so angry with that man; he really was dead to me. I did not want him in my life or in yours. He had made me suffer, so I figured he didn't deserve to see his only child. Then as time went on, and I could see you were very much like your father in every way, even to your rebellious nature, I knew I did the right thing. If he had been in your life, I would have had no control at all.

Then you became a teenager and I found you were slipping out at nights to meet the boys and party. I tried to curtail that, but you were truly your father's daughter, even down to your devious ways. So then, you ended up pregnant. I had to earn a living so there was no way I could let you keep the baby and help you raise it. I also had to think of my reputation. What would all my friends think? Therefore, I sent you off to that Home in Calgary. Everyone thought you were staying with an aunt because she was ill and needed the help. That was the story I told everyone.

When your time came to have the baby, I had already made up my mind that I would phone your father and let him be stuck with raising your illegitimate baby. How did I know where to find him, you are thinking. From his letters to you, of course, the ones I never let you have. Of course, you told me that backfired on me, but I still got him because the child he raised and thought was his grandson, was not his grandson at all. I know right now you are a little confused but I will explain. You gave birth at the same time as another in the Home. She gave birth to a healthy boy, while you gave birth to a girl, who was sickly and not doing well. In order for my plan to still work, I had to come up with a healthy baby. So a nurse at the Home helped me to switch the babies. When I phoned your father, I told him you had given birth to a boy and it was his responsibility to raise it.

I kept in touch with the nurse who helped and she, in turn kept up with the little girl and me. She overcame her frailness and become a healthy, happy little girl. She was never adopted because she wasn't available as a baby. By this time, you were married and living in Calgary. I knew if you found out about the baby, you would claim her and I couldn't let that happen. You had mentioned that Dave Knight was the father of your baby, so I figured it was time he took responsibility and looked after his own child, so I started sending ads to his home, promoting adoption of older children. I found out that Dave's wife couldn't conceive, so it was perfect. I sent pictures of older children available in the Home in Calgary, but focused on Sarah. It worked! Next thing I knew, Dave and his wife went to Calgary and adopted Sarah. This was good for me because that way I could keep up with her progress.

Yes, I have been keeping up with everything in her life. I suppose I should have let you know what was going on, but I knew you would never speak to me again. I am not sorry I did what I did. If you had been a different kind of daughter, maybe this would never have happened. You didn't give me much choice at times. In spite of everything, I did love you and only had your best interests at heart.

Now to my donor card. I have signed up for my organs to be used to help others. I did this primarily to help Sarah. I got a test done and I am a match for her to donate a kidney. Don't ask me how I know. Let us just say the right people can usually be bought. I hope this will help her until another donor can be found, if mine is rejected.

So now, you have the story. What you do about your daughter is up to you but because she is my grandchild, the funds I have saved for my grandchildren's education will be divided with her. James will see to that.

If Shane wants to look for his parents, I believe his mother's name was Betsy Welte. I don't know where the nurse is that helped me. She may be gone now, but she might know where she is.

There. I think I have covered everything. I wish you had been different kinds of daughter so we could have been close these last years, but you went and moved away to that Godforsaken ranch and joined that church. I think you did that to hurt me. Now that I am gone, I forgive you. I hope you will not have your children do the same thing to you.

Your Mother

Amy set the letter down and sat back. She could not believe her eyes. Her Mother admitted everything, but didn't apologize for anything. In fact, she blames me for everything, Amy thought.

"How could she be so cold and calculating?" Amy voiced aloud. "How could she just switch the babies and never have a second thought? How about the other mother? She must have given up her baby, too. Would she have done that if the baby was healthy?" Amy shook her head. The letter was definitely not the letter she expected. She did know some of the facts her mother mentioned, but she certainly didn't know that she maneuvered Dave and his wife into adopting Sarah. When Amy thought about how many families her mother had touched with her deviousness, it made her angry.

She felt like ripping the letter up, but knew Shane would want to read it, so she put it back in the envelope and laid back on the bed. When Ivan returned, she would let him read it. She knew he was going to be irate, too.

Chapter 59

Regina, Saskatchewan

Sarah came home from the hospital on a warm day in February. She was doing very well and had recovered much of the old vigor and color in her cheeks. While in the hospital, she had developed a bit of infection, but with dedication from the staff and doctors, they managed to get it cleared up. Though she still had some pain from her broken leg, it was also healing nicely and the cast had been removed.

"Boy is it ever nice to be home," Sarah commented to her parents as they drove into the driveway. "What's for supper, Mom? I am really tired of that hospital food."

"I'm not surprised," Alice laughed, "I don't think I could take that stuff for very long either. We are having chicken breasts, lemon rice, buttered carrots and a green salad. How does that sound?"

"Fabulous! I am so hungry, I could eat a horse, but I'm glad we are having chicken."

"Now, that is one thing I will not eat," Dave remarked, "Horse is not on my list of edible foods. How they can eat that in other parts of the country, I have no idea."

"Well, I guess if a person is hungry enough, they will eat a lot of different things," Sarah rejoined. "I know in a lot of the second world countries, they eat a lot of strange things."

"Yes," Alice joined in, "but they don't have too many choices. It is either eat it, or starve. So far, here in Canada most of us don't have to make that choice."

"Thank God," Dave answered, "I guess we are pretty fortunate, aren't we, Princess?"

"Yes, we have been very blessed in more ways that one. I was blessed the day you adopted me. I couldn't think of two better parents."

"That goes both ways," Alice said, "We couldn't ask for a better daughter. Now, let's get you into the house and I can get that dinner started. Do you need help with that bag?"

"I'm fine. Can you get my suitcase, Dad?"

"Sure thing."

As soon as Sarah was settled in her room, she phoned Jesse. She had promised to let him know as soon as she was home. He had been coming to the hospital to bring her the course notes ever since her surgery. She really appreciated all the help he had been to her. Now that she was feeling better, she was hoping her parents would let her start attending classes again. The transplanted kidney seemed to be working well and she definitely had more energy. Her color was good and there was no swelling in her extremities. Things were looking good. She prayed it would stay that way.

* * *

Alice busied herself in the kitchen, getting the food ready, while Dave set the table. She had already made the salad, cleaned the carrots, and diced them before going to pick up Sarah, so it was only the rice to cook and the chicken to sauté.

"Sarah looks pretty good, doesn't she?" Dave made the comment as he set out the silverware.

"Yes, she does, but we have to be careful she doesn't overdo it. I don't want any more complications at this stage of the game."

"That's true, but wasn't that good news when Dr. Olsen told us the kidney is functioning extremely well?"

"You got that right. I am so grateful to the donor's family for making sure the donor's wishes were honored. I wonder if we will ever know who it was?"

"Do we really want to know? I'm not sure I do. It would be hard to face those people, knowing they have lost someone and we profited from it."

"Now you are starting to sound like Sarah. She had a hard time dealing with that idea. I think she has accepted it now, though so don't get her upset."

"Our girl is one tough cookie. She has been through a lot, but just keeps on going. I know she is anxious to get back to school and it is going to be hard to nix that idea when she is so gung-ho, but we have to make her understand that it is in her best interests to let it slide for a while."

"Well, good luck with that. I know she has been telling Jesse she plans to be back in school next week."

"Really? Maybe I will have a talk with Jesse. If anyone can persuade her, it will be him."

Turning the chicken in the pan, Alice voiced, "Do you think Sarah still has a chance to graduate with her class.?"

"I don't know. I do know, if anyone can do it, it will be Sarah. She is very dedicated."

"You're right. Well, everything is ready. Do you want to call Sarah while I dish up?"

Chapter 60

Southern Alberta

February turned out to be a very warm month. Both Ivan and Shane were busy with calves coming and feeding the stock. With the unusually warm days, the calving pen on the Johnson Ranch was filled with slush and water, so Ivan was forced to turn the cows out to the meadow until the pen dried up. It made more work for him as he had to ride out several times a day to check on the strays that tended to wander off when getting close to calving. A few times, he had to pick up the calf so he could get the cow to follow. That didn't always work if it was a young heifer. She would keep returning to where she delivered the calf, bawling and circling. That is when Ivan would bring the dog into play. He would soon have the heifer moving down the pasture and into the holding pen so she could mother up to her calf.

Then there were the heifers that deserted their calves. Those were a little harder to detect. It meant after finding the calf, riding through the herd, trying to find the heifer that calved. Once she was discovered, moving her to the barn along with the calf. Then the fun began. Sometimes, as soon as the heifer was confined with her calf, she would realize, hey, this is my baby, and start talking and mothering up. However, there were also the ones that were determined that the human was trying to pull a fast one and this is not my baby; no way, no how. Those were hard to deal with and took lots of perseverance.

As a result, Ivan was spending a lot of time at the barns. Occasionally, Amy would bundle up the kids and head out to the barns, taking Ivan a drink and a snack. The kids loved these excursions. Amy enjoyed them, too.

Ever since Gladys' funeral and their return from Medicine Hat, Amy's mind had been in turmoil. She just couldn't decide what to do about Sarah. She had heard from Shane that Sarah was doing well since the transplant. Shane also told Amy that he did not say anything about who the donor was. He didn't think it was his place and he was leaving that decision up to her. He also said as soon as calving was over, he was going to try to find his biological mother. Although Amy still had some mixed feelings about this, she realized it was probably the best in the end. She just hoped for Shane's sake he didn't get another rejection. Amy had no idea whether she would ever contact Sarah, let alone tell her who the kidney donor was. She also didn't know how James Wiggins was going to deal with the trust fund and Sarah's portion. She knew he was waiting until Sarah was well to do anything. Amy realized she was being a chicken because she was procrastinating about the whole issue. Ivan had enough on his mind with the calving, she decided. She wasn't going to complicate things by wanting to contact Sarah right now. There was lots of time when things settled down on the ranch.

* * *

Things were very busy on the Collins' ranch, too. Shane was kept busy moving cows around and making sure all the calves were healthy and doing well. When he had time, he headed over to help Ivan. Being as Shane's corrals were built on a slope, he didn't have the problem with build up of mud and slush in the pens. He accredited the construction of the pens to the smart thinking of his adopted father, Abe Collins. Though they were raising sheep at the time, it still was a smart thing to do. Lambs were no different from calves when it came to contracting infections from dirty conditions after birth.

With the extra warm conditions, it made it nice for calving, but messy in the barnyards. If the good weather held, most of the snow would be gone and the yards would dry up. Shane couldn't predict that the good weather would hold, though. He had seen many blizzards hit in March, but by that time, most of the calving would be over. He was really hoping things progressed quickly as he wanted to get things under control on the ranch so he could concentrate on searching for his mother. He had looked in the Calgary phone book, but found no listing for a Betsy Welte.

He really didn't expect to find one, but was hoping. His mother could be living anywhere and she could have changed her name through marriage or whatever. It was not going to be an easy task.

As Shane forked the hay into the feeder, he thought about Amy's mother and what she had done. He could really understand Amy's anger toward her mother. He would be, too. He just couldn't understand how a mother could treat her daughter that way. And that letter! What a letter. Her mother had a chance to make everything right finally and she actually managed to make things worse. Shane was in shock when he read the letter. Amy's Mom had blamed everything she did on her daughter. Shane set his hayfork down and leaned against the fence. Taking off his glove, he wiped the sweat from his brow and adjusted his cap. Reaching down to pet Lad, he commented, "Lad, old boy, I think the animal kingdom could teach the humans a thing or two about family and faith. No animal would treat their offspring like that."

Lad wiggled, whined, and tried to lick Shane's hand. "I'm glad you agree, boy. Let's say we go see what's for lunch. I am so hungry, I could eat a hippo."

Giving Lad one more pat, Shane headed for the house and the much-anticipated meal. He was also looking forward to seeing his son because he was still sleeping when Shane headed to the barns that morning.

"I am one lucky guy," Shane announced to the world, "I have a beautiful wife, an adorable son, and an adopted family. Now if I can just find my real parents, I will be forever grateful to God."

Chapter 61

Regina, Saskatchewan

It was the end of February when Dave received a phone call from the lawyer in Medicine Hat. He had just arrived home from work when the phone rang.

"This is James Wiggins, attorney at law. You are the parents of Sarah Knight?"

Dave answered, "I would like to know your interest in Sarah."

"Sarah Knight is one of the beneficiaries in a will I am probating."

"Who's will?"

"Her name was Gladys Stern."

Dave was speechless for a moment, and then he replied, "Okay, I am Sarah Knight's father. What are we looking at?"

"Gladys left her entire savings account to her grandchildren. As you probably know, Sarah is one of her grandchildren."

"This is a bit awkward, because Sarah doesn't know Gladys is her grandmother. So you are saying Gladys has passed away?"

"Yes, she passed away in January, but she wanted me to wait for six weeks before contacting you. She wanted to be sure the kidney transplant worked for Sarah and she was doing okay. I understand she is doing very well?"

"Yes, she is, but how did you know about that?"

"You didn't know?"

"Know what?"

"No, I guess you didn't, if you didn't know Gladys had passed away. She is the one who donated a kidney to Sarah."

"What?"

"That was her wish. She knew about Sarah's kidney problems and had herself tested. She said if Sarah didn't get a donor before she passed away, we were to donate one of hers. She knew she was a match."

Dave sat down heavily in the chair by the table. He was speechless.

"Are you still there?" James inquired.

"Yes.... Yes, I'm still here. Just a bit of a shock. I didn't even know that Gladys knew about Sarah. No, that's not right. I knew she would know her daughter had a baby, but I had no idea she knew Sarah was adopted by Alice and I. How did she know that?"

"Gladys was a very sharp and shall we say, devious woman. She manipulated things to suit her. I have known her for years. Anyway, back to the reason I called you. Sarah is named in the will to receive one third of her savings account. I understand Sarah is attending school?"

"Yes, she is in her final year for pharmacy. She hopes to graduate this year."

"Well, her share of the account amounts to $23,345.00. Gladys had stipulated that the funds go to further her grandchildren's education. I will be sending some forms for her to sign and then I will forward a cheque to her for that amount."

"Where on earth did Gladys accumulate that kind of money?"

"Through the sale of her house and good investing, I guess."

"I don't know what to say."

"There's nothing to say. I just wanted to give you a heads up about this money coming through. You will be hearing from me shortly."

"Okay and thank you for the call. I will let Sarah know."

After giving James their address, Dave hung up the phone just as Alice walked in. She had just arrived home from work.

"Who was on the phone?"

"I'm not sure you want to know."

"Oh, no. What's wrong? Is Sarah okay?"

"Sarah is fine." Dave sighed. "I might as well bring you up to date. This call was quite a shock. That was a lawyer from Medicine Hat, Alberta."

"That is where you grew up, right?"

"Yes. Anyway, he is the lawyer for Gladys Stern, who is Amy's mother. Gladys passed away in January. As you can surmise, Gladys Stern is Sarah's grandmother."

Alice sat down opposite Dave, "I guess that would be true. Why was he calling us?"

"In Gladys' will, she left Sarah some money."

"Really? How much?"

"Over $23,000.00."

"Wow! How did she know where Sarah was?"

"It seems she has been keeping up with Sarah for years. She also knew that Sarah had kidney problems. This is the part I was blown away by. She is the donor for Sarah's kidney."

"What? It can't be! They wouldn't transplant a kidney from an older person into someone as young as Sarah. Would they?"

"Well, the kidney was a perfect match. They are blood related, so it makes sense. Sarah is doing very well with that kidney. I for one am very grateful to Gladys Stern for making sure her granddaughter got her kidney. Now, I just don't know if we should tell Sarah that the kidney came from her grandmother. How do you think she would react to that news?"

"I don't know, but I don't think we should keep it from her. She would be angry with us if she found out later."

"I guess you are right. Will this ever end? We still have to deal with the Amy issue. I am surprised that Amy hasn't tried to see Sarah. I just want things to get back to the way they were. It is so hard to deal with all this. I was so happy that Sarah is doing well. She is back in school, and happy. Jesse and she seem to be getting close and I am happy for her. She thinks the world of Jesse. Though I had misgivings at first about my little girl finding a special man in her life, I realize she is growing up. Old Dad has to let go, I guess."

"Oh Dave, you know Sarah adores you. You will never be replaced in her heart. We have a very special gift in Sarah and we will always have that."

"I know. Are you all right with what I just told you?"

"About the kidney? Yes, I don't care who the donor was. I am just grateful that it helped Sarah. I am sorry her grandmother died and she never got a chance to meet her, but I guess that was God's will. I'm not very religious, but I do believe there is a reason for everything. Are you okay?"

"I guess so. Now I just hope Sarah will be okay with it."

"Me, too. Let's get supper started and think about how to broach the subject to her later."

"Sounds good to me. What are we having?"

Chapter 62

Southern Alberta

Due to a heavy snowfall in early March and a delay in getting the calving over with, it was well into the month before Shane had a chance to start looking into the subject of his parents. Amy had been doing some research for him, but had been unable to find out much. The Home for unwed mothers in Calgary had been closed years before and no one seemed to know where all the records went.

Amy had gone back to Medicine Hat a short time after her mother passed away and got all her personal effects. She donated the furniture to the Salvation Army, boxed up everything else, and brought it back to the ranch. After the children were in bed and Ivan was out checking cows, Amy spent some time going through things, hoping to find some clues to help Shane in his search. Though she still had several boxes to go through, she had not discovered anything of value to help Shane.

With spring just around the corner, Amy was anxious to get the search underway. Once the weather warmed up and spring work started, neither she nor Shane would be able to spend much time researching, much less traveling to follow the leads.

One evening toward the end of March, Shane arrived at the Johnson ranch, all excited. He had found some Weltes in a Red Deer phone book. He had phoned several of the names listed and though none of them would own up to knowing Betsy Welte, they didn't rule out that she might be a cousin or something. One man he talked to said that his father's cousin had lived in the Calgary area and he believed he had several children. He also said he would try to contact his distant cousin and give Shane's phone number to him. It wasn't much, but was a start as far as Shane was concerned. Amy tried to caution him that nothing might come of it, but she had to concede that it was more than they had at any rate.

Shane had showed up just as Amy finished getting Laura and Abe to bed so Amy asked him if he would like to help her go through some more of the boxes. Shane readily agreed and they settled at the kitchen table, each with a box beside them. As Amy opened her box, she could see it looked like her mother's bank statements, and other business papers. Sighing, she wondered if it would be feasible to go through all of it, but didn't want to leave anything to chance, so settled in.

Halfway through the papers, Amy pulled out a small notebook. It appeared to be very well used and when she opened it, she found it to be full of names, addresses and phone numbers. Her heart started pounding. As she turned the pages, she didn't recognize very many of the names and assumed they were people from her church as most of the addresses were from Medicine Hat. Disappointed, she started to flip through the remaining pages when a piece of paper fell out. Picking it up off the floor, she unfolded it. With a gasp, she shot up out of her chair.

Shane jumped, "What? What is it?"

Amy stared at him and replied, "I think we just hit the jackpot!"

She handed the paper to Shane and he quickly scanned it, then looked up at Amy and questioned, "I don't understand? How does this help?"

"See that name on the top?" Shane nodded. Amy continued, "That is the name of the Home I stayed in when having my baby. The part I am excited about is what is written below. The Home was owned by the Community Church and there is their address and phone number. Do you know what this means?"

"I'm not sure."

"They will have all the records from the Home after it was closed. With any luck, we will be able to find the information about your mother."

"If that is true, what are we waiting for? Let's phone right away."

"I think we should wait until morning and call during office hours. If we call now, we might not be received very well, calling this late at night. We have waited this long. One more day won't matter."

"I guess you are right. I am just so anxious to get this settled. Wow! Wait until April hears! And Ivan! Where is he, by the way?"

"He went to check on the neighbor. Pete was having some problems with his water well, so Ivan decided to go over and see if he could give him a hand. Now that we are finished calving, he started thinking about the neighbors."

"That's Ivan for you. A great neighbor. However, I guess I had better get home, so I can say goodnight to my son. Thank you, Amy. Will you call in the morning?"

"Yes, right at nine. I will call you after."

"Great! Good-night now."

Shane grabbed his hat and was heading out the door, just as Ivan drove in. He could hardly wait to get home so just waved at Ivan, jumped into his truck, and headed out.

* * *

At nine o'clock sharp the next morning, Amy was on the phone to the Community Church. The woman who answered the phone sounded rushed, "Good Morning; Community Church. How may I help you?"

"Good Morning. I am calling from southern Alberta. My name is Amy Johnson. I am seeking some information about a Home that your church used to operate in Calgary."

"What kind of information are you seeking?"

"I am trying to locate a woman who was in the Home about twenty-five years ago."

"I'm sorry, but all our records are confidential."

"I realize that, but after all this time, I would think there could be exceptions."

"What would you call an exception?"

"Well, let's put it this way. About twenty-five years ago, there was a baby switch done at your Home for unwed mothers."

"What? That is impossible! What on earth makes you think that?"

"I don't think; I know. My baby was switched with the baby from a woman by the name of Betsy Welte. The reason I know this, is my mother is the one that did the switch with the help of a nurse there. My mother passed away in January and confessed in her last letter to me."

The silence was so long, Amy thought the woman had hung up the phone. When she finally spoke, she said, "This is terrible. Why would your mother do such a thing? I don't understand. Are you sure?"

"It's a long story and I won't go into it now, but the reason I want to get hold of Betsy Welte is for her son. I always thought Shane was my son."

"Who is the nurse that helped your mother in this?"

"I don't know. My mother never admitted that. She probably doesn't want her to get into trouble. I don't want to see her punished. My mother was a very strong, domineering woman and probably talked her into helping. Shane just wants to know his real mother."

"Okay, I will check with Pastor Phillips and get back to you. This is indeed, very different circumstances. What is your number?"

Amy gave her number and said, "I will look forward to hearing back from you. Will it be today?"

"Most definitely. We want this cleared up as soon as possible."

"Thank you. I will await your call."

As Amy hung up the phone, Shane walked in the door. "I just couldn't wait. What did you find out?"

Amy filled Shane in. He was so excited; he grabbed her and hugged her. Laughing, Amy hugged him back and asked, "Calm enough for a cup of cocoa, or do you want to rush home and tell April the news?"

"No, I think I had better wait until we hear if they will open the records for us."

"Good plan. If they will, it looks like we might be making a trip to Calgary in the near future."

"Depending on where my parents are, I guess."

"That's true. Now I am getting excited too. Here, drink your cocoa and tell me all about Michael and what new thing he has learned to do this past week."

Chapter 63

Regina, Saskatchewan

"So that is the whole story. I hope you aren't too upset over all this," Dave said as he held Sarah's hand and explained all the lawyer had said to him.

Sarah had tears in her eyes and she reached up with her free hand to wipe them away. "Oh Dad, I don't know what to say. You are telling me a grandmother I never knew donated the kidney to me, but she never tried to see me?"

"I'm afraid that is true. You see, if she made contact with you, her daughter might find out the truth about everything. I knew Gladys Stern a little bit while I was living in Medicine Hat and she had a reputation for being a very bossy, controlling woman. Her daughter Amy, your mother, was a virtual prisoner in her home. That is why she used to sneak out at nights to have a little fun with her friends. Of course, that just made Gladys even more controlling. I am sorry you never will get the chance to meet her, but you do have a chance to meet your mother. I know you don't want to hurt your Mom here, but you have to do what is right for you. Your Mom and I will understand any decision you make. I am sure your biological mother, Amy is waiting to hear how you are doing since your transplant. Your classes will be finished soon. Maybe you should think about contacting her, even if just to say thank you. After all, it was her mother that donated the kidney to you. You can't thank Gladys, but you can thank her daughter. I'm not asking you to become fast friends with Amy. In fact, I would prefer you don't become friends at all, but that is selfishness on my part. Are you going to be okay with all this?"

"I'm okay, Dad. I just need some time to absorb all this. I find it so hard to believe that my own grandmother donated the kidney that may have saved my life. Wow! Things sure can be complicated."

"I agree." Dave gave Sarah a hug. "Your Mom and I decided that I should be the one to tell you all this. If you now want to talk to your Mom, she is in the kitchen."

"Not right now, Dad. I am going to go for a walk. Maybe when I get back."

"Sure thing, princess. Take your time. We love you a lot, but you know that."

"That goes both ways. You and Mom are the best. See you when I get back."

Sarah jumped up and headed to the hallway. Grabbing her jacket from the hall closet, she headed out the door.

Dave watched her go and breathed a big sigh of relief. He thought Sarah took everything very well. His girl never ceased to surprise him. Whether she would now decide to contact Amy was anyone's guess, but ultimately, it was now her decision, Dave thought. Heading to the kitchen, he picked up the evening paper from the side table.

* * *

Alice watched from the kitchen window as Sarah headed out for her walk. She turned as Dave entered the room.

"How did it go?" she quizzed him.

"Actually, it went quite well. She is a very strong and understanding young woman. How did we get so lucky?"

"Good genes," Alice smiled as she filled her coffee cup and headed to the table.

"Thanks," Dave answered as he also sat down and unfolded the paper, "She decided to go for her walk and think about things. The ball is in her court now. Whatever she decided is what will be done. I hope she accepts the money and puts it into some kind of savings account for her future. I know the lawyer said the funds are to be used for education, but that is all paid already."

"I agree. Someday, she will want to buy a house or a car. That kind of money could help her out a lot."

"I wonder how Amy feels about all this. I just can't believe she hasn't tried to contact Sarah."

"Do you think Sarah will contact her now?"

"That is up to her. I told her we would accept whatever she decides."

"I know it will be hard, but maybe she has to do this for her sake as well as her mother's. I won't like it, but I will never let her know. I made that mistake before and I won't again. I love her too much for that."

"That goes for both of us. And I love you, too. You have been so good through all this. I can't believe how fortunate I was to choose you for my wife."

"Who chose whom?" Alice laughed as she sipped her coffee and settled back in her chair. "It seems I had a hand in that, too."

Dave chuckled, "You surely did. Thanks for choosing me."

"You're welcome," Alice responded. "Anything new in the paper?"

* * *

Sarah kicked at a dirt lump as she trudged along the walking path. She was happy the weather had turned warmer so she could enjoy her walks every day. Her doctor had urged her to try to walk every day. So far, her body was responding very well to the exercise and she was feeling better and stronger than she had for a very long time.

"Thanks to my grandmother," Sarah mused. "Who would have guessed that it would be a grandmother I never even met that would be my donor. Life sure does throw some curves at us. Now what do I do about my mother? Do I want to make contact? Why hasn't she tried to contact me? Maybe she doesn't want to know me. Should I wait and see what she does, or should I be the one to make the first move? Decisions, decisions. Why are there always-hard decisions to make? Maybe I should just let someone else make those decisions for me. Would that be shifting the blame? Oh, what to do?"

Sarah paused and adjusted the collar on her jacket to stop the wind from blowing down her neck. Staring off into the distance, she could see the traffic starting to pick up on the freeway. Realizing she had been walking a long time, she reversed direction and started heading back the way she came.

Passing a couple of joggers, she waved and smiled. "Well, Mom and Dad will be starting to wonder so I had better get home," she voiced aloud. "I will have time to think later. I don't have to make any plans tonight."

Setting a fast pace, she was soon walking up the driveway. It was then she realized she was famished and was looking forward to supper.

Chapter 64

Southern Alberta

Pastor Phillips sounded like a kind and gentle man. He apologized profusely for being so long getting back to Amy. "I was in meetings all day and when Jill was finally able to contact me, I had to come back to the church to check out the records. And I must say, our records haven't been disturbed for a long time, so I had no idea where to start. Anyway, I did find your record. It says you gave birth to a healthy little boy, but it looks like the record has been altered. I can't read the signature of the nurse attending, but if I was to guess, it looks like Elizabeth Anger or something like that. I am still looking for Betsy Welte. If I find that record and it has been altered as well, maybe we will have something here. I find it so hard to believe that your mother would want to switch babies. Why would she do that?"

"She had her own agenda," Amy answered. "It seems that the baby I gave birth to was not very healthy at birth. She wanted a healthy baby. It is a very long story and when we have time, I will fill you in."

"Would it be possible for you to come to Calgary and bring the letter from your mother? I need to have some assurance that I am doing the right thing by opening these records to you."

"Shane and I can be there in a day or two."

"Shane?"

"That is the boy that was switched and I thought was my son."

"Oh. Then by all means bring him, too."

"Okay, we will let you know when we are coming. Thank you for all your patience in this manner."

"You're very welcome. We, here at Community Church feel responsible if such a thing happened in our care. Terrible thing; terrible. See you soon."

As Amy hung up the phone, she started to shake. She couldn't believe she was actually making some headway in finding Shane's mother. Maybe, just maybe things will be settled and back to normal soon, she thought as she headed to the kitchen to start lunch. Then she remembered and headed back to the phone to call Shane. He needed to make some plans to be able to go to Calgary with her.

* * *

Shane had just finished supper when the phone rang. "Amy?"

"Yes, it's me. I heard back from the Pastor. He wants us to come to Calgary and bring the letter from Mom. Can you get away in a day or two?"

"I can if Ivan will check on things here and do chores."

"I haven't talked with him yet, but I am sure he will. Do you think April would be willing to have Laura and Abe for a day or two?"

"I'm sure, but I will ask her. When did you want to go?"

"How about day after tomorrow? That will give us both time to get last minute things squared away."

"Sounds good. I will get things cleared here. Boy, I am getting so excited. I sure hope the trip will be worth it."

"Well, just a little incentive; the pastor did find my records and he said they looked to be altered, so if we find your mother's and it has been altered, then we will have more proof."

"Altered in what way?"

"I guess where it said baby boy. If it originally said baby girl, the two words are very different. He also said there was a signature of the attending nurse. That might be a lead. He said it was difficult to read."

"Maybe she didn't put her real name down if she was doing a switch."

"That's a possibility, for sure. Well, talk to you tomorrow and we will finalize plans."

"Perfect. Talk then."

Shane hung up the phone and went looking for April. He found her in the bedroom, feeding Michael.

"Was that Amy on the phone?"

"Yes. She heard from the Pastor of the church. He wants us to come to Calgary and bring the letter."

"When are you going?"

"That depends on you. Can you keep Laura and Abe for a day or so?"

"Of course. Ivan will do chores?"

"I'm pretty sure, but Amy was going to check with him. I am so excited. Just think! Maybe I will soon meet my parents. I can hardly wait."

"Don't get too carried away. This is just a first step. Next, you will have to find her and make contact. But yes, I am excited for you, too."

April finished feeding Michael and started getting him ready for his bath. "Can I bathe him tonight?" Shane asked. "That way, you can finish up in the kitchen."

"Great. Thank you. You are the best."

"And don't you forget it!" Shane answered with a smile as he hugged April and picked up Michael. "Come on, buddy. Let's get you all cleaned up and ready for bed."

Michael gurgled, smiled, and grasped Shane by the ear. April laughed as she headed to the kitchen. It was nice to see her husband and son having fun together. Some day, she was going to have to tell Shane her news, but it could wait until he got things settled with his family, but only if it didn't take too long.

Chapter 65

Calgary, Alberta

Two days later, Amy and Shane were sitting in the office of the Community Church in Calgary. Pastor Phillips had instructed Jill, his secretary to make them comfortable until he returned from his morning meeting.

Both Shane and Amy were nervous and the waiting seemed like forever, but it was only twenty minutes before the Pastor hurried into the office. Extending his hand, he welcomed them, "Sorry for not being right here when you arrived. I had a meeting I just couldn't get out of. I hope you had a safe trip."

"Thank you for seeing us," Amy took his hand and shook it. "We are very grateful for any time you can give us. This is Shane," Amy gestured toward Shane who rose, nodded his head, and then took the Pastor's hand.

"It is a pleasure to meet both of you," Pastor Phillips said. "I just hope we can be of service to you and help you in your search. I would like to read your mother's letter first, if I may."

"Of course." Amy reached into her purse and produced the letter. Handing it to him, she remarked, "It is not a nice letter to read, as you will understand shortly."

Pastor Phillips took the letter and settled back in his chair to read it. As he read, the expression changed on his face and by the time he was finished, he was actually scowling. Throwing the letter down, he rose to his feet and came around to the front of the desk.

"I don't know what to say. Never have I ever read a letter like that from a mother to a daughter. I can't believe she would write something like that when she was passing on."

Amy nodded, "I am not sure when she wrote this letter. It must have been after she found out I knew about my father."

"I feel just terrible that a thing like this switch was allowed to happen in our Home. I will definitely endeavor to help you all I can to find out who your parents are, Shane."

"Thank you," Shane answered, "Where do we start?"

"Well, our files are listed in alphabetical order. Unfortunately, the boxes are piled into the storage room, so we will have to go down there and sort through them to try to find the box with Betsy Welte's files. It was just by chance that your file box was near the front of the pile, Amy."

"How many files would there be in each box?" Amy asked.

"Oh, I would say, maybe thirty to forty. Everything pertaining to that individual while they were here is recorded. For example, their health charts, history, etc. I can't let you read all your files, but only that associated with the birth of your child."

"That's fair. Shall we get to it?"

"By all means. I am glad Shane is here. He can do the moving of boxes for us. I'm not as young as I once was and I have a bad back. Don't get old, young man. It's not fun."

"I will be happy to move anything that needs moved with the hopes of discovering information about my parents," Shane replied. "Lead on."

Pastor Phillips led them through the chapel and into a hallway that lead to the back of the church. There he opened a door into a stairwell and headed down the stairs, with Amy and Shane right behind him. At the bottom of the stairs, he stopped in front of a door with a sign stating File Room. Taking a key from his pocket, he proceeded to unlock the door. Reaching inside, he switched on the light.

Amy groaned. The room will filled with boxes. There were boxes of every size and shape. Amy knew it was going to be hard to know where to start. Over in one corner there was a table and two chairs. Overhead was a bare light bulb. This was the extent of the furnishings.

"I apologize for the lack of décor in here, but I hope you can make do. I will grab another chair so we all can sit down. Shane, why don't you start sorting the boxes. If you find one labeled W, we will start with that one. I'll be right back." With that, the pastor headed back out the door.

"Might as well get to it," Shane sighed as he shed his jacket and rolled up his sleeves. He reached for the first box, read the label and set it aside.

"This is going to be a long day," Amy observed as she also took off her coat and tried to wipe the dust from the table and chairs with her hand.

* * *

A few hours later and they were no closer to finding a file with Betsy Welte's name on it. They had found several boxes with W on the label, but her file did not appear to be there. This was very disappointing to Shane. He had hoped they would be able to find something to help in his search.

Opening up another file, Amy remarked, "Maybe this will help us a bit. This name on this file appears to be the same name as the signature on my file. I can read the name this time. It is Elizabeth Anker. Do you think she was a nurse at the Home? It was so long ago, but I vaguely remember a young nurse called Lizzy. She was the one that looked after me after I gave birth. Do you think she could be the one that did the switch?"

Pastor Phillips paused in his searching, "You know, she just might be. If we employed her, I should have a record of her employment. That file would be in my office. I will go and look right now."

"Great. Maybe we can come at this search from the back door," Shane commented. "We don't seem to be making any headway from the front door."

"Don't give up. We'll find something," Amy assured Shane. "Let's just keep looking while Pastor Phillips checks his files."

One-half an hour later, Pastor Phillips hurried into the room. "Wonderful news! We employed an Elizabeth Anker during the time you gave birth. She left our employ shortly after that, and did leave a forwarding address. I don't know if that will help you, but it is right here in the city."

"Do you think we should check her out first, or continue searching here?"

"Well, it is getting late and I would like to lock up soon. Maybe you could continue the search here tomorrow?"

"Okay," Amy reluctantly agreed. "What time can we come in the morning?"

"Oh, nine o'clock would be fine. Here is Elizabeth's address. I imagine if she is still in the city, you can get her phone number from information."

"Thank you for your time, Pastor," Shane said. "I am feeling confident that we will turn up something soon."

"You are welcome. Do you have somewhere to stay tonight?"

"Yes, we have friends in the city. Thank you."

"Okay, let's get out of here and call it a day. I for one am tired and ready for a break."

* * *

Elizabeth Anker didn't have a listing in the Calgary area, so Shane and Amy decided to just drive to the address and see if she was still living there. It was over twenty-five years since she had given that as her forwarding address. It was a long shot, but that was all they had at the moment.

They were a little shocked when they found the address. The place looked run down and almost deserted. There was a picket fence in front that had seen better days and the house was in need of a coat of paint.

"Do you think she still lives here?" Shane commented to Amy as they parked in front of the house.

"Who knows? However, it is the only lead we have. If she doesn't, maybe who lives here can give us some information."

"How are we going to approach this?" Shane asked.

"I have been thinking about that. I think I will go to the door, inquire for Elizabeth and say I am an old friend. See what happens."

"Okay, I will wait here."

Amy stepped out of the truck and headed up the sidewalk to the front door. Stepping close to the side of the house, she rang the doorbell. She didn't hear any peals inside, so tried again. Still no rings, so she knocked on the door. Inside, she could hear a dog barking and finally a voice commanding the dog to be quiet.

Hearing footsteps, Amy stepped back just as the door opened and a man peered out. "Yes; what is it?"

"Hello. I'm looking for Elizabeth."

"Lizzy, it's for you," the man hollered back into the room. Turning, he then said, "You might as well come in. No sense standing out in the wind."

Holding the door open, he gestured for her to enter. Amy glanced back at Shane in the truck, and then stepped into the room.

The man headed back to his TV in the living room, just as a small, grey haired woman appeared in the kitchen doorway.

"Yes? May I help you?" she asked Amy. Her voice was very soft spoken and Amy felt a nagging memory.

"Lizzie? Do you remember me? You used to work at the Home run by the Community church here in Calgary. I was one of the patients and you were very kind to me."

"I'm sorry. I don't remember you. What is your name?"

"My name then was Amy Stern."

Lizzie's face blanched and she started to tremble. "Amy Stern?"

"Yes. You took care of me after I had my baby. I had to give my baby up and you were very nice to me and consoled me. I have never forgotten that."

Lizzie's face crumbled and she started to cry. She turned and headed back into the kitchen. Amy followed and put her hand on Lizzie's arm.

"Is there something you want to tell me, Lizzie?" Amy prompted.

Lizzie sat down in a kitchen chair, and dried her eyes. "This has been eating at me every day of my life since I did that. If I had known how I would feel after, I would never have agreed. But she offered so much money and we were so poor. I couldn't see any harm at the time because both babies were being put up for adoption. However, I knew it wasn't right and I have paid for it every day since. Now I suppose you are going to have me arrested?"

"Of course not. I know what a tyrant my mother was and very hard to say no to. All I want from you is some information if you have it. Do you know where Betsy Welte is, the mother of the other baby?"

"That is the saddest part. Betsy married a few years later, but she was never able to have any more children. A few years ago, Betsy suffered a stroke and was paralyzed on her left side. I understand she is doing a lot better, but unable to look after herself. Her husband died in a car accident a few years ago. So she is all alone."

"Not any more. Her son Shane, who I thought was my son, is trying to find her. Do you have an address for her?"

"No, but I know she lives in one of those assisted places on the west side of the city. Her married name is Black. You really aren't going to charge me?"

"You have suffered enough. You are making amends now. Thank you for all your help. We won't ever forget this. Shane will be so excited if he finds his mother."

"Don't say anything to my husband. He doesn't know everything, you know."

"I won't say a word. Thank you again. I must go."

"I hope you find Betsy in good shape. Have you found your daughter?"

"I know where she is, but I haven't made contact yet."

"Oh, I pray it all works out for you. And I am so sorry for the part I played in all this."

"I know. Take care." Amy reached over and gave Lizzie a hug. She then headed out the door and back to Shane who was waiting patiently in the truck.

* * *

Shane was jubilant! Finally, they had a lead on his mother. "Do you think we are letting that nurse off too easy for what she did?" he quizzed Amy. "If she hadn't agreed to help your mother, things might have been a whole lot different."

"That's true. You would not have been raised by the wonderful parents you had in Abe and Laura Collins. You might have been in entirely different circumstances."

"I guess that is true. I will never be sorry that they adopted me. They were wonderful parents."

"So now let's just concentrate on the future and finding your mother. I think the first order should be to go to our friends and dig out a phone book and phone every assisted living Home in Calgary until we find Betsy Black."

"I agree. Besides, it is now six-thirty and I am famished. Do you think we are too late for supper?"

"Maybe we should grab a bite before we get there. I will call them and tell them so they won't hold supper. We sure don't want to be a bother."

"Yes and then we can get right to calling when we get there."

* * *

Amy hit the jackpot on her third call. The attendant said, yes, they had a Betsy Black, but she had retired for the evening and she was hesitant to call her to the phone at this time. Amy assured her that they would come to visit in the morning and asked what time would be best. They agreed on ten o'clock and Amy hung up.

Everyone was talking at once, excited that Shane and Amy had found Betsy. Shane just knew he would not sleep that night in anticipation of finally meeting his mother after all the years. For Amy, it was a relief-sorrow feeling; relief that Shane's search may be over and sorrow that it would finally be confirmed that Shane was another woman's son. She knew she would shed a few tears that night.

Chapter 66

Southern Alberta

Ivan had just finished his chores and walked into the house when the phone rang. He was in a bit of a hurry as he had to get cleaned up and changed to head over to April's for supper so he almost ignored the call. Checking the number, he could see it was unknown to him, but decided to answer.

"Hello. Johnson Ranch."

There was a pause, and then a female voice said, "Hello. Is Amy there?"

"No. I'm sorry; she is away for a couple of days. Can I take a message for her?"

"When do you expect her back?"

"Well, the kids and I are hoping for tomorrow. If this is really important, I can contact her and get her to call you. Who is this, anyway?"

"I'd rather not say. I will call again in a day or two."

That was when Ivan knew who it was, but he asked anyway, "This wouldn't happen to be Sarah, would it?"

"Yes, but how did you know?"

"Just intuition, I guess. The fact that you seem to be a little hesitate about everything. How are you feeling?"

"I am doing very well. Thank you for asking. I assume you are Amy's husband?"

"The one and only. I'm Ivan. Amy will be so glad you called. You will be sure to call again in a day or two?"

"I will try. Things are pretty busy right now, as I have just completed my courses and getting ready for finals. I was reluctant to make contact with Amy because I wasn't sure she wanted to hear from me."

"That isn't the case at all. She is dealing with many things right now, which I won't go into but I know she was planning to contact you in the near future. She wasn't sure how you would feel about her, either."

"I have no feelings, one way or the other. I would like to hear her side of the story when we have the opportunity to get together. With everything that has happened in the last while, I am not surprised by anything. The one question that has been bothering me is did she give me up because I was sick or because she had to?"

"I can answer that. I know Amy would not give up a child unless she was forced to. It would not matter if the baby were sick. She is very caring and compassionate. I don't know if you know, but we have two children, so you have a brother and a sister."

"Actually, I don't know anything about Amy. I hope we can rectify that. I will call again in a few days."

"If you want to leave your number, I can get her to call you."

"No, I think it is best if I call her."

"Okay. Thank you for making contact."

"You're welcome. Good-bye."

When Ivan hung up the phone, it rang again. This time, he didn't check the caller ID.

"You were on the phone a long time," Amy said, "Talking to one of your girl friends?"

"Hardly. How are things there?"

"Well, rather exciting. We have found Shane's mother. We will visit her at ten o'clock tomorrow morning. Therefore, we should be home tomorrow afternoon. Shane is so excited. I hope she responds well to our visit. She doesn't know who we are yet."

"Do you think that is wise, not to let her know the reason for the visit?"

"It is a long story, which I will relay to you when I get home, but I am sure she will welcome him with open arms. Her story is very sad. I was far more fortunate than she has been."

"I am so glad you had such good success. I miss you and the kids do, too."

"That goes for me, too. Are the kids' home?"

"No. I just finished chores and am heading over to April's for a late supper and to pick them up. If you are going to be home tomorrow, I will probably keep them with me in the morning. I don't need to do any feeding here until later and Shane will be home to do his."

"Better rethink that. It would be nice if Shane didn't have to do any chores tomorrow so he could bring April up to date on what went on. And it would be nice if we could just have some family time."

"Good thinking. How come are you always so smart?"

""Taking lessons from my husband. See you tomorrow. If something changes, I will call you on your cell."

"Okay. Love you and take care."

"Love you, too. Hugs and kisses to the kids, and you, of course."

* * *

Ivan hung up the phone and immediately dialed April.

"Hi; sorry I'm running late, but I am on my way. Are the kids getting anxious?"

April laughed, "Not really. They are in the middle of a movie and haven't moved for the last hour. Were you held up? I hope everything is okay?"

"Just fine. I was on the phone for the last while. I will tell you about it when I get there."

"Okay, see you then."

Replacing the receiver, Ivan headed to the porch and grabbed his jacket. The weather wasn't warm enough to go without one yet, though the forecast was for warmer days in the next week. He would be glad when he could shed some of the layers while doing chores.

As he started the truck and headed out the driveway, he thought about the phone call from Sarah. He knew it must have taken a lot of courage for her to phone and he hoped he had put her mind to rest on some of her worries. He thought she sounded like a sensible, young woman. "But how could she be anything else," Ivan voiced aloud, "Look who her mother is!"

He was sorry Amy had been away when she called. He deliberately didn't mention the call to Amy. She had enough to think about with contacting Shane's mother. She didn't need any more complications at the moment. Once she was home, he would tell her about the call.

As the Collins' ranch loomed ahead, he geared down, turned in the driveway and braked in front of the house. He was starving and sure hoped April had saved him a large portion. Then he would get the kids home to bed. He was tired and anxious for bed, himself. He never slept well when Amy wasn't there beside him.

Chapter 67

Calgary, Alberta

As the weatherman predicted, the sun was out and the day was warming up nicely when Shane and Amy made their way to the Home on the west side of the city. At exactly ten o'clock, they were walking into the facility.

"I am so nervous," Shane muttered to Amy, "What if she doesn't want to see me?"

"I don't think that is going to happen. It sounds like she is all alone, with no other family, so why wouldn't she want to see the son she had to give up?"

"I am so glad you are with me for support. I don't think I could do this on my own."

"I will always be here for you. You know that."

As they approached the front desk, the receptionist there looked up and smiled, "Good morning. Can I help you?"

"Yes," Shane answered, "We are here to see Betsy Black. We made an appointment for ten this morning."

"Oh yes, there is a note here. I will take you to her room. She doesn't get many visitors so is quite excited about your visit."

The receptionist beckoned them to follow and headed down the hall. Several times, she was stopped by one of the residents, but eventually stopped at a door and knocked. A voice said, "Come in."

Opening the door, the receptionist said, "Betsy, your company is here." Opening the door wide, Shane got his first glimpse of his mother.

Betsy was sitting up in a reclining chair beside her bed. She was dressed in a brown pantsuit, with a yellow top underneath. Her hair, though mostly grey, was once a golden blonde. She stared at Shane and Amy. Shane was staring right back. Taking the initiative, Amy stepped forward and extended her hand, "Hi; my name is Amy Johnson. We don't really know each other, but we did spend some time in the same facility here in Calgary a long time ago." Turning to Shane, she continued, "This is Shane Collins. The reason we are here today to see you is to find out some answers."

Betsy took Amy's hand and replied, "I am so glad to have company. I don't know what answers I can help you with, but I will try. Please sit down."

Amy took the chair closest to Betsy while Shane sat closer to the door.

"We don't want to upset you, Betsy, but we have some information that is of interest to you and to us. It is a long story and it is best I explain right from the beginning."

"Please do. I have nothing but time. Since I had my stroke and my husband died, I have all kinds of time. Sometimes, way too much time."

"I know. Okay, here goes. Many, many years ago, you and I were both in a Home run by the Community Church here in Calgary."

Amy could feel Betsy tense up and she seemed to withdraw into herself. Amy continued.

"During that time, you and I both gave birth to babies. You gave birth to a baby boy and I gave birth to a baby girl."

"Stop it!" Betsy whispered, "I don't want to hear anymore."

"But you must," Amy soothed, "This is for your benefit, too." Amy then went on and explained her mother's role in everything that happened and how she found Shane and always thought he was her son, only to discover that he wasn't later.

By this time, Betsy was staring at Amy and seemed to be in shock. Then slowly, she turned and looked at Shane. When she could speak, she whispered, "You are my son?"

Shane stood up and moved over to Betsy and knelt in front of her, "Yes, if you are Betsy Welte, then I am your son. I have been searching for my mother every since we found out that Amy wasn't. How do you feel to have a son?"

"I always knew I had a son, but I never told my husband about you. Then I had my stroke and after my husband died, I didn't want to look because what child would want a crippled mother?"

"I would. In addition, you also have a grandson. His name is Michael. My wife April and I are anxious to have you in our family."

Betsy started to cry and Amy put her arms around her, "Go ahead and cry. This is a lot to take in all at once. You have a very compassionate, caring son who has always been that way. When I first met him, he was eighteen years old and already responsible for a sheep ranch. We all live in southern Alberta."

"Oh, I love the country. I always wanted to move to the country, but my husband was a real city boy," Betsy wiped at her eyes. "I couldn't have any more children. My husband wanted children so there was no way I could tell him that I had a son somewhere."

"Because of the switch, it would have been hard to find me," Shane consoled Betsy. "I am so glad we finally have made contact. We have to go home today, but I will bring April and Michael to see you in a week or two. Would that be okay?"

"Oh, that would be more than okay. You have given me a new lease on life. Now I have something to live for. Many days while in here, I have wished to die. Now I want to live!"

Shane reached over and gave Betsy a hug. She hugged him right back. For the first time, a smile broke over her face. "I always wondered what it would be like to hug my son. Now I know."

"What about my father?" Shane asked.

Betsy's face darkened, "Your father left me in a hurry when he found out I was pregnant. He joined the army and was sent overseas as a peacekeeper. That is why I had to give my baby up. I had no way to support a child. I heard years ago that he had cancer and passed on. You could check it out through the military records, I'm sure. His name was Conrad Beam."

"I don't understand how any man could desert his responsibilities. I am thankful I didn't receive that trait from him."

"You don't look anything like him, either. I think you look more like me. You have my blond hair and blue eyes, and you are tall. Conrad was short and had dark hair and brown eyes."

A knock came on the door and a nurse poked her head in. Seeing Betsy had company, she said, "Oh, I'm sorry to interrupt, but it is dinner time, Betsy."

Amy glanced at her watch, "Oh my! I had no idea it was that time already. Betsy, we won't keep you any longer. We have to get home today. It has been such a pleasure to meet you."

"Likewise," Shane echoed. "I am so glad we found you, mother. I may call you mother?"

"Of course," Betsy clung to Shane's hand, "You will come back and visit me?"

"Try to stop me! I will be back next week with my wife and son. They will be anxious to meet you. Until then, keep well."

"I will. I have something to look forward to now. Thank you for coming." Turning to Amy, she commented, "I know this is probably very hard for you, being as you thought Shane was your son and I really appreciate you coming and bringing him to me. Have you found your daughter?"

"I know where she is and I will be making contact shortly. You take care and thank you for thinking about me. Now I know where Shane gets his caring nature."

"Hey, I've already got a swelled head, don't make it any worse. I am so happy about finding my mother, I could burst."

After many good-bye's, Shane and Amy managed to get away. Walking out of the building, Shane put his arm around Amy and commented, "She is right; you are a special lady. You have been there for me all along and I really appreciate it. You will always have a special place in my heart."

Wiping away her tears, Amy whispered, "That goes both ways. Let's hit the road. I am missing my husband and kids."

"I know what you are saying. I am excited to get home and bring April up to date on everything. And of course, give my son a great big hug."

"I think we need to stop at the Community Church first and let Pastor Phillips know about the meeting. I know we cancelled our appointment at the church this morning, but I'm sure he will be curious about the visit."

"You are right. Let's head there right now so we can get home in good time."

Chapter 68

Regina, Saskatchewan

Dave and Alice knew that Sarah had phoned the Johnson ranch in southern Alberta, but Sarah seemed reluctant to talk to them about her conversation. She did say Amy wasn't there and she had talked to her husband. Though they were dying of curiosity, they didn't ask Sarah for more information. With time, they both felt she would talk to them. She was in the middle of finals and studying hard. With the stress level associated with her studies, both Alice and Dave felt it was not a good time to push.

Dave was very busy at work too and he felt it was a good release for him. Ever since they had made the decision to urge Sarah to contact her mother, Dave had been struggling with his feelings. Though he knew it was the right thing to do, he was not happy about having another parent in Sarah's life. He could only imagine how it was for Alice. Keeping busy did take his mind off the whole issue and he hoped that once Sarah did contact Amy, things would settle down and get back to normal. Dave hated change. He knew Alice did too, though she handled it better than he did. With taking his medication faithfully, he had been feeling good. At his last check-up, the doctor said his tests were much improved.

* * *

Sarah had been disappointed that Amy was not home when she called. It had taken a lot of courage to make the call. She wasn't sure if she could do it again. For the time being, she was just going to concentrate on her studies and get through that. Afterwards, she could make some plans. She knew her Mom and Dad were wondering what she was planning, but she really didn't have any answers for them. Until she actually contacted Amy and talked with her, she had no idea herself what her plans were. Once she graduated, she hoped to find work somewhere in the city. She wanted to remain close to the hospital in case of complications from her transplant. So far, everything was great. Her last check-up showed that the donated kidney was functioning perfectly. Though she never met her grandmother, Sarah knew she would always be grateful to the family for seeing that her wishes were carried out. She certainly never dreamed that her biological grandmother would be the one to help her. Thank God for blood ties, Sarah thought. If not for a blood tie to Sarah, the kidney may not have been compatible. If not for a blood tie, Gladys Stern would never have requested her kidney be donated to Sarah. The more Sarah thought about it, the more she realized she had a lot to be grateful for to her biological family. Because of this, Sarah knew she would have to make an effort to contact Amy again. Once she finished her courses and exams and before she started work, she would definitely try to make another contact. Maybe Amy would contact her first, Sarah thought.

* * *

Alice knew that Sarah was torn between being loyal to them and being grateful to her biological family. Because of that, Alice was trying to make it as easy for Sarah as she could. Though she was torn up inside, she never let Dave or Sarah know her true feelings. To her mind, Sarah was her child. No other woman should be able to lay claim to her child. A child only needs one mother, and Alice was Sarah's mother for over twenty years. How does a mother let go, Alice asked herself? How long can I go on, pretending I am happy about everything? Do I appear selfish when I wish someone else had donated the kidney? Am I not being grateful that my daughter is well and healthy?

As all these thoughts were going through Alice's head, she knew she was being silly. Sarah would always be her child. She just had to learn to deal with the fall out from whatever happened with Sarah and her other mother.

"I can do this," Alice reminded herself. "I don't have to be best friends with that family. I just have to support Sarah. No matter what comes, I have to be here for her."

Chapter 69

Southern Alberta

It was a warm, sunny day early in May and Amy was out in her garden. The last of the puddles had dried up and Ivan had worked the garden for her in preparation for planting. Ever since the last rain, the grass was a brilliant green and Laura and Abe were thoroughly enjoying the sunshine and rolling around on the lawn.

Stretching her back from bending over to mark the rows, Amy glanced up at the hillside behind the house. Seeing something moving on the hill, she took another look. What she saw made her heart leap. There was no mistaking it. A black bear was sitting on the hill, looking down at the buildings.

Dropping her hoe in a hurry, Amy scrambled to the gate out of the garden, calling to the kids.

"What, Mommy?" Laura asked as she scampered up to Amy.

"Let's go into the house and have a drink. I'm thirsty. How about you and Abe?"

"I'm thirsty," Abe answered, "Can I have apple juice?"

"Whatever you want. Come on." Amy grabbed Abe's hand and headed to the house. Glancing back at the hillside, she could still see the bear, but he was on the move. It looked like it was heading down the hill to the creek.

As soon as Amy poured drinks for Abe and Laura, she got on the phone and called Ivan on his cell. He was in the lower pasture and she wanted to alert him to their visitor.

"Stay in the house and keep the kids there," Ivan instructed her. "Which way was he heading?"

"Down toward the creek. Do you think he has been hanging around for a while? The dog has been barking a lot at night."

"Probably. Springtime is when the bears are the most hungry. I sure hope he's just thirsty."

"You be careful, too. Are you on foot?"

"No. I have the truck down here and the rifle is in it. I'll be careful. I just hope to get him in my sights before he does decide to help himself to one of my calves."

"Me, too."

Amy hung up the phone and headed back to the kitchen. What she saw made her heart drop. It was empty!

"Laura! Abe! Where are you?" She yelled.

No answer. In a panic, Amy rushed outside. There was no sign of the kids.

"Laura! Where are you? Answer me, right now!"

Still no answer. Scanning the hillside, there was no sign of the bear, but she could hear Ivan's truck coming from the lower pasture. Rushing around the house and checking the garden, there was still no sign of the two children. Amy was beside herself. If it wasn't for the bear, she wouldn't have been so upset, but she had no idea where the kids were or where the bear was.

As she hurried around the front of the house, she thought she heard a giggle. Stopping short, she listened. Then she heard whispering, and it was coming from under the front porch.

Stomping over to the porch, she demanded, "Laura and Abe, come out of there right this instant!"

There was some scuffling and then the two crawled out from under the porch.

"Mommy, we were just playing hide and seek. Why are you mad?"

Grabbing both by an arm, she hustled them into the house. "I'm not mad. Just scared. I guess I should have told you why I got us all into the house earlier. There is a bear by the creek. He could be very dangerous at this time of the year. So now, you know why I was so scared. Bears are big and dangerous."

"We're sorry, Mommy. Is the bear still there?"

"I don't know. Daddy is on his way and he will check it out."

Just then, Ivan roared up in his truck and jumped out. Grabbing his rifle from the front seat, he headed around the house and toward the creek. Amy watched as he vaulted the fence and headed north, the dog with him. As he disappeared from view, Amy prayed he would be careful.

A few minutes later, there were two rifle reports and Amy could hear the dog barking. Abe and Laura were sitting at the table, finishing their drink, their eyes as big as saucers.

"Do you think Daddy shot the bear?" Abe asked.

"I don't know. I sure hope he scared him off at least."

"Daddy is a good shot. If he wanted to hit that old bear, he would. Right, Mommy?"

"You're right, Laura. Now, you two stay in the house until we find out what happened. No more hide and seek, okay?"

"Okay." Abe answered as he picked up his juice. "Can I have a cookie?"

"May I?" prompted Amy.

"May I, Mommy?"

"I guess. One won't spoil your lunch."

As Amy dug out a cookie for each of the kids, Ivan opened the door and came in.

"Did you get him, Daddy?" Laura asked.

"No, I didn't, honey. He was already going over the hill, but I shot at him a couple of times so he gets the idea he is not welcome here. I want you kids to stay very close to the house until we get this bear thing solved. Okay?" Ivan looked over at Amy for confirmation.

"I will see to it," Amy replied. "Could you tell if it was a young bear?"

"Couldn't tell. It has been a few years since I lost cattle to a bear. The last one was an old bear and probably couldn't hunt too well. Young bears are kicked out from their mother's at this time of the year, so it could just be a two year old, looking around. At any rate, I want you all to be very vigilant for a while."

"We will. Don't worry. I am disappointed, though. I was hoping to start walking with the kids into the hills, now that things have dried up."

"Wait a while on that. I will get some neighbors together and maybe we can track that bear and get him out of here. I am glad you spotted him. I would hate to think what could happen if he got down into the yard."

Amy shuttered. She didn't want to think about that, but definitely planned to be very careful for the next while. She would have to keep the kids with her when planting her garden.

* * *

Two mornings later, a neighbor to the west called Ivan to report sighting a black bear in his lower pasture. He didn't get a chance to shoot at it before it disappeared into the brush, but it looked to be a young bear. That was all the incentive Ivan needed. He started calling neighbors to plan the next move.

"With any luck, one of them will get a good shot off and our problems will be over," Ivan told Amy. "The bear appears to be moving to the west, but we can't be sure, so take care. I have to go to town today for supplies. Is there anything you need?"

"I'll make a list. We would come with you, but I want to get at my garden. Do you want to take one of the kids?"

"I can take both. That way you can plant and not have to worry about watching them."

"That would be great! Thanks. I will get them ready. When do you want to leave?'

"In about an hour."

"Okay. Love you. Laura! Abe! Daddy is taking you to town. Let's get you ready."

Chapter 70

Southern Alberta

Amy was on her hands and knees, planting a row of beans when she heard a vehicle coming into the yard and parking by the house. It didn't sound like Ivan's truck, so she stood up and wiped her hands on her coveralls and started heading for the garden gate.

As she came around the corner of the house, she spotted a young woman standing on the porch, about to knock on the door.

"Hello. May I help you?"

The young woman turned and immediately, Amy felt a tightening in her chest. This had to be Sarah.

"Hello. Amy?"

"Yes, I am Amy."

Coming toward her, the young woman held out her hand. "I'm sorry to just drop in like this, but I just couldn't seem to get the nerve to phone again. I am Sarah."

"I know," Amy whispered. "You look just like your dad."

"That is what people have always said, but being as I was adopted, I didn't believe it."

"I'm sorry. I must look a sight and my hands are filthy from the garden. Come in and I will get washed up."

"I hope you aren't upset with me for just showing up."

"Of course not. Ivan and the kids are gone to town, so we can talk in peace."

"Thank you."

Amy led the way into the house and slipped off her coveralls in the porch while kicking off her garden shoes.

"Go on in. I will only be a minute. Excuse the messy house, but I've been trying to get my garden planted, so the house takes second place."

"Don't worry about it. I didn't come to see your house."

As Sarah headed inside, Amy headed into the bathroom. She was in a bit of a frazzle. Imagine! Sarah just showing up on her doorstep! Washing her hands and face, she ran a comb through her hair while checking out her reflection in the mirror.

She found Sarah sitting at the kitchen table, fingering a place mat and looking nervous.

"Would you like a drink? Hot chocolate, juice, milk?"

"I could stand a cup of coffee."

"I'm sorry. We are Mormons and we don't drink coffee so I don't have any in the house. I still have a coffee pot stored away somewhere from before I joined the church, but no coffee. Sorry."

"That's okay. A glass of water is just fine."

Hurrying to the fridge, Amy poured two glasses of water and commented, "You must have been up very early to get here by this time."

"I spent the night in your little town. I drove there yesterday. I'm not accustomed to driving long distances, so didn't want to arrive at your door, all tired and road weary."

"How are you feeling?"

"I am feeling great. The kidney is functioning very well. I have to admit I was flabbergasted when I found out the donor was my grandmother. Did you know she had designated a kidney to me?"

"Sarah, my mother did a lot of things that I was not aware of until these last years. Moreover, I didn't even know she had signed a donor card until she was dying. She left me a letter that explained all she had done, but she never apologized for any of it. She was a very hard woman, my mother."

"She must have had some compassion to be thinking of me, her granddaughter."

"Yes, that did surprise me. But being as she was responsible for you being switched at birth in the first place, maybe she thought this would make amends with the big guy upstairs."

"Big guy?"

Amy laughed, "Sorry; I mean God. My mother had her own twisted relationship with God. I think she thought she could make amends with one little stroke. Don't get me wrong. I am grateful she donated a kidney to you. What I am upset about is the fact that she switched you for Shane and kept that hidden all these years. Then somehow, she engineered the adoption to Dave and his wife."

"Why did she switch the babies?"

"When you were born, you had some health problems. I had a very difficult delivery and I don't know if that was part of it. Anyway, she had made plans to have my father adopt the baby. My father had left her years before. But she figured that he would not accept a sick baby, so she got the babies switched."

"You are sure about this? Did she really plan Shane's adoption, too?"

"It seems she did. Someday I will let you read the letter she left for me. I guess I was the daughter from Hell."

"So where does this leave us? I wanted to contact you and thank you for honoring your mother's wishes. However, where do we go from here? All these years, I often wondered why my real mother gave me up. Then after I found out you were my mother, I wondered if you gave me up because I was sick."

"I had no choice. I was sixteen years old, controlled by my mother. I didn't even see my baby. That is why I didn't know if I had a son or a daughter. I only found this out after Shane went looking for his father and I told him Dave was his father. I knew that Dave was the father of my baby. I imagine you know the rest of the story. I always thought Shane was my son."

"That is so sad. How is Shane taking all this?"

"Actually, he just found his mother a while ago. He is excited to have her in his family and is making plans to have her come and live with him and April. She had a stroke a few years ago, but is doing very well and looking forward to moving to the country. I am so happy for them. It was hard for me at first, being as I will always consider Shane part of my family. So he is doing okay."

"That is good. I understand you have two more children?"

"Yes; Laura and Abe. Laura is coming seven and Abe is coming four. I was very fortunate to be able to welcome two more children. After I had you, I didn't know if I could have more children. It's a long story and I won't bore you with it."

"So where do we stand? Can we be friends and try to put this behind us?"

"That is really up to you. I would welcome you into our family in a heartbeat, but I do not want to cause any upset in your adopted family. How do your Dad and Mom feel about all this?"

"They are okay. Worried, naturally, but they know I will always love them and be their daughter. The thing is I'm not sure if I can be your daughter, too. Even though you gave birth to me, I have no attachment to you. Now, your two children are another story. They are my half brother and sister and I have always wanted siblings. Do you think I could visit sometimes and get to know them?"

"Ivan and I would want you to consider this your home, also. Laura and Abe don't know anything about your existence, so I would like to talk to them first before they meet you, if that is okay."

"I'm cool with that. Maybe in a month or two, I can make another trip out here. I am starting a job next week in Regina and will be concentrating on that for a bit. Thank you for seeing me today. Now I know what you look like and where you live. It is beautiful out here, by the way. I can understand why people move to the country."

"Next time you come, we will have a long talk about the family. Ivan will be anxious to meet you, too. You will like Ivan. He is a great person and a great father. I am so happy to have him in my life. I hope you will be, too."

"I'm sure I will. I have to go now and get home before too late. Can I give you a hug?"

"By all means. We are a hugging family around here. Be safe on the trip home."

"I will."

One big hug later and Sarah was heading out the door. Amy watched her drive out of the yard. That is when she broke down and cried. Throwing herself down on the sofa, she cried until there were no more tears to shed.

She was still there when Ivan arrived home with the kids.

Chapter 71

Southern Alberta; Two Months Later

Amy watched from the kitchen window as Sarah played with Laura and Abe in the back yard. It was so satisfying to see the three of them enjoying each other's company. Sarah, true to her word had returned within the month and met Ivan and her two siblings. In advance of her visit, Amy had sat Laura and Abe down and told them about Sarah. At first, Laura was a little confused, but agreed to meet Sarah. Abe, as usual was excited about having another sister and one that was older. Of course, Ivan was happy to welcome another member into the family. Amy knew Ivan would be right there and help with the transition.

Now, as Amy watched the three of them playing, she thought back to all that had transpired in the last year or so and realized just how lucky she was. Not only did she gain a daughter in Sarah, but maintained a son in Shane. Shane had been very careful to include her in all his plans and she was grateful for that. Since Betsy had moved in, she and Amy had become fast friends. Amy found that she thoroughly enjoyed visiting with her and sharing experiences in their lives.

Shortly after she and Shane had found Betsy in Calgary, April dropped her surprise on them. She was expecting again. Shane was ecstatic and Betsy was thrilled that she would have another grandchild. Amy was excited too, and considered it another grandchild for her, too. She didn't need blood ties to care about Shane and his family.

Since Betsy had moved to the country, her paralysis on her left side had improved a lot. April was a good incentive for Betsy and kept her doing little things to strengthen her arm. She was walking a lot better and only needed her cane now instead of the walker. She was even feeling comfortable holding Michael while sitting in her chair. It was a source of great joy to Betsy and Amy was happy for her. She could not imagine how devastating it must be to have a stroke and not be able to use your limbs. Now the future was looking good for her.

Turning from the window, Amy started setting the table for lunch. Sarah was staying for a few days, having time off from her job. In the afternoon, they planned to head over to Shane's and have a visit. Ivan and Shane had some time because it had rained over night and put the haying on hold. It would be like a family reunion, Amy thought as she set out the plates.

When Sarah had arrived, she had announced that she was engaged. Showing Amy her ring, she revealed that Jesse had proposed to her the month before, but she had been reluctant to accept, being as she had been advised to not have children. Jesse assured her that adoption was okay with him. Talking it over with her doctor, she decided to accept. Her Mom and Dad were very happy for her and she hoped Amy would be, too.

Amy chuckled to herself. Of course, she was happy for Sarah. She would look forward to meeting Jesse, but didn't know about attending the wedding. There she would have to face Dave and his wife. Oh well she thought, she always thought she had courage so that should be a piece of cake. With luck, maybe Sarah and Jesse would elope and she wouldn't have to worry.

Spotting Ivan down by the corrals as she glanced out the kitchen window, she thought about the bear problem. It was resolved when the neighbor to the north caught it in his yard early one morning. Two shots later and the bear worries were over. All the neighbors breathed a sigh of relief. It appears it was a young bear and had never learned to hunt properly so was looking for food.

As Ivan started up the path to the house, Amy turned and took the salad and cold cuts from the fridge. Smiling to herself, she knew she was one lucky woman. Who could ask for anything more; a great husband, great kids and good friends She also had her faith in God and was forever grateful to Him for all the blessings He had given her in the last years. She knew that no matter what happens in life, there is always hope. Her family had proven that to her. Blood ties or no blood ties, family were the most important thing. That was a lesson her mother never learned. Amy was happy that she did.

Going to the kitchen door, Amy called "Lunch is on. Come and get washed up. We don't want to be late going to Shane's this afternoon."

THE END

CPSIA information can be obtained at www.ICGtesting.com
Printed in the USA
LVOW041518271012

304648LV00001B/32/P